Praise for

High as the Waters Rise

"Prose with the brightness of poetry, in a splendidly lucid translation."
—Jennifer Croft, author of *Homesick* and co-winner with
Olga Tokarczuk of The International Booker Prize for *Flights*

"So beautifully written, Anja Kampmann's novel is one of those very
rare things: a debut of a literary master." —Ilya Kaminsky,
author of *Deaf Republic* and *Dancing in Odessa*

"There are difficult questions asked in this novel, about responsi-
bility, culpability, love, trust, and the weight of time and distance,
and there are no easy answers—instead, we are treated to the most
vivid particulars, the glory of specifics, the full human reality of a
character whose attempt to wander away from deadening grief only
reminds him time and time again of all the many ways he has and
does and can still feel alive." —Ilana Masad, author of
All My Mother's Lovers

"Kampmann and Posten write gorgeous sentences . . . The most vivid
and memorable character is the oil platform itself . . . Kampmann
brilliantly conveys the industry's reckless disregard for human life."
—Jane Yager, *The Times Literary Supplement*

"[A] poet's novel in the richness of its imagery and the exquisiteness
of the language. It's as if the protagonist were a modern Odysseus
returning to a home he no longer has." —*Library Journal*

"It is unexpected to encounter a modern-day *Moby Dick* with the same dangerous stakes, but, for workers under global capitalism, the sea remains as treacherous as ever. Capitalism's disregard for human life is as deadly now as it was on the *Pequod* . . . Kampmann uses her gifts not to make the ugliness of global capitalism palatable, but to resist it, in the tradition of Audre Lorde . . . This novel fulfills the essentially radical task of poetry."   —Fiona Bell, *Chicago Review*

"This is climate fiction—a genre that explores climate change in fictional narratives—at its best."   —Amy Brady, *Literary Hub*

"It is not easy to write about something as consuming as grief; it is even more difficult for language to enter right in the thickest dread of it, the incomprehensibility of it, the hopeless, elegiac nature of trying to bring absence into sharp relief. Yet *High as the Waters Rise* fills the great blank canvas of loss with a precision that nourishes the fine contours of emotion, wherein sadness is a thing of many shapes and colours, following a love that has no nature but wherever and whenever the lover is."   —Xiao Yue Shan, *Asymptote*

"The beautiful English-language debut from German poet Kampmann tells the story of a middle-aged oil rig worker's emotional crisis after the death of his friend . . . As Waclaw digs up memories of his drilling throughout the world—in Morocco, Mexico, and Brazil—he ruminates on generations of workers who must eke out a living by exploiting the earth and its resources. Kampmann captures the visceral uneasiness that arises from second guessing one's past."
—*Publishers Weekly*

"In her debut novel, German poet Kampmann touchingly and intimately illustrates the fallout of capitalism's dependence on oil. The true tragedy here is that Waclaw's story is not unique. His plight is a perfect vehicle for Kampmann's lyrical descriptions, which reach from dusty Moroccan cities to the brass-colored balustrades in a Budapest hotel . . . This is a haunting exploration of the devastating costs all kinds of gig workers have to bear to feed themselves and the belly of the beast."   —*Booklist*

High as the Waters Rise

HIGH AS THE WATERS RISE

A Novel

Anja Kampmann

Translated from the German by
ANNE POSTEN

Catapult
New York

This is a work of fiction. All of the characters, organizations, and
events portrayed in this novel are either products of
the author's imagination or are used fictitiously.

Copyright © 2018 by Anja Kampmann
English translation copyright © 2019 by Anne Posten
First published in Germany as *Wie hoch die Wasser steigen* in 2018 by
Carl Hanser Verlag GmbH & Co. KG, München

Hardcover ISBN: 978-1-948226-52-3
Paperback ISBN: 978-1-64622-082-3

Cover design by Nicole Caputo
Book design by Wah-Ming Chang

Library of Congress Control Number: 2019957069

Catapult
1140 Broadway, Suite 706
New York, NY 10001

Printed in the United States of America
1 3 5 7 9 10 8 6 4 2

The translation of this work was supported by
a grant from the Goethe-Institut.

There's a new continent at your doorstep, William.

—ARTHUR MILLER

High as the Waters Rise

The storms out there are no place for men. If one were to approach from afar, there would be darkness and more darkness, the waves would swallow the rain, swallow the lightning, it would smell of metal and salt, but no one is there to smell anything. There are no eyes. There would only be sea, piling up and up. There would be no north or south. The water would swallow even the cries of the storm, which no ear would hear. A darkness, planes layering upon each other, waves that break in utter darkness, and somewhat farther, farther on, is a flickering of distant light, swallowed by waves, just a moment, a light.

Cantarell

They followed the long lines in the asphalt. Mátyás walked on, and the wind from the rotor blades pressed their clothes to their bodies as if there were no weariness and no doubt, just the drone of the machine, and far away, beyond the airfield, he saw the white tip of a mole against which the waves beat and, way off in the distance, broke in a great roaring light.

The clouds had thickened that morning, a storm front from the Faeroes had stopped over the Atlantic off the coast of Morocco, where the air had been heating up for days and weeks, and they lay tired on the long benches in the heliport and knew nothing of it. The light of the Coke machine shimmered over the linoleum, and they had a long wait for the helicopter.

It was the first time he'd seen the heliport of Sidi Ifni in anything other than the gray five o'clock light in which they'd departed on the other mornings. Before the sun had even risen the waiting room had been full of men shoving their bags in front of them through security, the smell of coffee hung in the air and no one said much, some had landed in Rabat only that night and then continued on south, and when they arrived, the ocean was still gray and wide and the wind so strong that they happily went back into the little room to smoke, as if they were already on deck in the closed container, where the table and benches were screwed tight to the floor.

Mátyás was kneeling next to Waclaw, looking for something in his bag, when the first helicopter finally landed and men and more men came through the glass door, which silently opened and closed, its edges giving off a bluish gleam, like a precise blade.

The men carried their bags on their shoulders, some wore sunglasses, and their steps were heavy and cold in the glaring light of the waiting room. Waclaw knew only a few of them. They'd been drilling for two months, the Atlantic raging past them toward the North African continental shelf. They'd drilled through sandstone and basalt, eighty miles from the coast, for nothing but mud and rocks. The oil—if there were any—would lie very deep, they'd been told. But until something was found in at least one of *these shitholes*, the mood remained tense, the work seemed more laborious, it wasn't like in Mexico, in the Bay of Campeche, where all they'd had to do was stick more straws into the bulging bubble of oil, Cantarell, to drink for a few years, like wasps feeding on the last rotting fruits of autumn.

This wasn't Mexico, and the men were tired and high-strung when they got to land. A piece of luggage came flying through the air, a bag, big as a porpoise or a stuffed boar, *Hey, Budapest.* Mátyás had only just raised his arms when the bag crashed on the floor in front of him, his curls bounced. They looked at each other for a moment, *Hey, Texas,* before the huge mountain of flesh came to him and wrapped him in an embrace.

It's a bitch out there, Trevor said, not something you want to be sailing in, that's for sure, they'll close the harbors if it keeps up.

He chewed a piece of jerky, his English rough, like someone unloading a ton of rocks.

How's the new guy? Mátyás asked, and Roy joined them. Suddenly a circle was formed of those arriving and those leaving, of weariness and the smell of sweat and the tension that overcame them all before things started up. Waclaw sometimes thought of the starting gates of big races, the nervous trembling of the horses, each led by three trainers while the jockey just crouched on top, or the steel bars crowds hid behind as the bulls ran by, the smell of sweating livestock.

He's a pussy, Roy cried. Have you ever seen anybody out there in a tie? Not in thirty years. He looks like he needs—he raised his eyebrows and snapped his fingers a few times. The men laughed and a few clapped, shoulders were slapped, but Roy remained serious. I mean, what are we supposed to do with him, he said, when we really need him, what is he going to do for us, some calculations? He'd spoken softly, and his eyes had wandered to Waclaw. They're young, he said, they don't know what it means.

They stood together a moment, then the glass door closed behind those who were still there, waiting.

I

Westerly

The sea at night is the darkest thing there is. Behind heavy storm clouds the moon was invisible, and the horizon hard to distinguish from the blackness where the waves piled up, drawing breath again and again as the wind whipped all it could muster of froth and spray over the crests. Far below, the platform swayed on its long steel mooring cables, tugged at the meter-thick piles sunk deep in the ocean floor, and threw its bright light in a compact radius on the churning brown.

It was the eighth hour of the shift. On the narrow monkey board, he braced himself against the harness, holding on to the bars of the derrick with both arms. The salty wetness surrounded him like an all-embracing undertow, and for a while he'd been expecting the signal that meant work was over. Pippo would have called them in long ago, but the new rig manager didn't seem to care, he'd sooner let them drown than interrupt the drilling. Waclaw felt the blows against the jacket legs—back then they would have evacuated the platform, he thought, but not now, now they'll just wait—while the rain drove near-horizontally across the floodlights, and the sea tugged at the welded joints, dashed against the platform like some crazy herd, the waves fled the storm, everything coming toward them.

Far below on the rotary table he saw the men, they were calling something, he saw how their mouths moved, but the only call was the call of the storm, the spray, the futile flapping of a seagull, the light undersides of its wings flashing a few times.

It was almost half an hour before the signal sounded and work ended. He had simply held out, braced himself on his narrow platform and waited. The other roughnecks went in, someone opened the heavy door to the cabins, he saw the strip of light, the first men entered. There was only this coldness in his limbs and he moved his feet in single movements, stiffly, his legs knew the space between steps, every single wet rung. The water had long since crept under his oilskin, and Waclaw was chilled to the bone and kept on gripping the bars once he finally came to stand on the floor of the platform.

Inside, the light was glaring, the warmth friendly, even in the little room where they put their boots on the rack and hung their coveralls to dry. He felt almost cheerful now, coming into the warmth with the others. It was a new team and there were only a few, like Albert, who was in charge down on the rotary table, whom he'd known for a long time. The storm had made his mood even worse. Silently Waclaw stuck his feet into his flip-flops and walked down the hallway to their cabin. The light was on, but Mátyás's bed was empty. Their blankets lay on the lower bunk and for a moment he thought perhaps Mátyás was under them, but there was no one there. The headphones dangled toward the floor, the Walkman was next to the pillow. He wound the cord around his hand. Mátyás? he said. Without waiting for an answer, he opened the door to the bathroom. It was four in the morning. He turned on the hot water.

Barefoot and still wet through, he stood in front of their bunks. He pulled both blankets over himself, over his still-damp skin, and suddenly the storm seemed very far way. He waited. The warmth made him sleepy, and he'd not eaten anything since evening. This was new, too, for the drilling foreman to put them on different shifts.

As always, his skin looked strangely pale under the parallel lines of the neon tubes. As he entered the mess hall, the men who sat at the table in front of the counter fell silent. He felt their gaze behind the sticky plastic sauce bottles, shadowing his movements as he looked around. Next to them, off to the side, sat Francis, pallid and somewhat absent. A sick seabird, fluffing his feathers for a few last days. He sat erect, ignoring the jibes that the crane operator was bellowing from the next table like a fat pig. Shane showed off for the new guys, barking at the floorhands to put more chemicals in the drilling fluid, to bring him water, or to hose down the deck again and again. Only when they sat weak and exhausted next to him, enduring his crude jokes, did his face take on the air of absence that for him signaled satisfaction. Then he could sit there as if his eyes were made of glass. But when the door swung open his face had brightened, and Waclaw heard a scornful, beckoning whistle. Hey hey, Shane mocked, who might we be looking for. His voice sounded dull and deep, like that of a very fat man, but he was scraggy, with a hawk nose that had followed their every step since they'd met him for the first time two years ago. His arms, all of him, were still coated with a greasy film. Outside on deck he wore yellow work gloves that made his hands look like claws. It was the usual talk. Waclaw never paid any mind when people stared after them.

Francis sat next to them, silently drinking two glasses amid their noise. Waclaw was annoyed that Mátyás wasn't there. He took two ladlesful from the warming pot, dunked in some nearly transparent toast, and ate. Here, too, the light was too glaring. The soup too brown, skin too pale. Gradually, the mess hall began to fill. After work ended, they either came here to eat or lay down in their cabins to sleep.

In the hallway the storm seemed nearly silent, the swaying, everything felt as if it were some ways away. He heard voices from the movie room, and his own steps, growing quicker, as he passed the plastic-covered doors with aluminum knobs. He went down the long hall to the last door, the room was dark save a small electric candle in the corner that flickered no matter the weather. They'd met here sometimes: just a few rugs turned toward Mecca, hardly anyone came to pray. Mátyás? Would he have been surprised to see him leaning against the wall, laughing his soft laugh? A stream of light fell into the darkness as the door opened. The room was silent. Only an unreal silence and the rugs. He went back to their cabin. Through a cracked door he saw Andrej lying on his bunk, phone on his shoulder like a little bird—his paunch peeking out and his pale, threadbare pants. The song he was listening to sounded like *reshushshickshurroo*, and he would be listening to it all night long.

The smell of socks and sweaty tank tops, the thin walls. Five thirty, maybe, at night, normally he'd still have nearly three hours out on the iron bars of the derrick, and it should have been Mátyás's last hours of sleep before his shift. Perhaps he'd felt sick. The night was still as dark as it was possible to be, not a streak of light. Once, the door to the deck hadn't closed properly and the water had flowed nearly to their cabins. That was long before he'd known Mátyás, before the weeks out here had taken on a certain temperature, almost like a color, which he recognized in the way their things formed a disorder that was familiar to him.

He climbed over their bags into his bed and stretched out on his back. He left the light on for Mátyás and tried to close his eyes. The platform was dependable, you could trust that it would float, that it was high enough, twelve meters above sea level, that the water couldn't simply wash over it, but what could you really trust, it was floating steel. The *Ocean Monarch* had spent years in the North Sea before it had been towed down south, a semisubmersible, a colossus that was getting on in years, the wall above Waclaw's bed shone with the greasy headprints of other workers. Countless nights, way out. Mátyás analyzed the drill cuttings, he knew about the rock chips and traces of sediment, he could tell what kinds of forests grew on the seafloor in prehistoric times. Waclaw had never heard someone laugh so much, an almost childlike way of dealing with the weeks at sea. From the first day, his expression had reminded Waclaw of old playing cards, a joker in yellow garb. While the instructor in the big halls where they were trained laid his American *r* under every sentence like the base of a platform, waxing lyrical about the unbounded freedom of the oceans and the company's oilfields, Mátyás just stared off through his curls and held his tongue. His father was Hungarian, some uprising or other had led the family out of the heart of Budapest and into the countryside, where he had been supposed to become a blacksmith on a large farm: hooves, steam, young mares and whites of eyes, endless drives through the countryside and the smell in his uncle's car that made him sick.

For six years they'd shared a cabin, and it had been one since they'd left the Gulf of Mexico. What raged outside now, this booming spectacle of a night, was none other than the Atlantic itself, and here, near the continental shelf, off the coast of Morocco, it felt furious and open. He reached into his bag and pulled out a sweater, suddenly cold. He thought of Pippo, their old drilling foreman, confined to bed for weeks on end by vicious bouts of malaria. Some said it wouldn't be long before it got to him, made him not quite normal. It was the platforms near the coast, the Niger Delta and the mosquitos that flew out from the swampy banks, the lack of wind and the heat, the fact that no one could long stand taking the tablets that prevented infection. How long had Pippo been out? He knew Mátyás liked him. But when they had gotten back to the platform there was only Anderson, who didn't even bother to introduce himself, and the glow of the few days they'd spent on the coast was blown out.

He must have dreamed, but when the alarm shrilled he remembered only shreds, trees in a landscape, some hills. It was Mátyás's alarm, only a few minutes left before his shift. The light was still on, the air stuffy and damp, he'd forgotten to close the bathroom door.

Mátyás wasn't there. Wind pressed against the cabin wall, it was quiet in the hallway. They'd keep work suspended for a few more hours. He turned on his side and stared at their things. All was unchanged, even his pack with the soapstone that he always carried—it lay where it always lay.

Waclaw pulled the blanket tighter and thought he had just closed his eyes when something startled him awake, dull and distant, not the clatter of steps on the walkway, something other than the piercing signal for work to continue. The unease was unexpected and strong, it seemed to emanate from the bright wall, where the sudden daylight traced a clear line. Mátyás's warm fleece still hung in the closet.

So he brought him the sweater. The morning was clear, heavy clouds moved across the early blue as if in a hurry, in the distance a silvery shimmer still lingered. He carried the fleece for Mátyás and he carried it like a plea, while the running of the machines suddenly struck him as unreal. Here we are, Petrov said as he came around the light blue tank behind which they extracted the drill cuttings.

He saw the familiar pans with the sludge, the stones and muddy earth, saw all the things that were familiar to him, the shaker screens, the monitors and hoses, saw Petrov with his good-natured smile, but he did not see Mátyás. Where's your friend this morning? Petrov took off his safety goggles and looked at Waclaw in the same way Waclaw was looking at him.

Petrov had wanted to wait until Mátyás came by himself, work had gotten off to a slow start after that night. Waclaw didn't have to remind him of the darkness of the sea. They looked. It only occurred to him later, after they had searched every room, the whole deck, every corner and step all the way down to the boat landings, the gym, the mess hall several times and several times their own cabins, after announcements were made, after the drilling foreman subjected the workers to a standardized round of questioning, the sky broke into a radiant noon, while nothing of the day and none of the seabirds that flew over the water could possibly be real, radio messages went out, someone brought him a hot drink and he scanned every jacket leg with his eyes, the water's surface with its crazy shimmer, after they tried to drag him in and finally left him to sit between the tanks and an even, round sun sank into the water, only then did he notice that his fist was closed around something, which only then, in the evening and before the flat horizon, turned into something that had once been Mátyás's fleece.

On this evening the moon seemed scarce, hovering as it did above the swaying sea. In his bed, Waclaw still wore his boots, a few feathers escaped from the pillow. Some huge being had ripped everything away, everything that had been, only yesterday. He stood in the cabin and regretted winding up Mátyás's headphones. He thought about it, about the fact that he'd picked them up, that he couldn't hold any of it off, that it was now evening, and the storm was over and it had grown dark, as it always did. He heard steps outside, the men ambled into the mess hall in their sweaty T-shirts. They were hungry, the food smelled, he couldn't stay in the cabin. He went out. The sea was almost calm. Now and then they sent someone to come and check on him, at some point Petrov came and offered him cigarettes, and Waclaw watched as he sat next to him, wordlessly smoking.

They could cost you your job, Waclaw said, and Petrov laughed softly, took one more drag, and looked straight out at the sea.

They'll be asking you, too, he said.

They're not going to send anyone out to look for him, are they?

No, Petrov said. They most certainly won't.

They were silent awhile. Gas was still being flared, a seagull flew past through the floodlight, sometimes they came over from the tankers.

What will you do now? Petrov asked. Where will you go?

They looked down at the water, as it grew dim and a light sheen rode the swells.

Back, Waclaw said.

Where is that?

He thought he saw a smile in Petrov's eyes.

What about you? Waclaw asked finally.

Wife and kid, Petrov said. Fucking hell. They think it's good money out here. That's what they all think.

The last light came from far away and fell on the gray stubble of his chin.

Drops fell, echoing behind them on the empty tank. The wind picked up, rubbing against the bars and cables. Petrov put up his hood.

I can't let you stay out here, Wenzel. Come on in.

He put his arm around Waclaw. It was an arm that knew that the next days, too, would taste of rain, of rain and clouds, and of their passing. He couldn't stand to be in the cabin, he said *dobranoc* to Petrov and went to the mess hall. Fat Lúkacs stood behind the counter, and he wrung his chef's hat between his hands when he saw Waclaw, as if he saw a shadow beside him. And he heard how they lowered their voices. Mikael and Ray and Steve, someone pushed back a chair.

Wenzel, do you want to join us?

Thanks, but I won't stay.

But then he sat anyway, a long line, with an instant lemon tea, lukewarm in its paper cup. Enough silence to make their forearms stick to the tabletop. Have you guys seen these T-shirts? Bright red and green, Ray was wearing a washed-out sweatshirt with a manga print. A princess and a sword. A few feet separated his table from theirs. He noticed how they looked at him, how their eyes wandered surreptitiously over, as if it were his fault that no one was getting out the cards and they couldn't yell across the room to Lúkacs, who absently wiped at the glass as if he'd only just noticed the film of grease on the divider before the shimmering meatballs.

He wasn't sure it was the same room. He told Lúkacs to fry him up a couple of eggs, and ate them with some cold potatoes. Suddenly he was hungry. He was careful not to scratch the plate with his fork. It was no longer their mess hall, but it was the same room. At some point a new decade had begun, and they'd sat here and played, with all the strength of extinguished firecrackers. Mátyás, young enough, lively. Never before had Waclaw spent a night at these tables, never had he loved the sudden distance that surrounded them more.

The smell of cabbage and fryer grease hung in the air.

The door opened and Eugen stuck his head in.

Waclaw, they're looking for you, they're going to send a Super Puma for you, first thing in the morning, it's coming over from the mainland. Just for you. A Puma!

He heard the voices rise and knew they'd start talking about helicopters now, weighing the pros and cons of particular models, among which the Puma's superiority was unchallenged. He sat there and listened, Lúkacs was shoveling down some kind of food, then his gaze fell on the clock over the door: XI, what did that mean, eleven at night it must be, he looked at the face of the clock and felt something rising in him, he could still hear their voices, made it to the hall and into the cabin, to the metal toilet bowl where he vomited, and it was night, simply night, and he sat there and saw his hands shaking as if they were someone else's, like this night, in which he didn't belong.

Everything that followed seemed too clear and yet somehow blurry, frayed images, their edges ungraspable. After an hour-long conversation, Anderson the generous rig manager had given him the last four days of his shift off. While he spoke, Waclaw thought of the birds that imitate rain to lure worms out of the soil.

He didn't have strength to ask him. Through the window of Anderson's office Waclaw saw the men continuing to work, saw the rotary table, the colored work clothes and glaring white helmets, the water had grown still, lay there, flat, and no one came and threw a wreath in the water, a speech, anything. There was no place in his brain for a farewell without dark restaurants and brown sauce. He thought of the steel mills of the Ruhr, what he'd been told as a child about men who disappeared in the middle of the day, a white-hot heat after years spent between Carnival and grain alcohol, after the misery of the war came the silence of oak sideboards, the cramped miners' estate, lives turned to less than ash in the boiling steel of the blast furnaces. As a child, he'd carried within him the image of locker rooms, street shoes never worn again. He saw the choir at St. Cyriakus, widows lined up in their heavy suits. A parish hall filled with pies, fruit from infinite allotment gardens, black shoes smooth as washed plates. Children singing songs in Polish and German, collars starched. The waves had died down. Not even the colors were right: T-shirts, colorful helmets, hairy calves, the sea bright all around them.

Anderson asked several times if he wanted to go home. Several times Waclaw told him that the address he had listed as his emergency contact no longer existed.

Anderson said it would be good if he went back to land soon, and didn't hesitate in reporting the loss to headquarters. He held the phone to his ear. He said Mátyás's name in the middle of sentences that sounded like a list of things that were no longer needed. Perhaps he didn't understand what he was saying, perhaps he was trying to stay businesslike and matter-of-fact. From the wall gleamed a photo of some unknown crew taken with flash, the reflectors on the arms and legs of their red coveralls shining more clearly than any face. Waclaw tried to guess how old Anderson was, surely fifteen years younger than he, mid-thirties, maybe. Anderson's checked shirt slid back a bit and revealed a light, fatty hand. Everything about him was pale and hairless, and his voice had all the energy of a stick stirring up a lukewarm puddle.

He didn't know the tears Alexej had shed, missing the birth and short life of his son, he knew nothing of the languages in which each dreamed his private dreams. He spoke evenly, nodded a few times, then hung up. He reached for a yellow leather case, pulled out a fountain pen, wrote a few words, and looked at Waclaw as if he'd done something important.

He would do his best to make sure that Waclaw was transferred to another platform after the weeks on land, Anderson said.

That would be a relief for you, surely?

His smile.

What about him? Waclaw said.

Anderson looked at him in astonishment.

What about him?

He shook his head slowly and then pointed to the chart on the wall.

Mr. Groszak. You do know what these shadings mean?

For a moment they both stared at the topographical map where the test drillings and the platform were marked.

Yes, he said, absently.

Either the waves pushed him against one of the steel pontoons—he balled the fingers of his right hand briefly into a fist—or the undertow swept him away.

Anderson looked out. His mouth was also soft and he avoided Waclaw's eyes. Waclaw missed Pippo. He wondered what Pippo would have done. Pippo had hairy hands, and they could smoke together when something was wrong. Pippo knew his people. When the others laughed loudly, only a faint smile would cross his face, but his voice could get hard as the spiny fin of a perch, you could hurt yourself on it. He would never have talked with this secretary like a little puppy dog.

Anderson nodded toward the door.

The men will let me know if they see anything unusual outside.

He leaned back in his chair.

We'll be in touch. Your shuttle will be here around three.

And it was only this sudden rage that made him stand up. There was the curve of his seatback, his thumbs boring into it, and the fact that Anderson fell silent when he saw him standing like that, yes, frightened, but more the way one is frightened by a bug or by an unexpected noise, as if he might suddenly jump at him. Waclaw just stood there and stared.

Don't be stupid, Anderson said softly, biting his lip. I mean it.

On the way to the cabin Waclaw suddenly felt heavy, as if he hadn't slept in weeks. He tore open their closets and threw their things together, stuffed them into the bags, then carried them out, both bags, on deck, into the sudden sea air.

He climbed up to the helideck, and the drilling continued, they pumped more drilling fluid into the depths to keep up the pressure, the Puma wasn't there yet, and the bags were heavy. Only Petrov accompanied him to the landing deck, he stood bent like an oak and spoke little.

Waclaw leaned against a wall, saw the others continuing to work, the crane swung around, the wind was still cold, his face felt hot, his eyes welled up. Behind him he heard steps on the stairs, saw Francis, still filthy in his overalls.

Wenzel, he said, taking a breath. What did they say, where are you going?

Francis took off his gloves and let them fall next to him like two dead fish. Waclaw could see the line of his boots under his pant legs. Everything seemed too big, the clothes, the helmet, Francis reminded him of an animal whose fur had gotten wet, making it look suddenly pitiful and sick.

What are they going to do now? he asked. What will they do with—he faltered, as if he didn't dare to continue.

With Mátyás, that's still his name, Waclaw said softly.

It felt wrong to play this role. As he talked, he listened almost curiously to his own voice, which sounded unusually firm.

They'll do nothing.

He could see Francis pursing his lips, his skin shone greasily, as if he hadn't washed in days. Do you remember that boat a couple years ago? Off Mehdya? They were almost to land. Three of them were never found. And divers—

Waclaw waved him off.

Are you coming back? Francis asked quickly.

He was nervous. The shift was about to start up again and he had to get back. Even after so much time he still had the feeling that he couldn't afford to make a false step in front of the others.

Of course. Waclaw clapped him on the shoulder. *Sure.*

Then he watched him climb back down to the deck and cross the bridge to the drill floor. It gave him a pang to see him like that, already back with the others.

The Puma didn't come till evening.

This isn't Mexico.

The sentence crossed his mind several times, but he didn't know what to make of it. This wasn't Mexico, and the ocean was calm, but Mátyás wasn't there.

✦ ✦ ✦

What remained that evening of the platform was a small light on the waters, a dark horizon that stretched and stretched. He leaned against the glass with double hearing protection, a sweaty survival suit, the motor vibrating above him. He saw the bright spots, the gas flares and illuminated structures far below, growing ever blurrier.

And as he looked at the bright spots, he had to think of his father, of the garret and the oval window. The tremor of his dust-eaten lungs as Waclaw sat with him, a fear in his eyes that couldn't be reconciled with the hand that stroked his arm comfortingly. He asked Waclaw to tell him of another ocean, one that was nothing like the Baltic, with its dim cutters and cabins. He let Waclaw tell him of the sand that the Saharan winds carried over the water, which crunched between their teeth during the days, and Waclaw named coastlines, dunes of the finest sand right on the ocean. They spoke of traveling, to places where no one would follow them. *Iść tam, dokąd nikt nie idzie za tobą*, his father whispered, and Waclaw nodded. *Go where no one will follow you.* He tried to be strong, as he'd always been strong, and then they sat for a long time in the half-light of the room, which was so small that lying in bed he could touch the far wall. A few times his father drifted into a light sleep, then opened his eyes and said Waclaw's name.

The helicopter lurched through this sky, the helicopter would find a coast and land where a boat would bring him to the nocturnal harbor of Tangier.

The crouched running under the rotor blades with two duffel bags. The bags lay next to each other on the back seat of the taxi as the car drove off in the direction of the cutter. A light rain ran in red streams through the dust on the windshield. They drove. Low barracks with wire fences, now and then he saw the barred windows of workshops with car lifts behind them bathed in cold nocturnal light, a few well-secured warehouses. It was one of those industrial areas near the coast that looked like they were used only for scrap metal and car dealerships. He was tired. Next to him, the driver was chewing something, and he heard the sound of the windshield wipers. They drew streaks across the glass. And there were raindrops that lit up in these foreign streets, they got wiped away, and no one noticed. New ones would come.

2

Tangier

The ocean smelled of salt and oil, the slight rain had only increased the odor. Engines and outboard motors lay between the tin huts and from behind a high fence he heard the whimpering of two dogs who were meant to keep watch at night. From here it was only a few hours to the harbor of Tangier, a trip Waclaw knew well. It was a small cabin cruiser and the driver paid him no mind. There was a pain in his back again, and he tried not to think about it. The buckles on his bag were worn and dull.

The boat steered through the bay into the fishing harbor, agleam with yellowish light. The driver reduced their speed, and as they chugged softly past the other boats, Waclaw saw flies and moths dancing like white shadows around the floodlights of the harbor, strangely beautiful against the dark night. The shimmering of all the years that added up to nothing, surfacing without order in the narrow cone of light.

There were endless rows of little fishing boats moored close to one another. The driver let the boat float in until it stopped with a jolt against another. Instead of throwing a line, he held on to the other boat with both hands and gave Waclaw a nod. Waclaw hurried to heave over the two duffels, following them to the other side with a last long step. A bit of light fell between the two boats on the otherwise oil-black water, voices came from the shadows under the low concrete buildings. His helmet, which hung from the duffel, gave a distinctly hollow sound as it hit the side of the boat. That morning Waclaw had searched everywhere for the big *Thunder Horse* sticker—a red horse on the plastic—but Mátyás's helmet was nowhere to be found. Only his headband, still damp, which Waclaw had hurriedly stashed with the other things. He was barely to the other side when he heard the motor start. The shadow of the boatman had slipped back behind the steering wheel, Waclaw saw him maneuvering carefully through the rows of ships, and soon the boat could no longer be heard.

In the fishing harbor everything was as it had always been, the lights were dim, and it seemed far from the customs area, where the sound of yapping dogs hung permanently in the air. The mood here had changed since they'd rented the room a few years ago. Merchants on the streets sold cheap synthetic blankets that people draped around their shoulders like the shepherds in old pictures. They'd spent New Year's here, among too many faces who didn't know what a new year would mean for them. They'd stood between them on the cliffs to watch the distant glow of fireworks from across the strait.

The pier swayed, and he avoided looking to the side at the dark shadows under the awnings until he had the harbor behind him. The mild smell of tobacco filled his nose, soon he reached the street and walked up the hill to the city wall, accompanied by the sound of his own steps. This was the beginning of the alleys, which opened and branched for so long that it seemed all the haggling and noise of the merchants was just a distraction, a curtain before a picture whose depth one can only occasionally glimpse.

✦   ✦   ✦

The streets were still alive: small, windowless shops with merchants sitting out front. A woman shelled peas in a small, dirty storeroom, next to her a boy slept on a crate. Waclaw knew the way. It was a room they'd rented in a colonial building at the edge of Tangier's old city. It was one of the few places they had together—determined primarily by the accident of its proximity to the airport and water— and it was their first place after Mexico, after Katrina and the storms, and for a while there were rumors that here off this coast, as in Brazil, one had only to bore through the salt crust to reach a massive oil reservoir. All that had been found was some gas on the mainland. They'd kept the room anyway. A port of call where they could leave whatever there was no room for in the lockers, whatever didn't fit with the bright shine of the water, where they were forced together with the others for two, three weeks, once again.

Mátyás called the room Haven, after a tanker that had sunk off the coast of Liguria, and in fact it was like a place that occasionally suc- cumbed to the waves, when they came back after weeks to switch out their things and then lay themselves down behind the closed shutters to sleep for a long time. It was still warm. The sound of a few last Parchís players drifted up from the café, he saw their outlines in the bluish neon light. Waclaw heard the dice hitting the glass, otherwise all was nearly still. He let both bags fall, only the hinge creaked loudly as he leaned against the door. He took the steps quickly, without turn- ing on the light.

The bathroom in the hallway belonged to their room. As he passed, he thought he saw a bare shoulder behind the yellowish ribbed pane, someone was changing their clothes, but it couldn't be Mátyás.

He opened the door to the room. Some light fell in from the

streetlamp, outlining the low grate on the outside of the window. There were two large wardrobes, one on each side of the room. Both were closed—last time they'd had a few extra minutes to tidy up. The mattress leaned against the window. He dragged it to the opposite corner, laid it next to the wall.

Then, a bit later, there was soft music coming from the street, still the same darkness. He was no longer someone who belonged to the left-hand wardrobe or to the right, he stood up, went to the window, then out, and stopped where the alley grew steep, stood a long time, searching. Soon they would just be two wardrobes. High above the whitewashed façades he saw the stars of the Big Dipper tipping forward, and he wondered why people wanted to see a dipper, of all things, in these stars, and why the dipper was empty.

He had been lying awake for a long time when he reached for the little floor lamp next to the mattress. He sat up. The two bags lay in front of the wardrobe. He thought of Petrov, who had held the second bag for him, the dark tobacco stains on his teeth, the zipper of his overalls that didn't close all the way, the graying chest hair underneath. The cold on their skins that had reminded them both that they were still there, while the Puma flew around the platform, lower than usual, for a few moments its searchlights slid over the water like the anxious scribbling of a child. Just the noise, and the fact that Petrov stood next to him, the Puma coming to rest on its skids, both of them yelling something, pressing the hearing protection to their ears.

It was hot. He took off his second sock. On his sole there was still a brownish mark from their cabin. Dust and sweat.

+   +   +

It was still dark when he pressed open the door to the roof. A cottony fog lay in the distance over the bay. He was so tired and groggy he could hardly keep his eyes open, he didn't want to sleep. He wanted to be far from himself. To shut himself out, like one shuts out a dog begging for the last piece of meat. The outlines of the room had been too sharp in the darkness. He felt the cool air where the blanket didn't cover his arms and ankles, the frame of the metal chair pressed his sides. His head nodded to his chest a few times.

It grew light slowly. Above him the hurried bellies of the birds, the bright lines they drew taking off from the steep walls of the Portuguese fortress, down over the antennas and nested roofs to the harbor. The dirty gray-white of the air conditioners, the cacti in pots on the roofs. Dew lay in small drops on the tile table. The light was not yet warm, the air in the distance white and foggy.

It had been almost a ritual. Every time they returned, they met on the roof, lay stretched out for a long time listening to the muffled sounds of the streets, children in sandals and the rattling of handcarts, not needing to do anything. They'd stay here in the mornings, talking little, feeling the sun growing warmer on their skin.

Now the palm trees were swaying and he wanted nothing to do with it. He heard steps on the stairs, someone opened the door from inside. A shadow followed a large basket, and he saw Darya, carrying wet laundry against her hip. She hauled the bedsheets up to the roof. Darya was short and thickset, and dark hair fell messily out of her braid in front.

She wore the long, embroidered shirt that Waclaw knew, sequins that reflected the sunlight. She laughed easily. He could sense her gaze, gliding over him and farther across the roof. He closed his eyes. She was Rasil's sister and helped to rent the rooms. At thirty-two she was still unmarried, and it had started to seem like she was always waiting for their return; she would stand near Mátyás in the courtyard when he sat smoking on one of the benches. She'd certainly heard the key last night.

He concentrated on the reedy green in the old wall, on the fig tree, clamped between two boulders. Darya set down her basket and looked over at him through the clotheslines. He pulled the blanket tighter around him and closed his eyes. From somewhere below came the smell of fire, lit in some small workshop. He began to sweat under the blanket. He kept his eyes closed as if he were just tired after a very long shift, as if everything were as it always was. Out of the corner of his eye, he could see Darya stretching to fasten the clothespins. For a while he heard the steady clinking of her bracelets. He lay there as if just dozing under a sun that was barely high enough to warm him.

There was no one. The air hung in the whitewashed alleys, the room lay in twilight behind closed shutters, outside he heard people on scooters, smelled the clouds of exhaust, a bluish smoke, he didn't move. There was the hollow space under his ribs, his hand lying atop it. It wasn't hunger. The water jug next to him was nearly empty, the blades of the ceiling fan sliced evenly through this day as if it were merely a thought; nothing offered anything resistance.

They had seen each other cry, they had seen all these countries, but measured against that, what kind of farewell remained? A brief moment by the boot room: shift change, Mátyás took off his oilskin, gray as a spider, the night had left its shadow on his face. All the others surrounded them, the smell of the drying rooms, the clammy oilskin, and Mátyás in his sweaty long underwear, his skin still warm from work, where was that now? The hurry, he had to go out, a quick hug, his overalls were damp and musty. *It's getting stronger*, Mátyás said, they hugged quickly, then Waclaw laid a hand on his warm, sweaty shoulder. Everything was steaming.

It was afternoon when he left the room. He felt the long worn-out linen shoes and the fabric of his trousers against his skin. The stands: black olives and pistachio pastries, a man next to him testing an orange with his thumb. Waclaw took money from his pocket and bought groceries just as usual, he carried the bags in his long arms and felt the weight as he walked. In the night he had remembered the Finn's accident on the *West Capricorn*, the nights with Sharam, and he'd asked himself what Sharam would have done if he had been there, and he felt like a thief, lost in the long, shady halls of his own life. The days with Sharam had lain before him like a delicate painting that had to be kept out of the sunlight. He'd taken his old telephone from the wardrobe and thought of what people had started saying about Sharam, the Persian, that he was nothing but a sad drunk, as if all that had happened twelve years ago, when everything was just beginning, had no meaning. He didn't even know which country the first numbers of Sharam's telephone number belonged to.

He sat under the high palms on the Grand Socco, a square of light stone with a fountain and palms, a flock of birds luffed up the hill where a patch of green grew among the metal workshops. He walked in the shade along the narrow street: goat and buffalo horns in big braided baskets, the dull smell of red-hot metal and coal, low walls, then the green, Mátyás on the green, his hands interlaced behind his neck, no different than last time, clearer than anything about this day he lay there, and he walked, Waclaw walked along Mendoubia Park to the calls of the muezzin from the nearby mosque, he saw the men hurrying to prayer, he walked, left it all behind him, the dirt-red minaret, stands with cloths, bags, the big rubber-like trees, the sun-bleached wooden electricity poles, old Mercedes models with long noses that slowed down next to him, *Taxi*, a few times someone called out to him, the hand of a merchant touched his arm, he walked, walked farther, carrying what he'd bought, tossed a few bits to a stray, its fur eaten away by some kind of mange.

Without meaning to, he reached the coast. Far away, the dirty gray-white of the huge hotel complexes, a few boys were playing football on the beach, their thin bodies running back and forth before a goal made of two planks, they kept missing the ball, kicking a proportionate spume of sand into the air, they rubbed their eyes, kept playing. To walk. The outline of a camel on the beach had once made him happy, long ago. And perhaps just because he was gone, he saw Mátyás's face next to him plain as day, his curls flying rebelliously in all directions, tired only in the eyes, his slightly crooked teeth. He heard his voice, but it was different, as if out of tune, the slight sunburn on his forehead.

The same man as last time sat in the darkness of the kiosk, his large-pored skin between the rows of tobacco and newspapers. Waclaw put down a few dirhams and pointed at one of the papers. On the front page, a soldier in a khaki uniform saluted, two swords crossed on the front of his peaked cap. The vendor looked at Waclaw.

New president. Egypt.

He laid his big hand over the coins.

You read Arabic? Only Arabic.

He held the newspaper in the light.

No English, he said again. He waited. Waclaw could see the man's lower lip protruding under his mustache.

Then the vendor pointed to the yellow packs that Waclaw usually bought for Mátyás.

You want?

Waclaw hesitated.

One, he said softly, and pointed to the brand.

He didn't need the cigarettes anymore. He stuck the pack mechanically in his pocket, as always. Sometimes, early, when it was already light, they'd stood here. They were on the way back, without a single chip left from the casino, and the waves were a net being cast, briefly shimmering, in vain.

Farther west the road turned away from the city, toward Rabat. A few high bushes grew there under the cliffs, their leaves already the same ocher and yellow-gray as the sand. The spot could be reached only by water. Here in summer the light multiplied into a blaze, a narrow strip of sand, and years ago Waclaw had discovered a pair of eyes in the bushes. Later Rasil had told him that half the city knew about it, that she was a hermaphrodite and had lived there for years, people brought her food and money because they believed it brought good luck. Once in winter Waclaw had seen her by the dumpsters, just a pair of shy eyes, the skin hardened from the sun. He'd thought about it later, sometimes, when he and Mátyás sat close on the warm rock, as if the light, this onslaught of light, could drive away all the weeks on deck. A seagull sailed over. It probably knew about the little gifts people brought.

A strange smell rose from the rocks as he set down the bags of groceries. He didn't try to make anything out in the shadows in the underbrush. He didn't know if it was true what people said, and he didn't care. But as he left, he had the feeling that someone was watching him, and he walked slowly, in a straight line through the sand. For a moment he saw himself, a long line, with bulging pockets, the forward-leaning gait that gave it all away, the lower vertebrae, third and fourth, he kept walking. When he finally turned around he could see only the bushes where he'd set the bag down. Just the seagulls in low circles over the cliff. Waclaw walked. The narrow strip of sand ended and he was on the road again. It was too loud to call Sharam. There was hardly enough space to walk at the side of the road, he saw his own reflection in the bright paint of the little car. The coastal cliffs here were made of bright calcarenite, and he noticed how the word made him reel. A warm, salty wind came from the sea.

It was a memory, this walking, streets punctured with potholes, unlit courtyards. He knew this smell of piss in the stone corners of the streets, the grimy house fronts, bark peeling from the trunks of the trees. Around the next curve the white dome of the radar station emerged from the green like a faded soccer ball, a pale cap stuck on the top of a tower, the cliffs and trees looming, observing everything that moved on the strait.

He walked up the hill to where the wide street led past the stadium, where the overgrown graves of the Muslim cemetery lay behind a long white wall. A group of young men stood in front of the stadium. They looked toward the center of the circle they formed, taking no notice of the thin man who hurried by, bent forward as if walking into the wind.

In the evening he'll no longer know what he was doing there. The street was empty, the first villas crouched behind sprinkled lawns, an ornamental seam before the land fell steeply to the sea. Narrow paths were hewn into the stone between the villas, slippery on rainy days but now it was fine, the blue opened wide to the Atlantic where a few fishing boats bobbed, great distances between them. They were tiny, and his head throbbed, clouds had gathered, it was getting hazy. The smell of freshly cut grass wafted away over a wall.

The path ended, and he climbed slowly down the cliffs; a few times he slipped and had to hug the stone to keep from losing his balance.

Waclaw sweated. He had to jump down the final few yards and the wet sand hardly gave. He let himself fall forward and stayed lying there. The water approached, he felt the cold on his hands and forearms. The waves slapped loudly against the stones and split. Some trash danced on the water.

To scream. To simply lie there. His vertebrae, the third, the fourth. He saw Mátyás before him, the unfathomable exhaustion with which they'd sat here before the shift had begun, heavily clad in rain gear, here on the beach, Waclaw's legs stretched out, Mátyás's head on his shoulder, and then later, once he'd fallen asleep, on his thigh, the wind so strong it seemed to be working to make a place for them, the grainy sand blowing over the edge of the little depression in which they lay. He saw the waves lapping, the endless patterns of froth when the water withdrew. And Mátyás slept, heavy on his leg, slept off the weeks he'd spent up there, for the third time now, on the North Sea, the dampness in his clothes and the boundless need for sleep at four in the morning, when the body had long since cried out that nine hours in the icy wind was too much, knowing that the three to come as the first light dawned would be infinitely more difficult. Waclaw had spent the time in a little village on the east coast of England, he'd waited for him, in a town that seemed to consist only of rough men and identical gray stucco houses, and he'd been happy to have him by his side again, Mátyás, who took extra shifts, restlessly, and he didn't need to explain to Waclaw the exhaustion that had pressed him into the pillow for nearly three days, in something like a coma. When he'd woken up they'd gone out to eat or had ordered the warm, overcooked rice that counted as Thai food here. They'd laughed about it, and Waclaw hadn't mentioned the cans of baked beans that had kept him alive in the previous dreary two weeks. Every night he'd silently cursed his back and the vertebrae, but he never spoke of it. He needed rest, the doctor he never asked would have said. If it weren't for Mátyás he would barely have left the house. Mátyás had told him little of *Troll*, the new platform, other than that it was a dingy hole and that his roommate was a solid, dry family man. Seven photos, Mátyás said, and neither of them laughed.

People told awful stories of the North Sea platforms: that the rust spread more quickly than four men could fight it, and that the exhausted oil fields left cavities, unstable areas, it was possible for the casing in the borehole to break off, and then no drilling fluid in the world could stop the hot gases that surged upward through the porous layers next to the standpipes. Once more he felt the warmth of their bodies on the cold, deserted sand. There was nothing, no store or café open—the locals were all holed up in the warm corners of their houses. There was only the two of them, his arm on Mátyás's body, and the damp that had slowly crept into their clothing. They'd spoken little. For a while he'd closed his eyes and felt his arm on Mátyás's rib cage rising and falling.

Behind him the rock face rose in a mountain of light yellowish stone. He sat up. The air was dismal and milky, suffused with the smell of seaweed. *Northern Dancer.* A huge freighter edged along the continent toward Gibraltar. At first he'd tried to remember the names of the ships, as if they held some great promise. *Neptune Voyager.* Waclaw had just walked a little way when something dark began to grow visible on the shore. From afar it looked like a long, shapeless sack. It was pushed just far enough up on land that the waves no longer touched it. A body, strangely heavy and distorted.

As he approached he saw that the dark skin had burst, it was stretched tight across the body. The eye had already been pecked away, the dorsal fin hung listlessly to the side, and only the mouth formed a familiar line, a kind of wave that was traced in a curved row of tiny, perfectly white teeth. They still seemed to be smiling.

The wind was warm. He saw the sand on the skin that had torn over the mouth, blisters had formed, the carcass lay on its side. The sea spit out what it no longer needed. They'd often seen porpoises on the crossing, they came up to the boats in little groups.

He tried to breathe slowly, to suppress the nausea. There was a tug in his jaw, and his stomach cramped as if everything wanted to squeeze itself out of him. A cloying hum mingled with the smell of salt water. He turned away. For a second he saw an afterimage of the body, then he walked a bit farther and leaned against the cliff. The stone was cool and Waclaw could hear the waves.

He stood there awhile. Even the cliffs behind him seemed to be looking at the spot. He saw the water reaching for the tail fin, for the unmoving weight of the body.

Something pressed against his leg. He dug out the pack of cigarettes and threw it into the sea. It didn't go far. Even while still in the air, the wind drove it back toward him. He saw the men's bright T-shirts. He saw the way everything continued: the crane, the pounding of

the pipes. He thought of Sharam. How the others would have re-
acted if he'd been there. Or someone else. He imagined some crisis
manager or other making a phone call to the village in Hungary,
and he thought of Mátyás, who always spent a long time listening to
messages from home before he came up to Waclaw on the roof. Suddenly Waclaw was in a hurry. The strip of sand between water and
cliff was so narrow here that there was nothing to do but climb. But
he slipped, and the seabirds watched him as they drew their big lazy
circles, while every haul of his arms drove a nail deep into the spot
between his vertebrae. He couldn't make it. His fingers searched for
recesses in the rock face, one time he slipped down, waded knee-
deep in the water to try a less steep route. The sun had nearly sunk
by the time he reached the upper plateau. A few shards of light, the
stone was still warm. There was a stabbing in his lungs, and the salt
water burned his skin.

Far below him lay the smiling corpse in the sand.

The sea had grown softer. The sun had sunk below the horizon.
The last light was only an inference, an afterimage of something long
gone.

There was a knock at the door. Rasil, in his eternal plaid shirt. He
peeked through the door into the dark room and asked if he should
make breakfast.

Tomorrow? Two?

Darya had clearly sent him, and clearly the question was not just
meant for him. No. No breakfast.

He looked out absently.

You need anything?

Waclaw didn't answer.

A short time later, Rasil returned.

For your hand.

He passed a bandage and a little bottle of antiseptic through the door.

Help? he asked.

No.

Rasil must have seen him on the street, a line with scraped hands under the orange trees. Only now did he notice the red welts; the old cloth pants were completely torn over his knee. The stone had been rough.

He awoke in their room. Mátyás stood there in linen shoes and shorts, but with that silly hat on his head. He must have known how beautiful he was.

3

Ahmad

Ahmad greeted him with surprise when he entered, grinned from ear to ear, then looked past him toward the door as if expecting someone else. When no one came, he continued spooning ground beans into the metal hopper. Behind him stood an ensemble of five Bunsen burners on a board blackened from coffee and heat. In the corner hung photos of him with people from the movies, men and women with puffed-up hairdos who wandered here for a few days, for whom the harbor and the body of water that divided the continents had retained something of the old exoticism that had once attracted Western intellectuals and filmmakers to its hotels like flies. They were still happy to overlook the fact that this stretch of land had changed. The café had five high arched windows, through which one could look far out to the bay. On one side gleamed hotel behemoths, the sand before them dirty by contrast. A few young people smoked. Waclaw sat by the window. Next to him a young couple drank mint tea from tall glasses while in the back, in the darkest part of the café, three young guys threw dice. One of them sang along to the melody that came through the speakers. Wisps of smoke hung in the air, and Waclaw ordered a coffee without looking Ahmad in the eyes.

Still tired?

Ahmad smiled widely as he set the tall glass with its nearly black liquid on the table before him.

This will help.

I'm fine. It just takes a while, you know how it is.

Waclaw could see from the way Ahmad was looking at him that he must look more exhausted than usual. They'd often sat here, gazing at the green roof gardens that fell toward the bay in an endless progression of smaller and smaller boxes, until the white of the highrises beyond the stretch of sand began to shimmer, and they had slowly come back to the normal rhythm of days, as the voices mingled with the music and the afternoon light settled on the folding chairs and dinged tables.

For some time there had been large screens in the corners that played BBC Wildlife films; these had always bothered them, but now Waclaw was grateful for the scenes of feeding and stalking, boa constrictors in waterholes and herds on the move, oblivious to the flat backs of the predatory cats crouching in the flat grass of the savanna.

Waclaw sat there, watching predators shaking their prey to death, and then orcas playing paddleball with half-dead seals. The films were silent, but Waclaw felt he could hear the precise sound of the bones breaking.

He avoided looking at Ahmad and kept his bandaged hand on his leg under the table. Then he stared into the smoke and drank his sweet, dark coffee.

When he stood up, an unfamiliar pressure shot through the inside of his temporal lobe. For a moment he saw the brown of the waves before him, braced himself on the table. He laid a bill on the counter for Ahmad and held fast to the handle as he opened the door. Ahmad called something after him, his voice cracking like a disappointed child's.

He walked, and he noticed how thirsty he was.

In the moment when he felt a hand on his shoulder and saw the face with its high cheekbones thrust in front of him, two impulses pierced his thudding headache: one was called flight, and urged him to run down the narrow steps into one of the alleys where the weavers spun their threads; the other, at least as strong, had no name but resembled the sleep that travelers plunge into after great exhaustion, a cold wind going through him. Together, they simply slowed him down until he stopped, as if he had vertigo and needed something to hold on to.

Immediately all the energy seemed to drain from his body, and he heard Ahmad's voice.

You guys will come tomorrow, right?

There were Ahmad's high cheekbones and the noiselessness of the steps they stood on. Flowers twined on the opposite wall, their blossoms confusingly bright.

Wenzel, what is it?

He's not coming anymore, he said.

What's wrong? Ahmad didn't let up. Will you come tomorrow?

He felt his pulse and a soft roaring in his ears.

Work, Ahmad. Don't you know. Mátyás—

He shrugged his shoulders, as if any further words would be useless.

He wasn't even sure whether he actually spoke the word *accident*, which surely belonged to the sentence, or just thought it.

He saw Ahmad's helpless eyes, felt himself pulled toward him and his whole torso briefly compressed, and heard a soft voice in his ear saying: Come back tomorrow, Wenzel.

Then Ahmad slowly released him and watched his long, uncertain steps descending the stairs, the bandaged hand that hung loose at his hip. Waclaw still felt the strength of his arms on his sides; he continued on in a daze. Alleys with leather goods and engraved brass plates, all the tea that no one would drink. Markets with their prodigal colors, scents so intense that he might once have thought they could make up for everything. Now they stood there like uniform gray boxes. Strands of glass beads in the restaurants, rattling as they were pushed aside, one after another. He moved through the woven fabrics and the rubber soles of the tourists, and all the smells of cumin, anise, and urine in the shadowed corners of the walls soon became merely the smell of a new strangeness that was spreading through him, as if he were nothing but a plain full of dry grass.

When he woke, it was already dark. He lay on the mattress, covered only with the unbuttoned shirt that he'd thrown across his back.

The lights in the street were colorful, groups of people hustled past the small shops, the light on their shoulders, fat and steam, the smell of spices in the air. Voices. Tables were set up, tiny cups of tea between the plates. Waclaw walked. A man bumped into him. He thrust past Waclaw with a heavy sack; Waclaw could see feathers under the canvas, a bit of light fell on a tan wing.

They had tried to get rid of it, to get all that filth out of their bodies— steam baths, sauna. Mátyás's urine test had already been positive for amphetamines once before their shift. Usually they had little bottles in their pockets or got someone else to give them urine, but sometimes the tests came unannounced. They'd sent Mátyás to land for four weeks: forced rest that left him surly, like an animal in a cage.

They were in Madrid, Hotel Gran Meliá, an oval lobby with low upholstered furniture and illuminated lampshades. It was like stepping into a picture that claimed to be nothing less than one's own life. Everything attained. They rented a jeep. They had four-wheel drive beneath them as they chased through the Jerte Valley: cherry blossoms, a beauty like the white face of a porcelain mask. The fields were laid out in terraces; to Waclaw it all seemed artificial. They raced along as if something were after them. As if it were a rally. They drove down from the street and up a bank, until they couldn't go any farther. Then they could lie exhausted on the washed-out stones of the river, slopes with trees and shrubbery to either side, ocher sand. They could swim where the water was still ice cold, they could laugh. Waclaw remembered how Mátyás ordered for them with his few scraps of Spanish. As if a world lay open before him. Somewhere he was going alone.

In Tangier they'd always gone to the same business hotel, the bar looked like a spy film from the nineties. Avenue du Front de Mer. That evening he walked in the same direction, this time to another of the hulking white buildings on the beach. There was a roof deck with glass railings, keyboard music that reminded him of Barbra Streisand.

Everything was too sweet.

He drank a whiskey sour and gazed at the cherry in his glass, the same the world over. The waiter hesitated for a long time before clearing his plate. Waclaw hadn't touched the food. Usually it was different, the body recovered everything that had been done to it— too little sleep, too much sea, the cabins where it could never relax, the harsh noon light between the curtains. But now the body, too, wanted nothing, as if something were different now, more final, as if nothing more were coming. He lined up plastic-colored cherries on a toothpick. Then he drove back.

The key scratched in the lock. Again, he had the feeling that Darya had been waiting for Mátyás's arrival and not his. For days he'd been buying the clothes he wore, cheap shrink-wrapped shirts from stands on the street. All just so he wouldn't have to ask her to do his washing, all because he couldn't bear the silence that surrounded her jangling bracelets.

He had decided to take a different room, and for a while the idea electrified him. In the current of the streets he once more had the feeling of going toward something. He'd scrutinized the signs advertising *Aircondition* or *B&B*, watching the guests who came unassumingly out of their doors. And he'd kept on, looking for a place where he could stop in with his heavy shoes, until the feeling he'd left with melted away.

In the harbor, the long rows of fishermen on the jetty. Finally he'd reached the freighters. Workers slept on the heavy ropes after unloading the cargo, on the decks of the tankers or on the docks. They lay in the filth of their overalls, in the pileup of days, they lay where at night the tomcats patrolled their territory, where the seagulls turned their dirty-white circles, where the ships with their unvarying loops and knots had to be moored, slack and exhausted in a fleeting shadow, and what woke them was not daylight or the distant yapping of the customs dogs, but a disquiet that lay deep beneath the smell of the clammy fishing nets. Or it came from the fishermen themselves, as they once again sanded their wood, revarnished it, and gave their boats names that would fade as quickly as they were painted. It was enough to wake you up, this disquiet.

On the way back, Waclaw walked uphill through a narrow alley: prowling cats, tall, closed doors, and two boys who ran after him and kept trying to give him their left hands. They laughed. He was one of many. He was too tired to react, and continued on, until an older man came and chased them off. No room in the world would change things. He couldn't stay.

4

Whalebones

In the square where children played during the day it was now dark, and people were sleeping in the lee of the low walls. He heard voices. Beyond, the wall that surrounded the west side of the city towered precipitously. High up, a silent orange light shimmered peacefully, for itself alone.

Birds blustered in the rubber trees of the Jewish Cemetery. The fountain lay in darkness, no one sat there any longer. It was already light over the Grand Socco as he took his telephone from his pocket and turned it on. Sharam, the Persian—they'd laughed at him when he talked of the Gulf War as if that's where the story had begun, *That's where you're from*, he'd say, or *That's where we are from*, and no one wanted to hear it. But back then, when it began, he'd kept an eye out for them, and the mere fact that everyone knew it had protected them from all kinds of trouble. Waclaw didn't even know what country this number belonged to, how late it was there, morning or night—night, like here.

Sharam picked up.

His voice was deep, as it had been back then.

Have you heard? Waclaw heard his own voice echo in the connection.

Who's speaking?

It's me, Wenzel. Have you heard?

He heard his echo again, and then a heavy breath, as if someone were sitting up in bed.

Wenzel? What is it? What should I have heard?

Sharam's English sounded clumsy, as if he hadn't spoken it in ages.

Don't you know that Mátyás—he wanted to take a breath, but instead continued on quickly—that Mátyás is gone?

Sharam was saying something but Waclaw still heard the echo of what could be said so easily, in one word, *gone*.

Wenzel, Wenzel, are you there? Them bastards! Wenzel? Where are you?

Sharam was awake now and Waclaw heard him curse, as he always had. It was no relief, he didn't know what he had been hoping for.

Sharam, he said, I'm tired.

And hung up.

As he let himself fall on the mattress in the corner of the room, he wondered if he'd ever been so stupid as to give Sharam their address in Tangier.

The beacon on the far shore of the bay flashed steady and white. Through the curtainless windows he saw three young girls shaking their hair, sparring with one another in pink sweaters, arms whirling in the light, last games before bed. There were voices like a dull roar, a few engines, and beyond it all, the shimmering distance of the bay. He was restless. The weariness was like a lacquer over everything. Even the noises sounded more muffled. He saw the two big bags. He hadn't touched them again. Nor did he want to open the wardrobes, but there was this rage whenever he thought of Anderson and the calls from the company headquarters, where they would never say anything except that their hands were tied and that one had to wait and see, personal negligence, they'd think up something to keep the financial damage to a minimum, as if that were all that was worth talking about. But in the village, they'd want to have a few of Mátyás's things. Not the expensive shoes, not the fine shirts, what could he bring with him to this hole in Hungary that Mátyás had so rarely spoken of. He packed a rattan ball, a few clothes, a bullwhip from Mexico, papers, a calendar. Waclaw brought everything that he'd need for himself back on deck, and then last of all, the animal from the windowsill. Then, quickly, he shut the wardrobe.

Let no one in. I'll pay for it—no one.

It was still early, and his voice sounded harsher than he'd meant it to. He was loud, but Rasil just smiled as if he hadn't quite understood.

I have to take care of something, Waclaw said. I'll take the key.

Rasil nodded. Your hand, good?

He could have shaken him, just for some reaction other than that smile. Rasil had always denied it, but a few times they'd found the room altered when they came back weeks later. They'd fought about it: It's only a room, Mátyás had said, and couldn't understand why Waclaw's voice cracked with a kind of blazing disappointment. No, actually, it's not. Perhaps Shane, with his clawlike yellow gloves, had understood far more quickly what the room meant to the two of them.

Rasil had returned to staring at the little screen, a yellow curtain behind him repeatedly granted a glimpse of the inner courtyard, two white plastic chairs.

He stopped by Café Baba again, but this time he didn't submit to an embrace. You tell the girl. He said goodbye to Ahmad and walked out of the half-light and the strong smell of roasted coffee. And yet as he carried the things down the hill, amid the ferocious odor of fish and the yapping of the border mutts, he had a feeling, as if he all he could do was head toward him, nothing more, just hold a course that was already blurry. He had an hour before the ferry left.

It was a few years ago, when the great bubbles of real estate speculation had just burst; on television people were staring at their now-worthless driveways, and the *West Capricorn* lay a scant hour south by plane from Houma, in the Gulf of Mexico. Summer had begun. Mátyás was new on deck, and there'd been the incident with the Finn. It was one of the last platforms where spinning chains were still used on the drill pipes, the Finn got an arm caught, it all happened so fast.

They met after the shift in the back corner of the gym. It was a matter of carrying on somehow, oil prices were stable, but on land people were being fired all over the place, and none of them could afford to lose a job. The official story was that the Finn had gotten dehydrated and lost his concentration, like a hiker on the descent. He'd simply been spun away: like in an epileptic fit his head had been dashed over and over against the structure, his legs got wedged against the rotary table, and his mouth—after a short break they'd gone back to work, and only followed Sharam to the gym that evening.

Five young guys, the new ones still shaky after that afternoon. Sharam was the oldest, and Waclaw, too, had been at it awhile.

The Finn had long since been transported to land, and they sat with a lemon one of them had injected with vodka before departure, squeezing drops of it into their mouths.

There was something ceremonial about the meeting, the room was different, the smell of sweat still hung in the air, they sat behind the treadmills and barbells, and Sharam laid something silly in the middle—his helmet—and Philippe, who'd shipped on from Madagascar, placed his telephone beside it, glowing, and when it went out they'd push another button, so they had a helmet and a glow and the circulating lemon between them. The telephone played a song, they listened to it at least three times before Sharam began to speak. He pressed his curls down with the flat of his hand, but the ends frizzed up, and his temples were bare with age under the strands.

The mood was solemn as he prepared to speak, like in church.

The land we're here for is covered with whalebones, darkness, and silence.

He turned his eyes to the floor, as if trying to keep from laughing. Then he raised them. Now he looked them all in the eye.

You're here because a few crazy-ass engineers invented the best drilling technology in the world.

He paused and looked around. Philippe smiled at him, but Sharam didn't seem to notice.

But not for you, he continued.

They were hanging on his every word. As if all the warmth of the deck were concentrated here, a bright spot, the only one for nautical miles. They knew the stories that were told about him. Iranian speedboats had shot up his platform in the days when Saddam Hussein's poison gas crept over the northern plains, scaring back an army of five hundred thousand poorly trained Iranians. He'd lived through the Gulf War from beginning to end, had seen the Kuwaiti oil fields go up in flames one by one, Minagish, Burgan. He knew the names of the blasters who used extinguishing explosions to deprive the flames of oxygen. Sharam was one of the last of the true blues, a driller they looked up to, someone who could say things like: you're worth nothing—and they endured the long pause before he continued—if you don't stick together.

He talked of the oil fields and of the wars. Why is it our company drilling out here and not another? They listened. Only Philippe interrupted him. I'm not going back, he said. Even if it gets harder.

He saw something like rage flash in Philippe's eyes.

Where should I go—on a fishing trawler, to harvest the sea? The Itremo mines? Really?

Philippe pulled his hood over his baseball cap and drank another sip.

Sharam shook his head slowly.

I'm just saying that *we* are all we've still got out here. And this platform has a history, just like us, and if we don't know it we're fucked.

Francis laughed. We're fucked either way—that's the deal.

And how they fuck us. Philippe burst into laughter, fluttered his eyelashes and started to dance, wiggling his hips wildly. Sharam's *no seriously, seriously* could be heard a few more times, but even he seemed content with his chewing tobacco and his legs stretched out in front of him, flip-flops, and all of them leaning against the walls, as if they were on a journey, as if they were on a boat or a trip, just setting out together. Eventually the night grew long, and they stayed there until they had to sleep for the next shift.

The next morning, they stood in front of the rotary table a quarter of an hour before the beginning of the shift, helmets under their arms, facing east, where at a quarter to seven all the light was already blazing.

They never spoke much of that day, but from then on, they met in the corner of the gym, behind the fitness bikes—Philippe called it a *gated community*—and the meetings were a homecoming. They saw new images of soot and burning oil, flares in the dead of night, and perhaps it was only because of the narrowness of their cabins and the continual weariness that they saw only the gigantic flames in the center, dark orange and sooty. They squashed the wads of tobacco under their upper lips and lay there, bits of dirt stuck in their ears.

Waclaw had thought so often of these gatherings with Sharam

that the memory felt hollow and spent, and even Mátyás had rolled his eyes in annoyance when Waclaw brought it up. We're not a fucking club, Mátyás had said in a voice that sounded brittle and exhausted. Three times they managed to all work together. Philippe was the first to break away, then the Bosnian from Tuzla, finally the well was finished and they had to move on, and the next time they came on deck, twenty miles to the north, only Sharam was left. It was winter before they saw Francis again, pale and haggard. He kept close to them as much as he could. They tried a few times to revive the meetings, but it seemed that they were all too tired and worn down. The Sharam of today had none of that. His voice had sounded like nothing.

The boat left around ten thirty. From the stone steps beyond passport control Waclaw had looked at the new town, at the huge white high-rises, stuck in the scorching hot earth by some European architects in the seventies. Gigantic masses of hot concrete, fluttering laundry and the absence of color. A friend of his, Akhil, lived there with his family on a floor with narrow rooms, endless kitchens where sweet fruit juice dripped onto the floor.

He watched the waiters, busy selling potato chips and drinks to the passengers. They'd checked his passport twice, and then a third time on deck. The ferry would reach the Spanish mainland in less than two hours. And while the coast out the window became a distant bright strip, he thought of the traces of glaciers on the ocean floor, of the continents moving toward each other at the pace of a fingernail's growth. He thought of birds of prey that drop their victims down deep canyons, there to finish them off, of inflatable boats made of porous rubber. Somewhere out there he heard the dull smack of Darya beating the laundry dry. Only inside him was it quiet.

5

Budapest

The hotel exhaled the severity of the previous century. Express trains from Vienna, champagne drunk from crystal glasses, silk-lined suitcases with heavy clasps. Brass-colored balustrades. One gives one's luggage to the porter rather than dropping it in a corner as Waclaw did. The porter looked at him questioningly and he forced a smile. Then he glanced at the door as if someone else were still coming, but no one came.

A single room? Do you have a reservation? What must he look like—grimy and worn down, one didn't travel to such places with a duffel bag, and the light of the chandeliers was too sharp. Two nights, he said, not knowing how he planned to get there, to this countryside, *bald like old fur, the hairs ripped out*. That's how Mátyás had described it, this land, Bócsa, the village: a hole from which he had only ever wanted to escape. Waclaw traveled with these words, like an extra language, different from the ugly Texas English from the platforms that sounded like barking, a language to keep others away. He climbed the winding stairs and knew that Mátyás would have called the balustrades *golden*; the Danube beyond the high window, wide and summery and sluggish. He unpacked the animal and set it on the window. It had been with him for years, *zsírkő*, Mátyás called it—lard stone—*but it's the only fatty thing about you*. This animal, with the head of a lion and frog's feet, with which it would no longer hunt in any country on earth. He heard it snarl.

The previous evening he'd seen the glow of the great Gibraltar refinery, the lights of the harbor on car windows; he'd sat in the parking lot and stabbed his fork into the last bit of tuna in the can. In the darkness, the cranes moved in the container port, and he stayed and waited, until at five in the morning the Boeing's engines started drawing in air and jet fuel was injected into combustion chambers.

From above, he'd seen the Danube between the hills, eating through the land with its innumerable twists, an early light falling on it. He'd schlepped the bags through the streets, crossed the Chain Bridge, and saw the lion on the left side leering at him. He wasn't sure if he belonged here, in this Budapest that Mátyás had told him of, as of a beautiful woman with a cough.

A bottle of mineral water stood on the dresser next to his bed. He poured the whole thing into a beer glass. It was the first time in ages that he'd heard the bubbles bursting, the first time it had been so quiet. The sound reminded him of the clinking of tiny ice particles that Mátyás had told him about, at night on the *Ekofisk*, where the snow drove almost horizontally against the floodlights: silent, huge flakes. He lay on the bed until it was pitch-dark.

He went into the bathroom. For a while he stood on the warm tiles, hesitant. Then he turned on the tap, unwrapped a small piece of soap from its paper, held it under the water, and drew it along the underside of his left arm until the few armpit hairs were lathered. In the big mirror he saw the clear lines of his collarbone, above which stretched a strip of bronze skin, burned again and again over the course of countless summers. He saw his long neck and the beginnings of his shoulder muscles, the length of his arms, on which few hairs gleamed, his flat chest and the corset of his ribs. He propped himself hesitantly on the bathtub before plunging his head in the water. The slight scent of chlorine pressed into his nose.

It was night when he left the hotel. The Erzsébet Bridge was illuminated, seagulls circled through the lights and disappeared screeching into the darkness. Far away on the hills down the bank were several buildings; the lights should have made them look bigger, but the night swallowed them, like dust motes on a school stage.

The Danube flowed darkly past. Below, the water was an old, sluggish murmur against the concrete foundations of the bridge. The eddies swallowed themselves and glided by, fists that couldn't close, but were silently torn away.

In the morning, he stood at the open window. Below the Gellért, the lit yellow trams drove along the riverbank, bringing the first round of people to their jobs in bakeries and ticket kiosks, a bit of the warmth from their beds still living in the narrow space between neck and collar. It was almost a relief to see the little women in their padded jackets, their short steps, the mundane trips over these bridges. The day arranged itself along the river, the bells tolled, the stoplights changed. He left the window open to hear as much of it as he could.

But as he walked through Budapest, the thrashing and chasing within him hadn't subsided. He took the small streets parallel to the river; shop window dummies looked past him and it seemed unreal, everything, the whole last few years. As if he were already far from it all. Or as if somewhere deep within him the time with Mátyás was intertwining with another disappearance, for which he'd long lacked words. It was a throbbing, dull and distant, as if he were leaning on a dam and hearing the stormy movement of a few stones against the ground on the other side. Like a hollow space that, between all the new places, he'd failed to notice. He thought about this as he sat on a stool in a Budapest tailor's tiny workshop, watching him sew a blind hem in fine woolen cloth.

He didn't know exactly why he'd stopped in front of the workshop. He'd sought shade by the walls of the building, where little rivulets flowed from terra-cotta pots over the paving stones, and since morning he'd been walking around aimlessly. He'd sat in a café where a large painting hung on the wall: two three-masters in full sail, a raging sea with a tremendous tentacle coiling out of it, while beyond, scaly heads emerged from the water and opened their maws in various directions. At the lower edge were creatures with long tails and fangs, and in the upper left-hand corner, a single lighthouse was painted in the clouds.

He knocked back his coffee.

The heat on the streets was like a wall.

He was in no hurry to get to the village. He stopped in an alley. It was as if what he saw had slowed his steps. Nothing more than a shop window displaying a single suit jacket; it hung on a wooden dummy, and there was something so inexplicably calm about it that he gazed at it for a long time. He thought of the men's colorful T-shirts, the glow of the work clothes. The heat hung between the buildings, and the movements of the passersby were reflected in the pane, passing across the glass, behind which lay a deep, indistinct space.

After a while he noticed a movement farther back in the workshop, where it dropped down to a lower level. It was the first time he saw Jány, with a pincushion clamped on his arm. He looked up from his fabric and came slowly to the door. His fine white hair was combed back, and the scant light of the street was reflected on his forehead. *Jány. Úriszabó* was written in white letters on the window; from inside it read backward.

The tailor brought him a glass of water. It was still in the room. Waclaw looked at the dark cloth, nodded a few times. He'd need five days, Jány said, for a jacket, trousers, and vest.

Do you want a vest?

Waclaw nodded. For your size—we'll plan an extra foot and a half. Four running yards.

Waclaw chose a nine-ounce fresco in dark blue with oxblood stripes. When, after placing his order, he continued to stand in the room, Jány pointed to the stool by the window. Waclaw sat. It smelled of heated wool and horsehair, and he heard the crackling of evaporating water from the bottom of the heavy iron. He saw Jány's slight hands under the bright light of the table lamp. The tailor measured again and again, his eyes assessed the length of Waclaw's arms as if they might manage to poke out from the bottoms of the sleeves if he didn't pay close attention. Adventitious shoots. That was the name for the shoots plants form in darkness; they grow quickly toward a light they hope to find farther off. They are pale shoots, thin and prone to sickness, and they start to form leaves only when there is enough light. Waclaw had always been thin. On the gravel paths at the edge of the mines, beneath the dark smoke that discolored the windowsills. Even in all the years at sea his upper body had never developed anything in common with the rounded shoulders of the other men. The tailor measured again and again, as if he couldn't trust his measuring tape. Waclaw stayed on the low wooden stool as if he had no other place in the world.

It's very good cloth, Jány said. What do you need the suit for?

Waclaw said nothing. He looked out. He looked at the frothing brown in the floodlights, the rainy light over the sea the next morning, the water that grew dark far below.

Jány pushed the scraps of cloth into a heap, considering. A woman walked by on the street, the afternoon light on her felt hat, she carried a bouquet of flowers. He saw how she set her walking stick carefully in the depressions of the cobblestones.

It was an accident, Waclaw said finally.

He said Mátyás's name and spoke of a sea bright as a blast furnace.

It had rained. In the evening, the sun appeared in long rays; a crow landed before him on a streetlamp, the soft noise of claws on metal. He had walked to the island in the Danube, a yellow bridge. Beyond it a man lay on a park bench, his backside hanging over the edge, his hair long and gray. He held a radio up to his ear. This thing with music, even on the water: as if they'd always been somewhere else, already on land, and the interruptions were only dreams.

Jány was proud of his gabardine. Waclaw was waiting for him the next morning in front of the workshop, he watched as he hung his tweed sports coat on a hanger, breathed on his glasses, and disposed of yesterday's coffee filter with his sharp fingers. On the stool, Waclaw could feel the pain in his back increase and disappear, he saw the platform as it grew smaller beneath him.

Around midday, the brass bells over the shop door jingled urgently: three men in coats, with briefcases. One of them was a bit older, with a wide jaw, big solid ears, an almost aggressive healthiness. He wore expensive buckled shoes and he stood there as if he could appraise it all in a single glance: Jány, the man on the stool, the unswept corners with scraps of cloth, the half-light, the worn wood of the mannequin. He spoke the name of the London tailor from Savile Row where he had shopped, drawing it out with luxurious pleasure. Then he looked at some jackets, and Jány pulled out his best fabrics, the Scottish ones. Finally, he wrote down prices on a squared notepad, and then scrawled bigger numbers after it. The future was a tall, slender figure, and it could hurry past. Waclaw heard Jány persuading the man in quiet Hungarian. His companions leafed through books of fabric samples, bored, Jány talked faster, and on his stool Waclaw looked at the floor, because he knew that it was only a few steps to the street and there was no need to look back. Soon afterward they were gone, and only the bells chimed after them.

The tailor returned to his corner, picked up the iron, then set it back down again. He leaned on the trestle with both hands. His narrow nostrils trembled. Suddenly he seemed tiny between his dummies. I must ask you to leave now. Come back tomorrow. He remained standing like that until Waclaw had left the store. The light on the street was too bright to make out anything inside.

That evening at the Gellért he walked barefoot up the stairs to the baths connected to the hotel. Mátyás had told him of the colorful tiles and the steam. On the way to the pool, in front of the tall lockers, and amid the distinct smell of chlorine, Waclaw stopped. Through a window in the hallway he could see the bathers below, the paddling of white legs in greenish light. It made him think of manatees. At a zoo. He wasn't ready for other bodies. He took a hot bath in his room, but he couldn't sleep. He shoved a pillow under his back, but even that didn't help.

6

Chips

The thin man had hardly moved from his stool for the past five days, and he barely spoke unless spoken to. He had seen Jány coughing secretly into a napkin, seen how his fingers occasionally trembled. He wasn't in a hurry, Waclaw had said.

He had long since lost track of what the individual pieces meant. And as he watched the tailor join the padding, the horsehair canvas interfacing, the pockets and all the seams, watched him bring the blind stitching and layers, from right to left, into their proper form, where all of this would remain hidden inside the jacket, he wondered whether one day a moment would come when someone would flip over a life, and all the individual layers would finally form a whole. Whether Milena would be one piece, and Mátyás. And whether someone who was missing would still be a part of it, like padding that remains in place forever.

They were in the middle of a fitting, the future seams still run through with basting thread, when Jány looked up.

His people. The people here. They probably won't believe it was an accident. They won't accept it. Jány pierced the cloth, and as he talked it looked as if he were walking through his own personal landscape, as it was because he made it so.

What they believe won't change anything. Waclaw's voice was rough.

You just ought to know.

To prepare myself?

Jány shrugged his shoulders.

I don't know. People here react differently. Too much has happened. Why do you think it was an accident?

Jány was supposed to sew: the lining with two-toned thread, a ticket pocket deep enough to keep his key in. An ivory nut button. Nothing more.

And Waclaw was uneasy, restless before the sparkling riverside promenade. Everything he saw was like a question: swift water, the couples, the boats, what had Mátyás told him, what else were these streets but his words, what did it mean that those words remained, at six thirty in the morning when his alarm went off, the night's shadows still on his face, sometimes Mátyás would lie beside him for a few minutes before they had to go out. He walked, the puffy-faced homeless people in the Astoria subway tunnel, he rode to the other side, walked up the hill, a big church, hordes of tourists in cheap ponchos, it had started to rain, he walked, farther, the City Park, the Danube to his left, the parliament, the rain hung like lead, heavy over the plain, he felt his shoes getting soggy, the leaves had begun to drip, then statues that seemed to be wrestling with each other, marble-white, gleaming, a black swastika scrawled on a forehead, already half washed out by the rain, he walked, his shirt stuck to his skin, and by the time he reached the Gellért he was cool.

He took a hot shower, then it was night and he was drunk, the alcohol was wasted, it helped nothing. Waclaw called a taxi, rode along the river and along the other side. He slipped through the darkness once more, not knowing whether it was an accident. He got out of the car, the flashing letters on the door spelled *Tropicana*.

The ceiling of the casino was unexpectedly low. He wanted gambling to be like vomiting, vomiting grief, vomiting love, he didn't want to win, he wanted it to get quieter, wanted to lose himself. A woman smiled at him, withered palm branches hung on the walls, everything breathed the air of a desperate trip to the tropics. Bodies, too tired for the sudden heat, drifted in the light, got stranded in the net of slot machine lights and the tinkling of one-armed bandits and reels, in the light of a world that quickly kept turning. His bed was empty, *what makes you think it was an accident*. Waclaw stood at the bar and swallowed it down, Jány hadn't sat with that overgrown child who explained the storm to him and the depths, the ocean floor, where the epochs and particles drifted down like snow. The room had nine tables. The croupier at the first table wore a shirt that made his arms look strangely short. Next to him, a Japanese businessman followed the game with concentration; perhaps for one brief moment he understood the secret law of the numbers.

Waclaw placed three black chips on the square. The wheel spun, a shimmer like mother-of-pearl, no souvenir, nothing that could be brought back, a life left behind. The ball sought its number, stopped, no one bet on numbers, numbers were a waste.

He saw Mátyás's tense face, *come on, six, come on*. The tension was physical when a lot was at stake. What they lost justified every further week out there, a rhythm of land and sea, carpeting that swallowed their steps. He looked at the chips, the ball came to rest, he didn't care.

Thirty-five to one for the gentleman.

The croupier pushed the chips toward him with an elegant motion.

For you, he repeated. Are you placing a bet?

Waclaw looked at his hands.

Everything they went out for.

Sir? Then I must ask you to step back from the table.

The rake again, this time the croupier pushed the chips toward him with emphasis. He took them. Right, Waclaw, you take them and leave. Take them, take them away.

He didn't want them. They lay before him on the bar. He drank. With a chip he bought another drink, clear and strong. His eyes watered. At the next table, someone was losing. Mustache, threadbare suit. The unhappiest eyes of the whole night. A thin student, looking lovelorn, stood beside him and pushed small amounts back and forth between the squares. It was too early for the real players.

The hallway to the toilets was decorated with dry palm branches as well. For a moment he saw the churchyard, St. Cyriakus, the heavy old women, singing children, Palm Sunday. He had to smile. He was drunk. The chips in his pocket pressed against his leg. He would place them, he would keep them, it didn't matter. He laid them on the sill of the small grated window at head height. The room was tiled, it stank of urine. He heard a voice at his back. Someone stood behind him, grabbed his belt, he felt a hand. The breath of the stranger smelled of large, empty apartments, he couldn't move.

I'll take 'em. And pull those pants up good, *Dákó*.

It was a stabbing pain, he heard a few chips bounce along the floor. A hand grabbed at them, while at the same time someone hurled him against the wall: the small figure from the table, the yellowish beard. Waclaw's hands found his lower jaw and he ran forward, ran the short man against the wall where his back crashed against the tiles and he sank to the floor. He wanted to kick the man, Waclaw did, he kicked his kidneys, connected with the short ribs, the man doubled over, shielded his head with both arms, fell on his side.

And Waclaw left. Without picking them up, without looking to see if the man was still trying to collect them, shards, chips. He went out, walked on the long, gleaming yellow promenade. The Danube with its quiet promises, all the lights that touched it, almost tenderly, a bit of light on a great cold body.

And he knew this twitching in his eyelid. He saw Jacek, who brawled and started fights out of a sense of honor—they worked a summer together, Alto Adige, the fruit harvest in the Tyrol. It was in the time before he'd started to work on the water; they'd set out from the little village in Poland, and why did he feel so bad, Waclaw, was he more taciturn than usual when he brought Jacek the water? Because he'd lain on top of and sweated on Jacek's honor, on Helena's flowered dress in the muggy summer air of the pergola, where she'd hit her head on the wooden back of the bench because she wanted him, because she wanted him for an afternoon and for the time it took the cherries to ripen and because he, her Jacek, was on the road trying to scrape together at least a bare minimum of money, and so Waclaw can't cool his friend Jacek's cheekbone, not with schnapps and shared jokes. Because he can't bear Jacek's look, he leaves him woozy in the barracks and slaves away all day in the valley. Dark red apples, it's the loss of one workday, it must be hot in the hut, he knows. They lay close in the night, their bodies exhaling sweat through the hatch windows, mosquitos in the valley, those tiny days in the valley, the card game on the heavy wooden table, and the indifference of the waiter, who had seen too many like him already.

✦ ✦ ✦

In the morning his cheekbone was swollen at the fitting, painful to the touch. Jány eyed the scrape on his lower jaw as he moved around Waclaw. The spot was slightly swollen.

What happened?

They've stopped the search.

Waclaw put on the half-finished jacket. A woman's voice had called him, he said. Eight days had gone by, now all they could do was wait.

He tugged nervously on the edges of the lapel; it was hard for him to keep still.

Careful, said Jány, fingering the seam.

That's just how it is, they never looked for him. Waclaw's voice was husky. And now they claim they did, but still, there's a difference.

Jány had stopped sticking pins in the fabric.

I am sorry, he said, and shook his head slowly.

Get some rest. And ice that.

Finally there was one day left to work on the eases of the sleeves, on the vest, the buttonholes. Then Waclaw could feel how the suit made him stand taller.

He let Jány give him two yards of lightly woven wool to wrap Mátyás's things in. Leftovers of a life, the cocoon of a moth that had long since left it. Where to? In the evening he lay on the hotel bed, looking on a map for the tiny village near Bócsa where Mátyás had grown up. Perhaps in passing, you sense it, you look over your own shoulder.

He took the seven o'clock train, which carried him southwest: grass, fields, a bit of brown, and little gray stucco farmsteads. The corn hadn't yet been harvested, and the sun was already high.

7

Bócsa

The horizon here was so even that one could get the feeling that the sand, all of it, stretched toward nothing but itself. Occasionally a power line cut through the sky, and even the clouds seemed to say that the wind came from far away. The turnoff for Bócsa was one of those crossroads where the endlessly straight tarred road, the 54, was crossed by two dirt paths. A light stucco bus shelter with a sheet-metal roof, three green mailboxes close to the road, and, with no further signs, two dirt roads leading into the bare grassland. Only far in the distance could he see a bit of green.

It was that direction the bus driver pointed in, not before warily eyeing Waclaw's suit and the dirty duffel. The bus smelled as if it had been smoked in a great deal in the past; the light fell almost vertically on the aisle through the two oval skylights. Hand straps dangled on long rails, rows of faux leather seats, a door that opened on both sides. The bus driver pointed again toward the dark rise in the distance, poplars perhaps, perhaps some water.

Then only the grimy metal that he watched recede. The road was dusty. Everything seemed to shrink under this light. He headed for the distant point. It ought to be a road one walked every day, not his flat hand running over his thighs again and again, a country lane, the extended line of a burning sun. Finally he saw a few poplars, a small farm, fenced pastures. And what was he supposed to say, since he could explain nothing.

The house was gray stucco, with a large wooden veranda at the front. As he got closer, he felt the shade of a few trees on his skin. It was still. The whole country was still. At some point he heard a radio, and a dog barked and began to run around him in wild circles, as if it wanted to nip his heels as at a sheep that had strayed too far on the long line of a dyke.

The dog received the full attention of the woman who came out of the house. When she grabbed the black-and-white fur at its neck to pull it away, Waclaw heard Mátyás's voice in his ear telling him over and over again who she was.

He had only the bundle of cloth that he placed in her arms, and her mouth narrowed as she realized what it was. He felt keenly that he should say something, but he didn't know what. He looked again at the dog, then turned around and left.

She was the woman with the broken pen, or at least that's what it had looked like, the words were notched deep into the paper, and Mátyás often left the letters unopened for weeks in front of the wardrobe.

She called after him.

Did they send you?

No.

Then she came after him. She was shorter than he, and he knew the long braid. Back then he'd seen her from afar, and it was against their agreement that he'd stayed there in the little airport shop in Rome, near the arrival gate. She'd linked arms with Mátyás, and he'd watched them both go by.

Where are you going now?

Back.

On foot?

She looked at him awhile. Then suddenly her voice was so soft and gentle it surprised him.

Come on.

She pointed to the house with her head.

She spoke broken English. Just the dry wood, a house that seemed long forgotten. Patrícia took a ratty cushion from the bench under the window and put it on a chair. The slight smell of varnish hung in the air.

She brought water. Crickets chirped.

Could she see the sweat streaking his forehead, the mark of the helmet? The rusty footlocker they'd sat on during breaks? Only the wind, and the way their heels hit the rust?

She'd painted the railings, she'd wanted to do *something*. In the days before, Waclaw had tried not to think of her. His image of her had been erect, almost royal. But now a thin, exhausted woman with a firm handshake and smoker's voice sat before him, her shoulders falling forward. Her curly hair fell out of the braid: a black horse with silver creeping into its coat. She was Mátyás's half sister, ten years older than he; she had watched over him in these meadows. Later that evening when she cries, she'll press her fists to her eyes, a childish gesture. No one will see it. She smoked. Then she laughed in agony, it was the laugh of a mother.

What did you do? What were you doing all that time?

Then she spoke quietly, as if to herself.

Is this what you have to bring from your new world? Just this, and no explanations?

Her gaze rested quietly on him. For a moment she seemed to have sympathy with this tall, tired man, sitting there in his suit. But then the harshness came back to her face. I won't do anyone the favor of keeping quiet.

That night he slept in a narrow chamber that lay across from Mátyás's old room. It was a converted stable with exposed beams and single-glazed windows. Between the light beams, the dark seemed to be composed of many parts, but where Mátyás had been there was only a throbbing darkness. It was quiet. The bed was so short he had to lie diagonally.

It smelled of wood, and he stared at the ceiling. He thought of insignificant things, little games they'd played to pass the time. Imagine, Mátyás said, it's winter on land, nothing in bloom. And then there was this peculiar warmth in their cabin, which was created simply by replacing the world out there, the lack of even one single branch, with a world they told themselves of. By listening. By his listening to Mátyás's voice as he spoke.

They'd met seven years ago at the company's training site. Outside, a warm wind blew over the fields, and hundreds of people were hurrying across the grounds, the sirens droned like they did on deck. Those were days characterized by euphoria for most, the kind of expectation that was usually attached only to things that would turn life in an important direction. They were young guys, they *wanted* to believe what the short-legged Texan was telling them, they drew a connection between the unfurled world map and his sentences, between the exploration wells, the great oil fields—Libra Field, Jupiter, Kingfish—and their own boundless desires. They were all protagonists in a story that hadn't been told yet, heroes, movers and shakers, a story that began here, somewhere just around here. They'd earn good money for a while, and none of them could imagine how the skin over their elbows would grow leathery, and the time at home, and any possible return, would fade.

It hadn't been long then since Waclaw's accident, his arm was still slightly numb, even if he didn't want to admit it. He had to take this damned safety course, together with the beginners, that was the only condition. He'd been *fucking lucky*, they all said to him over and over.

Now they stood there, the instructor twanging away. Perhaps he was vain enough to think it was *him* the men were listening to with such determination, it was him in the center of this circle, him with his speeches on creeping gases, explosions, and hydrogen sulfide, while really they were all only waiting for *themselves*, themselves in this new world.

He's a cork, Mátyás said of the instructor, and it was one of the first sentences Waclaw heard him speak. They walked from the workshop back to the containers; everything here was arranged just like at sea, only here you could smoke. Mátyás walked along the high fence with him. Waclaw had already noticed him that afternoon— he'd done for Mátyás the few maneuvers that he hadn't yet mastered, perhaps because he knew that someone like him would have it hard enough out there. Mátyás's curls, which sprang right back when he took off his helmet, two eyes that might have been the two brightest points in the whole workshop. But now he'd begun to speak.

He's a cork, Mátyás said again, he doesn't swim, he floats. He smoked, stomped out his cigarette. That's what everyone here wants, right? Out into the world, or at least out away from the old one. Look who we'll be out there with. But then think what could be possible.

There was that tone in his voice, and Waclaw stood still next to him. The *we* had surprised him, like a touch he wasn't expecting. He didn't know how long they stood there, but it was as if someone were poking holes in a wall that he hadn't even guessed was there. The wheat fields swished behind the fence.

In the half-light of the pitched roof he wasn't sure where he was at first. He saw the roof beams, in the first light of dawn he saw a slow sun rising through the window. He hadn't understood everything she'd told him yesterday. But she wanted him to stay, she needed to talk to him after work. He should feel free to have a look around. Hungary, southern landscape. He heard a car engine starting.

When he stood in the front doorway, everything was once again unfamiliar, it was late again, and he followed his shadow, erect and with level shoulder pads, through the dust, as if he would know what to do with that last bit of water, the twinkling coastline that he hadn't taken his eyes off until it had completely disappeared from view out the window of the Puma.

On the farm, a large sandy area and then, at a slight remove from the house, an old barn. The roof was sealed with tarpaper, bars of light fell through the rough-hewn slats. Waclaw stood in the open doorway for a long time. It smelled of hay and straw, and there was the shimmer of dust; it was so quiet that he cleared his throat. For a while he leaned against a bale of hay and stared out. Stretches of grass. A white poplar that he stared at until he realized that it reminded him of another tree. A shore, the smell of rotting fish, graffiti on the electricity boxes, beer in cans, the time just before Mátyás.

Patrícia returned in the afternoon, she was nervous, and he saw that there was something she wanted to say to him; she'd surely thought long and hard about it and was now putting it off even more by showing him around. Finally Waclaw followed her into the house and into a large room whose windows were almost totally overgrown. The window frames were bleached by many years of sun, but inside, the furniture had heavy round feet, and a large woven carpet lay diagonal to the walls, where countless family photographs hung. As if this weren't the country with its dust, as if this room could be reconciled with a life of silver cutlery and the huge women's hats in the photographs. Patrícia lived between these things, she rationed the light that came from outside with heavy curtains. A silver-plated bowl stood on a long table; behind it, a piano with yellowed keys.

The dark wood floor was scrupulously clean, and Patrícia wore a strong perfume, as if she could cover up the country smell, the tobacco, and the sadness in her shoulders. In the corner hung a pendant lamp from Morocco, lined with red glass. The merchant could say the price in five languages, and in all of them it was too high. Mátyás didn't care.

Patrícia gave him time to look around. Then she got something from another room, went out onto the veranda, and when he came out, she held out a telephone.

Coll, she said. Coll.

An open bottle of wine stood on the low round table.

Every evening when she'd come home from work at the hospital in Kecskemét she'd called a different number: she'd called the headquarters in Texas and all the offices responsible for the West African coast. She spoke her broken English, screamed and fell silent. She alerted the fishery authorities as well. But there was no one there she could direct anything at. There was a letter addressed to her on a letterhead with no one behind it. He saw Patrícia under the open blue of the veranda, she yelled into the receiver, her grief was harsh, like metal rods hitting each other, while at the other end, the voices had long since withdrawn, to a place full of platitudes and promises, where time was an unbreakable band. But Patrícia didn't live in that place. She was here, where the evening fell upon paths and wood that she'd known every day with Mátyás, since *the same old lies* had forced her mother to leave Budapest and move out to the country.

That you can just accept it. Who says a search wouldn't be worth it?

She didn't want to see the charts.

That's paper, she said. We have to keep asking when the others give up. That you can be so calm.

Around her the shadows had begun to leave the bushes. Fluffy clouds, and the slight trembling of the poplars. A few swallows. As if someone had cut out this part of the world with scissors. Patrícia sat down, she stared implacably at Waclaw, as if expecting a reaction. He just sat there. He didn't speak and didn't drink.

What is it? he finally said.

You're already done with it, aren't you?

She looked at him again. He seemed not to notice.

He leaned forward and spat under the railings onto the dry grass. Then he looked out.

What do you see? he asked, indicating vaguely before him.

Then he traced the far edge of the grasses with his hand. He didn't look at her.

Do you see a line? He traced it again.

It doesn't go away. It stays there like a fucking black line. That's the sea.

A line that separates you.

It just imprints itself on your eye and doesn't go away.

He drank the glass that she'd put in front of him in a single swallow.

She looked at his hand, and then out again.

Sorry, she said softly.

He heard her accent clearly, even in just one word.

Genug jetzt, he said. That's enough.

He felt the alcohol when he stood. His back was tender, and he could see his feet below sticking out of the long legs of his trousers, taking steps, almost automatically.

8

Rotabyl

They hadn't needed all of this. For six years they'd needed nothing from this land, and they hadn't needed the woman with the heavy braid, either.

Later that evening Patrícia had knocked again on his door and asked him to come down. She sat in a big wicker armchair that was covered with sheepskin, and she talked a lot, though he'd asked nothing. Mátyás had always looked back with some scorn. That's behind us now, why else would we be here? Nothing but tragedy, Mátyás had said, do we need that? Now and then a saxophone inserted itself between Patrícia's sentences, and when the record was over, he listened for a long time to the muffled repetition of the last groove. Patrícia talked. Of her father, who had hidden in a boathouse on the Sava before he'd been found by the Soviets and hanged after a show trial. Stars that were torn off the town halls with long ropes. A thin layer of dust lay on the throw cover. As if it had been a long time since anyone had lived here.

And as she talked quickly on, Waclaw thought of the room in Tangier. What would she make it into in her mind if he told her about it? A labyrinth where they would be lost so long that time flipped over and Mátyás appeared in the middle? What if there were no middle? And they would just pick things up over and over again, things that promised or could deliver nothing, things that could undo nothing, as powerless as the Kossuth coat of arms that she kept mentioning, with stripes for the Danube, Tisza, Drava, Sava, with the Fatra, Mátra, and Tatra mountains. She said it like that, like a child, and it calmed her. Thirteen short days, she said, in which her father had raised the Kossuth arms while she'd sat at home, too young to understand, while her own story only began when he didn't come back. When her mother bought cigarettes at the Csepel kiosk, and they walked hand in hand back home, where he would be missed and they would be forbidden to cry: the beginning of a story in which mourning clothes were forbidden, and soon the apartment in Budapest would be cleared out too. His face would be retouched out of photographs as if he had never existed, or as if there had only ever been another, whose story was yet to be invented by the same people who had broken three of his ribs with heavy oars when they found him in his hiding place. But what were ribs. Patrícia was drunk, she talked of Budapest and he did not understand. The two of them had lived far from all that. And he didn't know what she wanted from him.

She looked at him like a woman looks at a man when she has lived too long alone on a farm, and it made him uncomfortable. Patrícia did not look like Mátyás; it felt a bit as if she were talking about someone else.

They'd had a different life out there at sea.

He stood up. But then he heard something and turned back around. It was almost the same sound, almost exactly the way Mátyás had said it. Night after night after night.

Jó ejszakát, she said.

He held on to the doorframe. It was almost Mátyás's voice.

He looked back without answering.

Just those two sentences: Good night. And: Leave some warm water.

In the night he went over. Held up a lighter in Mátyás's darkness until his thumb was red and hot.

In the morning the Honda was already kicking up a long cloud of dust behind it by the time he got to the door, and he stood barefoot in the early sunlight, undecided. Everything in this place where Mátyás had grown up was held together with an overflowing light, and yet Waclaw heard him running. He could hear Mátyás's soles running away across the gravel, over and over.

Mátyás had driven with his uncle across a countryside ordered by feeding times and seasons, where Patrícia's palpable accusations weighed less heavily. There was the silence over the straw they loaded, the splinters in their arms that quickly grew inflamed, the farm chickens, the sizzling in the pan, the grudging good mornings with no room for sadness, and the way Mátyás hurried to wolf everything down, the aluminum Soviet fork in his mouth and the compote that Patrícia pushed slowly across the uneven wooden table. He could live here in peace, his uncle had said, he belonged here. But Mátyás couldn't find this belonging anywhere inside him.

Around midday Waclaw leaned against a bale of straw in the barn. He'd put on only the vest. It was a bit shadier here, and he wanted at least to tell Patrícia goodbye. On his knees he held a picture book that he'd taken from Mátyás's room. Dinosaurs with stubby arms, volcanoes spitting their sooty clouds into a violet sky. *Bringing fossils to life.* He looked at the drawings: layers of sediment, foraminifera, the smallest particles, as incomprehensible as luck. As if all the mud and the noise of the shaker screens required another story, something that belonged to them and to their time out there. The fairy tale behind the oil. Mátyás had even filed away the name of the asteroid that had hit the Bay of Campeche millions of years ago, Chicxulub, he said, working hard on the pronunciation, imagine that. Waclaw leafed slowly, looking carefully at the pictures. Lizards, basking sharks, primeval forests, meter-high ferns. He didn't know what about it touched him so much. It was something different from the tons of chemicals they pumped down with the drilling fluid. Then he heard a sound. Swallows flew under the roof, and at first he didn't know where it came from. Something moved in the hay, and he heard a muffled fall.

Shortly thereafter a girl came over to him, brushing off her hands. She wore frayed cut-offs, her untidy hair hung just past her bony waist. She smiled. She seemed to know who he was and said her name so softly that he didn't understand it. Mátyás, she whispered; it sounded like a question. He shrugged. Then he nodded. She beckoned for him to follow her. She walked fast, he could barely keep up. She walked along the dirt path to a pasture fence that he'd seen only from a distance. Then she pointed through the wooden rails.

It was a stretch of yellow grass, where some horses were dozing in the distance. He'd already seen the image repeated endlessly on the bus ride.

He leaned on the wood.

How nice, he said softly, thank you.

What had he expected. There was nothing here but land and creatures, and he thought that it would have made Mátyás nervous. In the end he'd gambled so much in the weeks on land that it only made the next shift harder.

The girl looked through the fence at the animals. It was time to go.

Waclaw turned around.

Nem! the girl called.

She pointed to a distant spot. A single horse pranced nervously among the flies, a bit away from the herd.

Mátyás, she whispered.

As the girl rode off, the rack on her bicycle clattering, he climbed through the fence and sat on a rock underneath one of the meadow's few trees. It was an oak, the leaves were already yellow from the heat. He saw the herd walk to the watering trough, he saw spiders running through the dry sand. He stood up only when he heard the engine of Patrícia's car.

You're still here, she said. Her hair was combed back severely, and she felt in her bag for her cigarettes. Waclaw propped himself with one hand on the shed where she'd parked the car.

Did you send the girl? he asked.

The girl? She tried to smile.

What's with the horse? he asked.

She looked at him. Then it looked like she was going to laugh, and he wasn't sure whether she was laughing at him. He didn't want to stand there waiting, he had no patience.

The horse, he said again.

You don't know? Patrícia asked. He didn't tell you?

Matyi, the great horse breeder? For years we barely had enough money for milk, then he has some, he takes his dollars and buys a Thoroughbred that's completely crazy. Only his uncle, the old fool, made sure that no one messed with it.

She looked at him. He didn't tell you?

Waclaw shook his head silently. He said he was going to go and pack his things. But then he sat exhausted on the bed for a long time. It smelled of wood, and he thought of the Andes. Mátyás had wanted to take off around now. His slightly crooked teeth as he'd told Waclaw. He wanted to travel, he said, alone. The sand was on their shins, they were sitting on the coast near La Rochelle, the water was still cold. Mátyás, talking about his itinerary, fields on steep slopes, a railroad track on high trestles, a refined journey with a view of the ice caps on the Nevado de Acay. But it was as if the highest of these peaks had already been reached, in the exhaustion with which they listened to each other, with the breaking of night that made the distant villages float like buoys on the water. Mátyás wordlessly embracing him until Waclaw stroked his forehead like a child. How he paused after describing a peak, a valley, a city. As if the sentences reached far beyond what he was saying, as if it were here that the real distance began.

He was tired. It wasn't his bed. Out the window he saw a distant strip of green. He didn't go down. He didn't turn on the light. He lay in the dark and felt his back aching.

Moonpool. He'd gone again through the two safety doors into the interior of the *Ocean Monarch* that night, to the edge of the *moonpool* where the instruments reached down into the sea: a great rectangular basin, the noise of the machines and the sound of the iron bars. They'd secured the instruments because of the storm. From high above, Waclaw saw the waves sucking at the platform, pulling back, only then to pound loudly and violently again; bubbles rose, a slight sparkle, then the water broke on itself, sprayed up. Come back, he'd said, as if the whole ocean were before him. He'd whispered it, softly at first, and then over and over again. The waves broke fiercely against the artificial boundary and soon they came: workers, faces under helmets, they held his arms and brought him away, and on the flickering screen in the control room you could see how a tall, thin man who'd gone out without his work things, in only cloth pants and a light-colored sweater, let himself be led away, reluctantly, but then with his head lowered, as if he'd lost the fight and everything he'd staked on it.

He felt the arms of the men who held his sides and heard voices saying his name, and he had to think of the cameras that would record it all, and that it was true, what the little screen showed: that everything was blurry, his world, cut off at the edges.

He spent the day on the rock. He looked at this horse that hadn't existed. Rotabyl, what a strange name. In the heat, he could see the veins under its thin coat. It stretched its neck at little noises, snorted through the air, he didn't try to get it to come to him. He sat motionless. His arms burned. The *gulyáskrém* burned too, in his throat. He knew he would never get this dust out of his suit.

And here Patrícia cut bread for the evening and saw him in the meadow, and watched him coming toward the house, Waclaw with sunburned arms and only a vest on his skin and his trousers almost gray, the dust in his nostrils. He walked slowly. He had known nothing of this horse that seemed to him like a mythical creature. He went down two steps on the cellar stairs, the cold stone, the smell of fruit that was stored, bottled and preserved, fruit that pressed against the inside of the jars, colorless and soft, this sweetness, as if that were all that could be skimmed off from that time. It was cool.

He stood beside the shelves in the narrow, shady hallway; nowhere was the person who was still with him less visible. He wanted to cry with anger, there was nowhere he could still look, Mátyás's smile, which he could return like his own. He was a mirror without an object, he was the cellar stairs and the cool darkness of the cellar stairs, and he let Patrícia find him there, It's not a good place to say goodbye. She laid a blanket over his arm, and he walked with her through a wide, dusty landscape. It was the same grass, the land stretched away to all sides.

Thick tassels were sewn on the blanket: old curtain material that Patrícia spread out on the ground. There was the sound of reeds being pushed against one another by a dry wind. A small pond, maybe an arm's length deep. He watched her set out spicy sausages, peppers, and bread on the blanket. They drank a thin wine that tasted of resin. A small bush kept the sun away, but the heat seemed to rise from the ground. They didn't speak of the house and the cellar. A long time went by in which they didn't know what to say or what could be said. Then he saw her press her lips together, her face contorted slightly, and she wiped her eyes with the back of her hand and tried to smile.

Then she drew a line in the sand with her finger.

In our family there's a tradition, she said, and her voice sounded rough, and deeper than usual. As if there were no air, or she couldn't get enough of it to speak the strange English words.

In the morning after a death, someone draws dark lines with soot under the eyes of a child in the family. We say that all the tears that cross this line reach the person who is gone. I took coal, normal coal. Mátyás was eight, and I was already done with my training when our mother died. And he cried a lot on that day, and then never again. It was January and still cold, his uncle had his hand on the coffin as we walked through the village, as if he had to make sure that the cart reached the end of the street safely. In the evening Mátyás fell asleep with János's heavy hand on his chest.

She smiled briefly. János has that knack from working with the horses, he can calm anything. Patrícia drew her finger through the sand. With the same finger she carefully drew a line across his ankle. She didn't look at him.

Did he tell you about Ostia? she asked then.

He took another sip.

Yes, he said softly.

And he could see Mátyás taking off the expensive watch and the expensive patent leather shoes and becoming a different person to pick up his half sister from the airport. Waclaw had wanted to avoid the topic. The whole masquerade, all for this unknown woman. He wanted to go. His skin itched from the dust and grass.

The sun was already low, the little pond lay there like liquid metal, motionless. Slowly, he stood up.

She asked whether he would still be there tomorrow.

He didn't answer right away.

They could call me at any minute, he said. Then I'll have three days.

Patrícia sat up.

You want to go back?

She tugged on the cords of the blanket.

Come with me tomorrow, she said then.

The kitchen was full of tiny flies when they came back in. They circled under the lamp and drowned in the glasses, and Patrícia cursed when she turned the light on. *Átkozott!* Goddammit! She threw away the bottle of vinegar. Then she opened the refrigerator and stood there in the crack of light, and Waclaw could see her bare, bony feet, her buttocks under the fabric, some dust stuck to the backs of her knees.

On the way back, they'd spoken of the deep sea and of the black smokers. Mátyás had told her that in the future they'd look for gold *down there.*

Not yet, Mátyás had said, it was still too expensive.

Then she stopped.

Is it true? she asked. Hands on her hips, her face: narrow, serious. Maybe he found something. In one of the rock samples, maybe—

Waclaw could hear the shaker screens. In the middle of the vastness he saw the mud, and the workers in the mud, and the winter and the steam on the standpipes. Mátyás, standing there as if bewitched, the crude oil was hot in the pipes, then finally their voices, which sounded curiously clear when they came on land on a winter's night, standing at a crossroads, and for long moments not knowing which way.

He wanted to go, but Patrícia held his arm.

What is it? she asked. Whether he knew anything about it. She asked about *nuggets*, and he thought of the clay he'd dug in as a child, a dirty stream in the meadows, but all he'd found were leeches, they slid over his hand.

Nuggets? What did this woman want to hear?

He shook his head.

We never found *anything* down there, he said softly. *Nur Schlamm.* Just mud.

But now the narrow crack of light from the refrigerator was the only light, and where it stopped there was no shore for a long time, they were on a raft and the world had forgotten them. They were no prospectors, they'd found nothing out there. They floated on a very wide river, but unlike the heroes of his childhood adventure books they could fall, and those who fell did not come back.

9

The Station

He saw the dirty feet of the boys in their sandals above him, he followed them up the ladders. The wood was sun-bleached and covered with droppings, and they carried the heavy sacks of corn to the brightly painted lofts: turquoise, yellow, the colors gleamed high above the rooftops of Cairo. In the streets far below, cars honked: a perpetual rush hour, dust and garbage on the roofs around them, the endless satellite dishes. And the way the sky broke open as they let the pigeons out of the coops, and the birds flew their easy circles, far above the rooftops and the smog. The dumps in the distance, so many people in this city, even out there. It wasn't long since Waclaw's accident; he'd discovered the lofts one afternoon and had since then come again and again. He bought feed for the boys and they asked him nothing, and it was as if something different mattered up here, and he felt almost at home when he saw the boys pressing their birds' feathers to their cheeks—

Patrícia honked three times, the motor was running, she seemed to be in a hurry. He didn't ask where they were going. The landscape repeated itself: houses with iron fences, chickens in the gardens, one-story bungalows. The plains gaping beyond. Cairo was far away. He considered when he'd last been there. The morning when the boys knocked on his door, the dog they'd freed with wire cutters, half starved, the ribs under its fur. In the evening, Farangis's dress that left only her ankles showing.

She stopped the Honda in front of a sand-colored building. *Rendőrség.* The police station. As if somewhere there were an eye watching them after all. Inside it was cool, and they sat on long benches against the wall. A clock ticked. Patrícia rubbed her arms. They waited. He saw the chill on her skin, she pressed her legs together. The linoleum, the wooden bench. It smelled of floor polish. Dust wafted over the waiting room floor whenever the doors opened. Mátyás wouldn't have willingly spent a single second here, Waclaw could think that but not say it: his temples protesting, the bluish veins he knew so well. After a while an official came through the door, he looked flesh-colored, short and stocky. Patrícia jumped up, she spoke quickly and gesticulated with her arms.

Is it urgent, she translated, and turned to Waclaw as if expecting an answer from him, her eyes moist, Waclaw, is it urgent, as if he hadn't asked himself the same question for a week already, next to the window with sickly Mr. Jány, on the stool that threatened to cave in under him.

The official let his gaze wander between them, and Patrícia explained to each of the buttons of his uniform. Mátyás Pásztor, she said, over and over, until the official asked her to come in, behind the door, to the marine-blue uniforms. She turned around once more: Waclaw. He sat erect, hands on his knees, shaking his head almost imperceptibly.

He saw the door close behind her, voices, clacking walls. He thought of Jány. His family probably won't believe it was an accident. Waclaw hadn't known what Jány meant. He'd just stared at this spot inside himself that he'd discovered while sitting on the stool, a large, numb spot like a glass flask that was fogged up inside. He went to the foyer, breathed in the heaviness emanating from the polished stairs: old brown wood, banisters that seemed made for no one, treads shining as if they were made only of light. Quiet and dusty.

And like in a funhouse, the weeks at sea stretched and distorted into something gigantic, then shrank immediately back into something incredibly small. He thought of the ornithologist with his turquoise leggings, the Finn whose arm had been torn off, the Bulgarian whose back was scorched by a gas flare explosion, the jokes, always a bit too loud, and then again the pigeons over Cairo. It was like an optical illusion, in which he and Mátyás did not appear. There was just something that stretched, a hand that led him groping through the darkness without grasping anything. It was quiet. He heard the distant rolling of a desk chair, and something—a cabinet or a drawer—was closed. Closed, he thought.

When the door opened, he saw Patrícia's hot face, the cheeks red like those of a young girl's after playing in the snow. What is it, he said flatly. And he put his arms around her as if he'd always done so, and led her out and drove the red Honda against the glassiness of her eyes, against the silence and the unambiguousness of the police station, against the endlessness of these roads, which were followed by other roads, through the dust, to the calming noise of the stones hitting the bottom of the car, sudden and strong.

Who could they charge anyway, she said. There's no one.

Where is he registered? Malta? Malta?

But what had she expected from the short, pig-eyed man? He stopped at a restaurant: a main road, plastic flowers on the table, come, eat, Waclaw said, do me a favor and drink, two glasses, two more.

◆　◆　◆

He was awake early and looked at the unfamiliar body. The long slits in her earlobes. They'd left the Honda there and had gone on foot through the night, and Patrícia had first cursed the policeman, then forgotten him, and then she had turned on Waclaw. Just mud, she yelled, for some fucking mud? He couldn't hold her fists, and it hardly hurt when she hit him, though she was strong. Then he felt a tug between his legs, her voice grew harsh, and he realized that he wanted her, nothing else, just this short, hard rhythm, not her skin or her smell, not even for her to lean against his shoulder as they walked, and then he still did when they reached the farm. Her body was like a capsule: first something hard, her hands were rough and her knees dry, but when he came to her, she was like a small animal and pressed against him, and her rough voice, too, was gone.

She stayed lying next to him for a long time; it was growing light when she finally left. He heard her steps on the stairs, then he lay by the empty window, and the smoke of her cigarette floated up to him from below.

Then he lay there and waited for the sound of the motor, but it remained quiet. It would be a hellish day. The sun, though only just risen, shone hot over the land.

It was as if the whole plain had been emptied out.

He waited till midday. He thought of Sharam, and that he would have liked the story about the gold. That they all wanted something from him. And that Mátyás wasn't out here. Before he knew Mátyás, he'd sat for days on the shore, the Curonian Spit, it was the end of the year, only the pines were still green; a wind that rolled past and he didn't know where it was going. He'd lived with an ornithologist in a log cabin that was too small for two men who didn't get along. While working, the ornithologist liked to wear nylon pants that hugged his legs: turquoise and violet. And when Waclaw stomped through the yellow dunes, looking at a horizon where amber and washed-up phosphorus were the same color, it was years that lay before him, which crashed and crashed against the shore. It was the first weeks after Milena. He'd go early, before the banding, as it was growing light, through the finely woven nets. That was the hardest part, catching the birds in a swift motion without hurting them. He could do that. He felt the racing of their little hearts in his hand, though it was hard for him, since his arm was still a bit numb from the accident.

You're a different person, Milena had said to him. The water sparkling over the weir, the yellowish afternoon sun. The way she suddenly pulled her legs up to her body and started to cry. Weeks later he got her letter. The sea spray that followed him. That pursued him, like beaten egg whites, like something huge and ragged that he was growing more and more to resemble.

He folded things as he had learned to fold things, quickly and precisely, as if they were things that belonged to someone else. He left the duffel in the room and went out. The thought that Patrícia was watching him hastened his steps. Villages connected by a single street, a black band, few trees, this light. He had no name for this kind of vastness. Much later he saw a gas station in the distance with two vans in front of it; the markings on the asphalt were bleached from the sun.

The man reached behind him when Waclaw pointed to the cheap schnapps, staring straight at him as if he didn't have a stitch on, as if he could look right through him, at the ribs that stood out under his skin. Waclaw paid with a bill; he didn't wait for the change. A little later he reached a flat stream behind a shady cluster of trees. He saw fish, keeping still against the current, but they disappeared when he came close. He walked along the sandy bank and stuck the bottles of schnapps into the ground. The water flowed slowly, it would cool nothing. He just stood there. No one saw him, no one needed to see him, everything drifted past.

The crickets did not sing.

And this dry ground. As if they had given everything, what had they given, what lost, why had they seen each other cry, why the exhaustion, nights, by the bright windows of another chain hotel, why the ashtray next to the bed, and why did Mátyás ask him almost fearfully what he said in his sleep, as if there might still be something on his lips of what he shared with other men and women. Why this Thoroughbred with its prancing elegance that he'd never told Waclaw of? They'd seen the training tracks, the animals' steaming necks, their panting, their shadows in the morning, as if they'd come directly out of the night. They'd gone to the great races: Ascot, Baden-Baden. Now it seemed to him as if he'd only been seeing the front side of a picture.

The water was warm. And the stream didn't move, and the sun stood still. When he'd drunk the bottles, he could see the dust washing out of his clothing in clouds; he could stand there naked, looking down at himself, long and pale. A wind passed through the trees, and a slight dizziness through his head.

He didn't want to think of the coal dust, of the mine. His mother grew cacti on the windowsill: desert plants that pricked, needled, and bloomed, while his father descended underground, hacked ore in the darkness, bit into his *Kniffte* for lunch, all the way down to the soft whimpering of the trainees, who started to realize after the first weeks where it was they'd ended up. They lived five or six to a tract home with blackened windowsills, amid the cries of newborns and the green beans they grew themselves on the estate. The coal dust was as conspicuous as the peach fuzz on the babies' heads. Something told him that it was no different here. The same narrowness. And he could hear Mátyás running away, over and over.

He stumbled through the dry grass; his clothes were wet. He saw the gambling tables where they'd watched this plain of Bács-Kiskun turning away from them, this land and the land of the mines, and every promise of quietness, of morning love with a woman whose smell was still so familiar to him after all this time. The flickering black and white, as if it released them; Mátyás sniffed the stuff, a long leg with a high heel across his lap, and this was the whole stake: two men in shirts, dim lamps, and the secret feeling that there was nothing to lose, nothing that could really be taken away from them. That they were invulnerable. While Mátyás turned away to kiss Yala, her gap-teeth for a few nights, and then they were alone again. A little life to stuff in their lockers while storms with names like Ivan and Katrina laid waste to countless platforms. But they stayed, they endured it. It was years later, after the accident with the fisherman and the explosion in the Mississippi Delta, before they went back. Suddenly everyone was talking about oil. They saw the flames over the Macondo oil field, dark orange like the eternal fire temple of the Zoroastrians, black clouds, the growling of ancient powers. And then Europe, and the silence of Europe, where everyone was just watching a wedding: white veils, Westminster Abbey, the English royal family. It took them weeks to really arrive, as if something about this old continent had become unreal to them.

He didn't come back until dark.

He leaned on the sink and cooled his arm. The last bits of

intoxication were throbbing in his head, and he was glad to be alone in the kitchen, the water felt good. The arm looked like it had just come out of an oven. Coke, he thought. Freshly fired coke. The water on it.

Then he heard steps behind him. She stood there for a while and watched him.

You can stay, you know.

He said nothing, and kept cooling his arm. The water was loud in the sink.

Patrícia walked past him out to the terrace, to a large, octopus-like plant. He heard her cutting in the darkness, heard the leaf snap. She came back; sap was oozing out of the edges of the leaf, small, clear drops.

Take this, she said.

She watched him rub the leaf on his arm. It was cool and good. He still stood with his face to the wall.

You can stay if you want.

She said it as if he hadn't heard her.

For now. I mean, where else will you go?

He shook his head slowly. He rubbed the leaf over his arm.

You're burning, she said again.

He heard her go out; the plant cracking again.

There's a house, it doesn't belong just to me, he said.

The water pattered in the sink in front of him. His own voice, suddenly familiar to him like a silo that one could draw grain from, big sacks of grain and corn.

There was a place, there was a place once.

Close by there's a weir and a river. The river is named after a bird. In the winter the earth is heavy, and when you walk over the fields it clumps on your soles. Everything is wet, moist and heavy.

Blackberries grow on the riverbank, and there's frost on the leaves. And beyond it the water is as bright as the fucking sky. Like a promise.

And there are these birds that dive.

And when they dive, you never know if they'll come up again.

Maybe they don't know themselves.

You know, don't you? Everyone knows.

When they come up—the sky is the same, the bushes are the same, but the river is different—

He spat in his hand, rubbed the spit over his burned forehead, then brushed back his hair.

She stared at him. I don't understand when you speak German.

I know, he said, I know.

His trousers were wet, he felt the cold of the seams on his ankles. He took the second leaf from her hand. She'd peeled the skin off. The inside was a transparent, shimmering mass, like the vitreous body of an eye. Like the cow's eyes that he'd seen cut open once in the school in Wiórek, where he'd worked as a janitor. Slaughterhouse eyes: he'd found the clarity of the jelly strangely moving.

I know, he said again.

He left the leaf next to the sink, and went upstairs. She heard his steps. For a while she stood in the darkness, then she turned the water off.

10

Coral

In the darkness of the room, he'd folded his things on the bed. He sat under the tree, long before the sun was up. He heard the occasional stomping of the animals in the mist that covered the meadows. He walked over to the sleeping herd and spoke softly to them and stroked the neck of a bony old gray.

The land was still dark. The horse stood there with its eyes half-closed; he laid his hand on its flat head, and an image drifted up to him from somewhere else, an image in which only the horse's bones appeared. It was night, and the moon shone high and indifferent, just after the war. One of the men must have told him the story, back in the Birkeneck: Waclaw had earned his pocket money setting the pins back up. When they drank, the eras blurred, the long wooden planks of the bowling alley; the men seemed to roll their balls toward some other darkness. They watched the balls roll, and at the end the pins cracked, cracking bones, he soaked it all in, even when they said he shouldn't listen—it's nothing for you to be thinking about, son—but in his inner eye the bones grew, in the wide, empty farmland, like deep sea plants in the darkness.

He'd walked back in the dawn, up Gladbecker Straße, turning onto Aegidistraße, he passed the newly built bungalow and thought of the night out of which the men had come. Something told him

that the same thing awaited them down there, in Prosper, Rheinbaben, and Welheim, in the heat, six levels down, in the dust, through
which the men came in their columns, strewing salt and limestone
dust, as if they were afraid this darkness would rear up like a coal-
dust steed made of infinite parts, ungraspable, like a huge, empty
field. The gray stood still before him, he could smell the horse.

He pumped water into the old tub at the edge of the paddock, he
saw the herd approaching to drink, saw the water drip from their
heavy jaws. He watched them beating off flies, tail hair long as tinsel
on Christmas evenings, some dive or other, and they were hungry
for other people's stories. Mátyás, drunk, serious, *what do you see
out there*, freight workers, officers, reports of a sea swept clean, huge
expanses of filth, a white ocean, then the mirrored bars, the smell of
their sweat-drenched shirts. Tequila, gin, who was going home over
the next few days, no one, tequila, gin.

Mátyás was clammy and freezing when his mother found him at
daybreak. She had laid firewood in the oven, her hands shaking as
she tried to light the matches, she was barefoot and felt fluid running
cold down her thighs, and while she squatted and stared ahead, her
gaze wandered out to the first light and the apple tree with its thin,
knotted crown, and there was a shadow within it, her boy lay with
his head on the moss and his arms like claws around the branch
and didn't come down, not until after she had run up the hill in
a soundless line and grabbed him and didn't let go until the heat
of the bathwater reached his neck, and he finally fell asleep under
three down quilts and she looked at herself, furtively and *suddenly
old*, that's what she thought as she stood knee-deep in the leftover
lukewarm water, soaping herself until her hands were blue, and the

scent of the fine lavender soap drove away all thoughts of uniforms and boots in the night and the cold emanating from the soldier, of the hairy hand, after the door was closed and she just tried to be *quiet*, always *quiet, because of the children*, and on awaking a cold light, pale with rage, rose over the houses and the sheds, and only when she found her son clinging to the tree did she understand that the light wasn't angry but powerless, and her hair hung down in long strands in the lukewarm water, the soap helped nothing.

He'd waited a long time, and it was now noon. Mátyás's horse had come closer, it had run its nostrils over the dry wood of the tree trunk against which he sat. He could see the veins under its thin coat, the forelock, the eye. Something gleamed inside it. A deep brown that seemed to open into a wide, choppy landscape. There was the storm from that night, and he could taste the salt. Only the brown, and between the crests of the waves it sank again and again—Waclaw reached out his hand, the head jerked back, and in a few steps the horse was gone across the meadow. Maybe this horse was the only decision Mátyás had made in the last years—a buoy, a marker, a forgotten new beginning. He heard the waves hitting the jacket legs.

He went back into the room, too tired to leave or to stay. Simply and mechanically he took the sheet off the bed and placed it on a chair, the only piece of furniture in his room.

He was awoken by the noise of several cars. The darker light under the roof beams. He still had his shoes on, and the duffel lay next to him. On the floor, a beetle crawled in small circles; now and then it tried to spread its wings, but it couldn't lift off, so it reversed direction, crawled on, and didn't fly. Waclaw watched it for a while. Voices could be heard below, chairs were moved, glasses clinked.

He opened the window. Someone had rammed a pole with a lamp on it into the ground next to the path; there was a light wind, and he saw the quivering glow of the oil lamp on the terrace. When he heard steps on the sand, he pulled his head back inside. The mattress must have been filled with something scratchy.

He was awoken later by steps on the stairs.

She smelled of alcohol and said she'd been looking for him.

The room was narrow and small. Patrícia sat on the edge of his bed, she'd just said something. He was thirsty. His mouth was dry.

What are you doing here? he asked.

Emerging from sleep, he sat up. He heard her voice.

What did you say?

She leaned against the wall, the outline of her limp breasts visible under her shirt. She pulled her legs up to her body.

Didn't anyone hear Mátyás in the night?

What are you saying?

I'm asking whether no one heard him. She was speaking louder now.

Close your eyes, he said. He slid closer to her and placed both his hands flat over her ears.

Can you hear? he asked. He pressed his hands harder, her hair rubbed against the wall.

Can you hear! he screamed. The roaring!

He pressed her head against the wall.

That's what the storm is like!

She opened her eyes, but he held her even tighter, she gasped for air.

Stop it!

You asked!

A wave came over her body, she tore at his arms. Idiot! She struck at his wrists and pushed him away.

These are things that you know nothing of, he screamed, and his voice was hoarse. He was fully awake now, and he watched her hurriedly gather herself. In the doorway, she turned back to him once more.

There are friends here, they want to see you. Her voice was husky, as if she were fighting back tears. Waclaw shook his head slowly.

These people aren't here because of me, and you know it. He paused.

They called me, he said. I have to be back the day after tomorrow.

On the coast?

Patrícia turned away abruptly. He heard her steps on the stairs.

Then he lay there, and the voices of the guests reached him from below; it was late when he got up and went out. It was the first time he'd seen flames in the fireplace, from outside he could see their uneasy light against the windows. Patrícia stood by a long table where a group of older people sat; she had makeup on, and the rouge on her cheeks made her look like a doll. The vines were thick on the wall and the fire gave the faces sharp contours. Everything reflected, as if wine and schnapps and candles could breathe life into this old love. He didn't know why they'd made a fire—sweat was running into their eyes and their faces shone, he saw schnapps in the glasses.

It was three men and five women whose voices he'd been hearing since Patrícia had disappeared from his room. A few old men with honest eyes, livestock feed specialists with gray manes, perhaps

János was among them. Waclaw stood in the dark, not listening; he was the set of a Western, left standing though the filming was long over. They were both in over their heads, he and Mátyás, it was no longer a game they knew how to play. The lamp from the celebration stood on the windowsill, illuminating the darkness outside. He sat on the path. The smell of horse dung, the sand still warm, fluff floating down from the poplars, falling in inch-thick drifts on the ground, everything around him seemed brightly illuminated and in motion. He tried to think of Mátyás, of the coming departure, Rabat offshore, he'd go back to Morocco, and there was Milena's chin-length hair. But everything passed by, it was all just names of unfamiliar cities spoken into a pay phone, and the only thing that connected them now was the feeling of warmth in his back, the even movement of his abdominal wall, rising and falling under his hand. Hungary, too, would pass by, he'd seen too many places over the last twelve years, and it was only at the beginning that this distance had been a relief.

Waclaw lay still, everything fell upon him from far away. The pollen stuck to the dark cloth on his legs, the leaves trembled, then there were the sounds of the old people, still singing, drinking. Somewhere amid it all, an image of Mátyás, rocking slowly, a leaf on a river, whirling along before the water swallowed it. He had to think of the fact that he'd known a different Mátyás, but that the people on this tiny farm were the only other ones in the world who missed him. And that they loved him for far less than he and Mátyás had ever tried to be.

11

White Egrets

There was dust in the corners. The room seemed emptier than it had days ago when he'd seen it for the first time. He put the picture book back on Mátyás's bed, left the door open, and put on his jacket; he felt how the dark cloth made him stand taller. Outside it was already light, and the shadows of swallows crossed the thirsty land, he walked through the shades of gray and layers of branches until the bus shelter grew dimly visible.

It was a bus stop with a metal roof, painted green. The station couldn't be seen from the farm. *Falusi utca*, the sign read. Waclaw waited, long after the sun had risen. He heard noises on the roof. As if hundreds of birds were perched there, their claws scratching the metal. A few of them took off, flew in a circle, and landed again.

He could see them.

Egrets, after a long night on Cantarell in the Gulf of Mexico. They circled the *West Vencedor*, attracted by the artificial light on the water. They'd swarmed counterclockwise around the platform all night. A few of them had landed, exhausted, on the crane boom. The men jeered at them, it was shift change. Some threw little bits of iron up at them: screws, nuts, even a tool or two. After nearly two weeks on deck, the birds were a welcome change of pace. They'd never talked about it afterward, but on that morning they'd all stood there for a while, looking into the floodlight where the birds circled like a

silent oversized mobile. Then Shane had broken away from the group
and crossed the deck to the ladder. The others suddenly fell silent
while he climbed up, far out onto the jib. It was high, and the metal
swayed. The outlines of the birds seemed unreal against the night,
and Shane crawled on all fours and held on with his hands, wedging his work boots in the spaces between the iron struts. He looked
straight ahead. A few birds took off as he came closer. He waited.
And the men waited too, with all the tension of an NBA final. Waclaw heard a few of them whisper, making bets, maybe. Then he saw
Shane's stocky body shoot forward as he reached out for a bird, once,
and then again, until he caught one of the animals. He grasped the
egret's leg and the leg broke. He held the bird out like a trophy, its
head hit the iron. Then he held the egret up so everyone could see it
and began to swing the body around over his head like a lasso, and
the men relaxed and whooped, and the bird slid into the water head-
first like an arrow, without spreading its wings. Without a sound.

Waclaw remembered Shane's yellow work gloves. It was the time
before Mátyás, and there was no one there. Before it grew light, several
animals plummeted into the sea from exhaustion. Others left with the
first light, which freed them from the uncanny circle. White egrets.

It was an old-fashioned blue-and-white bus, and Waclaw hefted the
duffel onto his shoulders to make his way through the narrow rows
of seats. From the very back, he looked through a dirty window
at a country that was already becoming foreign to him again. The
windows vibrated to the noise of the engine, and he saw the driver's
bare elbows, and the blurry flicker of a tattoo. Maybe an anchor or a
name. He felt a mild pang. The radio played in a foreign language, in
front of him sat a woman whose bag had little sequins sewn into it.
They threw the light around like a thousand tiny mirrors.

The bus filled gradually. No one spoke. Everyone was still tired. They carried only the bare workday necessities with them. Waclaw had no image of the end of this journey, nothing he could head toward. Occasional smoke above factories. Highway. Empty land.

He bought some juice boxes at a kiosk and took the bus to Kőbánya-Kispest. The lemonade tasted harsh and artificial, and he saw dilapidated workshops, faded blue streetlamps with big silver numbers. Then the swinging hand straps in the subway. The light fell into the shafts as if through a sieve, yellowish, he sat in one of the long rows parallel to the windows. His suit, and then the duffel with his old work boots tied on to it. He felt the looks; his hands had grown brown, his body didn't speak the language of a business traveler. He left two calls from the company unanswered. As if where he was going were still undecided, as if it were just an early afternoon and he was on his way home. His own face was reflected blurrily in the subway windows. He'd sometimes wondered how Mátyás had seen him: spent, a bit stiff because of his back. Often Waclaw had found some excuse not to go out with the others, and instead had simply lain in the hotel room and waited. And for what. It had been hard for him to cover it up, the feeling of being forced to sit on a bar stool, unnaturally stiff. It was only recently that it had been getting so difficult.

In the distance he saw the façades of buildings, the tall windows, counted the stories. He imagined Jány, up there with his records, his composers, the big names, but none occurred to him. How Jány would look down at the old, summery city. As if the people were still dressed as they had been back then. As if clothing were something internal. He imagined visiting him—a brass door plate—but he remained sitting where he was. He thought of the tailor's cough, the bright light of the table lamp. The way one sews oneself into fabric, tenderer than we. There were the dark windows of the subway cars passing.

A light wind blew across the tarmac. He'd had to wait in Budapest, and in Ankara it had been a long time before the connecting flight arrived. He'd sat on the airport cushions, he'd stared at the screens. Tigers in rings of fire. Marilyn Monroe. He had no idea it was possible to be this tired.

Ankara shone in the hazy air of early evening. It was warm. He'd left Patrícia some money. He didn't know that she'd gone all the way from Bócsa to Rome to beg him, *come back, Matyi, what are you doing to us out here?* He didn't know what Mátyás had answered, he didn't know that Mátyás was playing for time, that he'd held her off, while Waclaw wanted to believe: in the key, in the door that could be locked, Haven, the shutters that kept out the light and the noise, and they could rest, finally rest, and lie down, and Mátyás's hand traced the whole length of his back, he wanted to believe in that hand.

The land was dark, they rode out across the tarmac, the illuminated white belly of the plane in front of him. On the gangway, the boy in front of him suddenly stopped and turned around. He wore a crocheted *takke* and a white robe, and he breathed in the warm air that blew over the tarmac. Waclaw was the last passenger after him, and the boy didn't seem to be in a hurry. He looked back at the distant lights on the horizon. Everything about him seemed like a promise. The day behind him was not ending, with his big, uncertain eyes he would remember everything. When he continued and the tall man followed him slowly, his steps sounded hollow, like big dogs barking in the dusk.

◆　◆　◆

They stowed the luggage over their heads and Waclaw felt his back. He traveled with only one duffel. In front of him the stewards acted out an emergency with yellow plastic whistles, as if the land and the water far below were a giant ear, and they looked indifferent, like village altar boys at an Easter vigil.

Waclaw sat up straight and slept sitting up straight, sinking again and again into scraps of sleep; once he saw Mátyás before him, laughing in the little room with the rugs, once a few bars of a melody came into his mind. His father had joined the newly formed choir of Ruhr Coal, Inc., as if he didn't know his lungs were no longer any good for singing. Melodies, interrupted by coughing.

The night was dark for a long time. A flight attendant woke him and asked insistently if he wanted a sandwich. Chicken or cheese? His face was young and clean-shaven, and Waclaw didn't know what to say. If the plane had some defect, his answer would be the last thing he'd ever say. Mátyás had been afraid of flying since two years ago a helicopter had almost missed the platform off Aberdeen. One runner had slipped over the edge, it wouldn't have taken much. But some nights Waclaw thought that the reason wasn't the helicopter or the fatigue, but something else that came and was with them always. Chicken or cheese. The boy next to him had pulled the blanket up to his chin. Sir? The flight attendant gave him something shrink-wrapped and soft, and he put it down in front of him.

Suddenly he had the distinct feeling that everything would be different, and also that this was a feeling he already knew. The plane was brightly lit; far below, little villages gleamed against the rugged landscape. The happiness of those years was like the tiny pricks of a needle. Promontories, studded with splashes of light. He flew on through the night.

12

An Orange (Sidi Ifni)

A couple came over to him, perhaps because he was the only other person on the beach far and wide, and asked for a photograph. Picture, they said. Waclaw pressed the shutter without looking through the viewfinder. The woman wore a long blue robe. He gave them the camera back and walked on. The Atlantic sent big, impatient waves toward shore.

In the hotel, the halls smelled of chlorine cleaner. An acquaintance, Victor, stood near the reception. They'd worked off Rabat together a few times; he saw Victor's hand and the chocolate bar in it sink when he saw Waclaw. Behind him shone the light of two vending machines, whose contents—little cakes and candy bars wrapped in plastic—he must have scoured for anything edible. There was something about the way he held himself that Waclaw had often noticed, cheeks that hung almost vertical, even over the places where talking and facial expressions usually leave marks. It was the ceaseless talking, conversations that no one heard, the men dragged these behind them like the train of a dress. On deck, Victor was a crane operator, an important position, and it was dangerous for everyone involved when the sea was rough and the supply boats danced beside the platform like broncos. But out here there was none of that, he seemed lost in the lights of the vending machines, his hands far too big around the shrink-wrapped chocolate. A buoy that had lost its tether, that signaled nothing, for no one. Maybe he'd heard already. Waclaw just nodded briefly and took the stairs up to his room.

From his balcony everything suddenly drove him crazy again. The weather, a landscape stripped bare, the feeling of being suddenly numb. A throbbing in his forehead. Nine hours before departure and he already had the rubbery stink of the survival suit in his nose. The new platform wasn't elsewhere, it was only a few nautical miles away.

A woman's voice had told him the time of departure from the heliport. She said: Sidi Ifni. Six thirty. He said: Yes. Then he hung up. She hadn't even mentioned Mátyás.

And he was tired. Somehow wrecked inside. He lay on the bed and thought of Victor, he saw his lathered head in the hands of a hairdresser, he thought of blowfish that travel slowly through shallow water, producing poison in their round bodies, some realm within them, black from being alone.

He lay awake all night, but it wasn't just his back that made him uneasy. He thought of the promise he'd made to Francis. Of course, he'd said, of course I'll be back.

Above him a frail old propeller circulated below the ceiling. *Sure. Sure.* For Francis it would make a difference whether he were there or not. They had both remained, maybe they should have gone long ago, Francis back when he'd grown skittish and had been overcome, in front of their overloaded plates in the mess hall, with hysterical fits of laughter, completely without sound. From the beginning, they'd teased him for his delicate frame, his swayback, and his mincing steps. Sometimes it looked like he walked that way intentionally, and he seemed to be the only one who didn't notice it. Yet when they saw him again after months away—Mátyás was brown and boisterous and they laughed a lot—it seemed that something had happened to Francis.

He'd only told Waclaw weeks later, and had pressed him back down into his chair when he tried to jump up.

Quiet, Francis had said. You won't do anything, promise me. Rage and panic mingled in his voice.

One morning Francis had woken up, he lay in his bunk, his pants were pulled down, yes, his buttocks were bare, and he lay on his back. He hadn't fallen asleep that way, it was still dark, he heard the first men in the hallway getting ready for their shift, and he felt down his body, his underwear was sticky with someone else's sperm, he was dazed, he couldn't remember. Shadows, not even a voice.

Since then he hurried to leave the drying rooms, and he didn't want to talk about it. He seemed underslept, tired in those weeks, wilted, while it grew hot, and the winds carried the sand of the Sahara all the way out to them on deck. Waclaw felt the fine grains between his teeth.

He hadn't slept. The sunlight rose early and soon fell evenly over everything: the mud walls, the few tired dogs roaming around the garbage cans by the parking lot, the sunlight on the salty sea and the pattern of the small, angled alleys that were suffused with weariness. He went to the reception and brought Jány's suit and the rest of the things to the luggage room, where many such bundles already lay. He heard voices, and it smelled of coffee and baked dough and spices, and he knew that Mátyás would have dunked the flatbreads in a lot of syrup.

He'd ordered the taxi to the back door of the hotel. When he got in, the driver's music droned in his ears. *Habibi. Habiiiibi.* Only when they were outside the city and he stretched forward between the front seats to turn down the old-fashioned black volume knob, did it get quiet, and the landscape passed by, torpid and shimmering under the early sun. A big, dry plain with a few streets running through it, just a few big cliffs and the hint of a sea that would soon glow beside them. A plain, as if it were made just for the light.

Since they'd found gas near Kentira, they'd searched like mad in this area. A few Austrians had even tried it in the Sahara. Waclaw had been transferred from Foum Draa to Sidi Moussa; their assignment, the exploration well, had a name that consisted only of numbers and letters. His breath grew shallow, and he ran both hands over his face; for a moment he kept his eyes closed and held tight to the door handle. He heard the motor, and something that must have been fixed to the rearview mirror swung against the windshield.

Stop! he cried.

He opened his eyes and grabbed for the driver's shoulder, for the tropical print of his shirt.

Stop, he said again.

The driver laughed.

Here it is nothing! He pointed to the road, which seemed to eat into a dusty yellow endlessness.

Nothing! He laughed and turned the music up a bit. Fifteen minutes, maybe, he said.

Stop! He was almost screaming. Stop here.

Deceleration. His bag. Even the early air was hot.

The driver waved, bemused, and drove slowly, as if he wanted to give Waclaw a chance to wave him back, to get back in. Waclaw had given him fifty dollars, he didn't want him to ask questions. Then Waclaw saw him turn, the taxi drove slowly by him once more, and then finally he heard it speed up.

Then the flatness of the land, and again the feeling of numbness. Not even crickets. Just many sharp rocks. To walk. The road remained invisible because it was built atop an embankment. Which sloped downward. Then a call, which he didn't pick up, another call, walking, the expanse.

I will not come, he said. And walked. The telephone stopped ringing. Leave it.

He was relieved, happy, until the thirst came. Fear of snakes.

He walked southeast, toward the middle of the land. In the distance the foothills of the southern Atlas mountains towered into shadows for which he had no name. But he knew that this sand merged into the Sahara. He'd seen it. He knew that around Chbika the dunes rolled to the sea. It was a nice image, when you were just imagining it.

He walked.

The ground burned. Blazing distance. Thistles.

Milena walked through the sand next to him, her steps bewildered by the expanse. She slid the tip of her foot over the ground.

You didn't call.

You didn't pick me up last time I visited.

Her laugh.

A visit, Wacuś! We wanted a life.

Then she breathed out and was gone.

All the wind in this vastness was like that exhalation, nothing stirred.

He carried the bag on his shoulder, the reflective stripes on his pants caught the sunlight. And in the midday heat, a smell emanated from the oilskin, the boots, the helmet: a smell of machines and oil and the mud of the seas, a smell he knew, a smell that had always been with them. What did it smell like. Like all the time they would never have. He dropped the heavy things, first the work boots, then the jacket. As if it were that easy, as if he could just leave it all behind him. The freezing feet at four in the morning, the sweat when the afternoon light came at them from every direction. He took out the water bottle, the screw top stank of alcohol: reserves for the last hours of the shift. They'd never have let him bring it with him on the platform.

The sun blazed.

The desert was an hourglass of infinite parts.

Lizards between the stones, dry shrubs. Beneath it throbbed the noise of metropolises, the beats, the brightly lit bars, no different than the unison of the desert, the stuff they snorted in the shabbiest bathrooms, the desert that lay beneath all of it, another desert, of forgetting. A desert where one could forget names, no longer speak a language.

He reached a few distant huts.

His skin was burned.

This is no hotel, one of the men said. Waclaw offered him money, and they rolled out a mat for him in a shady corner. He stuck his wallet down the front of his pants. And slept.

The images inside him were soundless, moments cut out of the course of time. Milena was strangely present. Here, too, the dancing of moths in the night. It was dark when he woke. They gave him lentil soup, squeezed some lemon in it. They sat around a fire. He with them; sparks flew, the wood crackled.

His thirst was powerful. They gave him something to drink. He wasn't the stranger who tells stories. He was no one at all. The dancing of moths, he had no fear.

The corner in the hut. Patterned rugs, he heard their soft voices.

A child with matted hair eyed him in the morning. Flat land all around, he must have walked far. He gave them almost all the money he had left. Breakfast: an orange.

Then he took the rest of his things and walked. The indelible smell of his work clothes. He dropped them. The helmet with the chin strap and the signatures that they'd scratched in the plastic for him when they'd thought that it would mean something, no matter what happened. It would fade in the sun, in the low shrubs. The desert floor began to glow under his steps. After about an hour he heard an engine behind him: one of the men, in a jeep. He let Waclaw climb up onto the truck bed, drove. Cliffs in the dry light. Reddish, whitish, grayish, yellowish. The sun celebrated itself, there was no distraction from it. The man let Waclaw out where the high-rises began. He hit Waclaw lightly on the cheek. You okay? Waclaw saw his tea-black teeth and his dust-colored cloth. He wished the man would have just taken him back to the tent. Waclaw could feel that but not say it. The man stood next to the jeep and watched as he climbed down.

Shukran, Waclaw said. And laid his hand on his chest.

Then again: a room, a ceiling, a propeller.

The reflective white of another unfamiliar shower stall. He lay naked on his bed, his feet on the duffel. This word: it caught at him every time, gave him an image of her chin-length hair. He didn't move. There was the village street where they walked together, the fog lay heavy over the fields, her face was cold and wet. They'd gotten off the bus, Milena hugged him quickly, carried his new duffel on her shoulder, laughing. They'd spent all of August getting his gear together, relieved that there would be something left in the account

at the end of the month, now that they'd even canceled the newspaper and barely left the house anymore. No going to the movies.
The school bell that made him nervous, the job as a janitor, and the
prospect of the worn steering wheel of the bus between the villages,
the seats rubbed bare.

Instead, they now had something else ahead of them. How big
is a platform? Milena asked. The length of three streetlamps: and
they walked up and down the stretch of village road, they stopped
and stood, Milena hugged him close. Three streetlamps, and then
the world ends.

13

Brent

Morning came like a foot stomping, as if the cities, Budapest, Grand Socco, the alleys, the walls, were nothing more than the land that he'd seen from the water: made only of light and wind and sand that could shift and layer again and again without a trace. He started when his telephone rang. He must have fallen asleep.

It was Patrícia.

Where did you get my number?

It was in Mátyás's things.

She said nothing. He considered what else she might have found, but nothing else occurred to him. Scribbles in Mátyás's papers, Hungarian, that he might have overlooked. There was a soft hissing in the connection.

Waclaw?

I'm still here.

Maybe there's something to it. The thing with the black smokers, with the gold.

Ich hab's dir schon gesagt. I already told you.

But why not?

He could see her, on the terrace, next to the wood varnish that would change nothing. All that light. The dust and the house.

He felt the light breeze from the ceiling fan.

What's it like there? she asked.

She spoke more softly now.

He thought that he didn't know.

He stared at the ceiling. He thought of the dusty, almost bare palms on the beach, the herds of goats in the alleys.

The shadow of the fan.

There's no one here anymore, he said.

A car door closed.

He hung up.

The apricot-colored walls of the hotel, the balcony with the seven iron bars on the courtyard and the sea. An ashtray next to the bed. The warning in small print next to the remote: channels above 72 would incur "extra costs." He saw Victor before him again, the movie room, the bored lust of the men who turned to the side in their bunks, as if the thin walls could swallow sounds. Those first times sharing a room with strangers.

Much later, one evening in the village, Milena had said that they were already calling her a widow. He was just packing his things. They sat silently in front of the stove all night. Alone, a person can become so angry or sad, it rubs their eyes dull.

This duffel: the feeling of being unable to get up.

He was awake in the dawn, occasionally he fell into a light sleep. He left the room once to get something to eat, he sat next to a dirty mop in the corner of a bar, over the dishes stood a rose, mounted in a frame of glass and silver, on it the greasy fingerprints of count-less summer days. Ornate scales forced themselves through a pair of computer speakers, droning up and down, *daaarling*, it didn't escape the notice of the young man behind the bar when Waclaw put a tough piece of meat back on his plate.

That afternoon he saw a stocky figure with a flat face and a checked shirt in the courtyard. His walk, as if he were carrying a heavy bucket in each hand. Troy had always been there a bit before them, he came when the fields and the bedrock were still being developed. He gave Mátyás prophesies about the depth at which the rock would become particularly hard, and he was always right. He came from Perth and had a reputation. Some said he could hear the rock. But he avoided the big drilling crews, and Waclaw rarely saw him. He limped. Troy had grown old.

And Waclaw knew where he could find him.

That night he took a taxi to the edge of the city. Sidi Ifni was small, and it wasn't a long drive. The bar was squat and stood at the edge of a cliff. Inside, there was a heavy wooden door, behind which the drinks were poured.

He found Troy out behind the bar on a low bench, his sharp knees pointing toward the sea far beneath the cliff. Here one could hear the waves smacking against the sand in the darkness, the gurgling under the cliffs that stood on the sides of the bay. Like large animals. Like something that waited.

Sit down, Troy said.

He smoked as he had learned to long ago in the army, he hid the glow with his palm. He lifted his chin as if thinking about something, and even in the semidarkness Waclaw could see that the skin underneath had grown slack. Troy's English was a friendly singsong.

Waclaw gave him a beer.

Thank you, mate.

He asked Troy what was new out there.

He said, not much. They've expanded the area. To hell, he said, it's steep. Like this. Troy tilted his bottle just slightly to the side.

If you ask me, he said. And waved the thought away with his hand.

They see it as a matter of area now. But the oil doesn't come from that alone. And then you poor devils have to go out there again.

It will be a while, Waclaw said.

But it will happen.

They were silent.

The night was clear.

The door swung open and closed a few times, people walked over the gravel to the parking lot, music played in a car.

I heard about your friend, Watts, Troy said.

Yes. He held the bottle as if he couldn't move.

Yes, Troy said.

They looked out. A distant freighter thrust itself slowly out into the night.

You know what I've never understood, even after all these years? Troy finally said.

You shoot the cannon, and the sound goes down and the reverberation hits the ocean floor. And all you do is wait for an answer. But there's something between the shot and the first signal. I don't mean just the time. No matter how short the interval is, there will always be a gap. You know, my whole life just revolves around that space.

It's strange that you guys are looking out here, Waclaw said.

They're looking everywhere.

Troy shook his head.

I could be somewhere else.

Waclaw stood up and went to the bar. He bought four more

bottles, and they were ice cold, and he carried them out, and they didn't clink them, but they drank.

I was one of the first on Brent, Troy said.

It was a night like this one, I was young and couldn't sleep. I went up onto the helideck. The moon was almost full, it was spring, still cold. Maybe something had woken me. The sea was blue and silver and ice cold. Northeast of Shetland.

He paused, as if he needed a breath.

And then I saw it. Their backs first, a whole family. There were a lot of them. As if they were bathing in that strip of moonlight. Watching to see what we were up to. I never saw so many again. Not a single one in the last few years. I guess they understood what we were up to. But when you see them, you believe that they were there much earlier. That we'll never have anything on them. And the oil fields, too. As if they'd been there for all eternity. But they die quicker than flies.

They sat. Chairs were put up in the bar, they could hear it.

Where to? Troy said finally.

We're at the same hotel, no?

No. I mean, where to, Watts? What are you going to do?

He felt the bench against his back. The air was warm, but he was freezing.

North.

You quit?

Don't tell them I'm here.

I won't. No.

Troy put his bottle down. The glass crunched softly against the sand.

Do you know that we learned it from them? The seismics, to use the reverberation?

They took different ways home.
Each through his own night.

A dog followed him for a while. It was thin, and its hind legs trembled. Behind the houses was the sea, and the horizon was dark and far and roaring. The night was clear. It wasn't yet light when he got the rest of his things from the luggage room. Sometimes he wished he'd never have to fly again, he wished to walk, with her, wordlessly through the fields, past the little river with the rapids. The dark wood of the footbridge against the snow. He remembered how the fog was so thick that it dripped from the trees, a flickering sound, like a plodding, in an otherwise motionless brightness. Birds squawked. Sometimes he'd still called Milena. She must have known it was him. They hadn't said a word, just stood there, an endless distance on the other side of the germ-covered earpiece of the platform telephone, where people were already lining up in the hallway behind him; now and then he heard her breathing.

Waclaw folded his things. He stood on the balcony and kicked against the railing, while outside the heat was already creeping over the parking lot. Sometimes the sound had calmed him out there, kicking against metal, as if this sound were a memory, his own ticking, not perfectly congruent with the running of the machines.

At midday he sat under an umbrella, bent over a tortilla, he felt gristle between his teeth, and the corn tasted sour. A woman watched him, she ran a hand over her belly, he couldn't decipher her smile.

He left Sidi Ifni by bus. He knew that the CEOs came by helicopter, their necks always freshly shaven, and they seemed pale beside those who had already been toiling out there for weeks. For the normal workers there were shuttles and taxis. Waclaw stood with the others in the concrete public bus stop. He was taller than most. A few women sat on the sidewalk, the men smoked in the shade a little way off. When he saw how the full the bus was, he turned around.

He went to the fishermen in the harbor and asked if they would take him. He offered money. Tomorrow, they said. And no farther than Tiznit. Airport, he asked, but they seemed not to hear him.

He waited for the night bus. It drove through the twilight. A woman sat beside him; her daughter sat on her lap and fell against him in her sleep. She slept against his chest. The lights inside the bus stayed on all night. He didn't move. It was warm.

When it was already growing light, he saw camels tied up in a row under a streetlamp, but he hardly dared to move his head.

The taste of salt was on his tongue when the bus entered the long line in front of the harbor; the motors of dented, overheated cars, the distant yapping of the border dogs, in the water the silent parasols of a few jellyfish. The border guards straightened their pants as they walked toward the bus. The driver had gotten out, and through the windows Waclaw saw bags being torn open, passports taken out and flipped through. The border guards stood silently and watched the driver hauling the heavy suitcases out of the luggage compartment.

The air over the parking lot was cool after the cramped bus. He still had a little splotch of the girl's spittle on his shirt when he took his bag and left. He knew this part of the journey. Freighters, the brackish water of the harbor facilities. This smell of rust and heat. He sat for a while on an iron bollard. His phone rang, and he listened to it with something like amazement. This sound: as if he were still important, as if he were still needed.

Behind the harbor a broad street ran toward the high-rises that flickered in the distance, like the asphalt itself. Laundry was drying in front of the windows, a few thistles bloomed reddish on the ground. He soon reached a stoplight. Merchants with coolers in front of their bellies ran through the cars selling drinks, sweets, stuffed animals. A few tall trees next to the street.

He was about to put down his duffel when he saw a woman sitting in the shade, wearing blue plastic gloves. Two girls, still very young, stood behind her. In her left hand she held a plucked chicken over a pot, in the right, a knife, which she stabbed into the cold bluish flesh. Then she looked up. As if he were disturbing her. As if he were witnessing something not meant for his eyes. Her look was brief and hard, and he saw her wide eyebrows. The girls stood there in embarrassment. They edged in front of their mother and tried to smile.

Waclaw continued on. He let himself be driven to the airport as if he were in a hurry.

14

Malta

The clasps of his duffel were worn and dull. Evening was falling when they reached the airport at Luqa. He'd had to transfer in Rome and had to wait a long time for the connecting flight; the doors of the gates snapped open and closed and he'd watched how everything arrived and continued onward, and when they took off, he looked down at Rome and at the Coliseum, and it wasn't the city he knew. He could walk again across the Piazza del Popolo, thirsty among the water fountains, Mátyás was with Patrícia and Waclaw wandered aimlessly, though he knew they'd see each other in three days. He'd sat on the Spanish Steps and not dared to call Milena, gelati, marble, nothing helped. From the plane it was no more than the outline of some city where they could no longer be found.

He didn't want to see any swimmers; he sat between the big rocks on the water and listened to the gurgling. A distant lighthouse whose nondirectional beacon didn't reach the spot where he sat. He avoided the artificiality of the promenade, the sounds of the tourists: the bored, slightly anxious forward movement of their rubber soles.

Malta, Patrícia had said to him. What did you two want with that place? You need something official for taxes, he'd said.

Malta, *stone of shimmering white*, the cupolas and hotels. He sat for a while on a bench near the quay. Yachts and yacht owners.

Cruise ships slid by like huge floating apartment buildings. From the top deck passengers were filming the departure from the harbor. *Valetta*, they'd write on their vacation videos. Maybe they'd discover him there, weeks later. A spot on the rocks. What's that? No, he's not hurt.

It was nearly eleven when he reached the alley. He went to the bar and sat down, she ignored him awhile before putting down her rag and coming over. So soon? she said. Bad? She smiled, gave him the key. There were still two guests in the bar. An older man and a boy in a faded T-shirt: *California*. He saw the man's leather shoes brushing the boy's shin and ankles. It smelled of aftershave.

The spiral staircase was narrow and steep.

He dropped his bag in the corner of the room, lay down, listened to the noises of the street. The room was in a side street off the Is-Suq covered market, in a few hours the first vendors would be setting up their stalls. Sometimes he'd watched the dark shadows moving between the stands as if setting up a stage. Irene came up the stairs, her steps heavy. He stood up and waited for her at the window.

She pulled the curtains closed while her hands were already unfastening his belt. She lay under him and let him do what he liked, she didn't meet him halfway, she didn't stretch toward him. He'd wanted to just lift up her dress, but she took it off completely and lay under him, a pale landscape. On good days she stood up against the wardrobe; then her body seemed more resistant, with more tension. Standing behind her he could imagine the woman who'd set out years before, who'd gradually let her body become exhausted by the Mediterranean sun. Her back still had the shape of a younger body, narrowing toward the waist. But her face, when she met him in the bar, had something so disappointed about it, her voice grated metallic over a background of cigarette smoke, and she left long pauses between her sentences, which she herself didn't seem to notice.

Sometimes he tried to imagine the faces that had accompanied her for a while; sometimes he was horrified by how little she expected of him. The smell of peach-scented cleaner drifted through the cracks in the bathroom door. It was a wordless darkness, in which they sweated without much excitement. Afterward she touched him, and he lay still until she was asleep.

He'd been coming to her for a good two years, and she asked nothing in return, just a present now and then, as if he did actually owe her something after all. After the fall of the Wall, she'd set out from a small town in Thuringia and ended up in Malta, the bottom edge of Europe, she said, where people like you and me wash up like animals after an oil spill. The thing that people have to lose is what we lack. Irene babbled when she was drunk, and didn't open her store until noon or so: shell necklaces that she'd made herself at first, then begun importing from China. Tourists booked island tours with her—to old film sets and far-flung coves, and he was sure she'd had a relationship with most of the tour guides at some point. It meant nothing to him to lie beside her, it didn't feel like betrayal, and even if he were to see Milena again, everything that happened here would be without significance.

He lay in the half-light until the noise from the market became intolerable. The traces had dried on his body, they often reminded him of salt, the dried edges of puddles that crystalize in indeterminate heat, salt lakes, dry landscapes where the light stabs your eyes. But while trailers rattled over the cobblestones outside, and an unfamiliar body turned over to the clatter of empty boxes, while merchants whistled and he looked through a slit in the window screen that fluttered in the light wind, and when he finally sat up, the bony shins and the residue of night on his skin, it made him think of a skim of ice that had spread to his rib cage and covered him. A new kind of ice, something that could have come only from inside him.

He dressed quietly and threw on a shirt, slipped his bare feet into shoes, walked to the stand at the corner of the square, and had them put together a cardboard box filled with ham and olives that he would leave by her door, as he had often done, without going in. The morning was cool, and the vendor looked at him thoughtfully. Everywhere, for years, people had seen at a glance that he was from somewhere else.

That there was something unfinished, something yet to be continued.

In the church several candles were burning on a wire rack. Maybe it was only the midday heat that had gone to his head, the wandering around an island, and the fact that they hadn't even mentioned Mátyás when they announced the termination of his contract and his summary dismissal to his voice mail. Two old women under dark scarves knelt in prayer closer to the front. The thick stone walls screened the heat, a few voices trickled through the streets like a light drizzle. On a pedestal stood a saint with a beehive at his side, everything was carved out of white marble. After a while, Waclaw looked up again without knowing what it was about the saint that bothered him. He carried an old-fashioned straw beehive. But there wasn't a single bee to be seen. And what was the point of a hive without bees? A structure for everything that had once been alive, now empty. Strangely contorted, the figure looked over his shoulder at a small round window that, if it had once been colored, had now been replaced with plain glass. He left.

+ + +

Closed shutters, mildewed limestone balustrades. He walked downhill, the light was yellowish. Somewhere was the sea that he'd once set out for, that had been with him even in sleep. But now there were only these smoking candles on an altar, and he saw the kneelers before him: countless pleas, hundreds of days, the wood soft as soap.

And there were the market flagstones that would stink of fish for a hundred more years, there were the fish, long as an arm, shimmering like aluminum, boys who schlepped the tubs full of water, red and bloody, a few meters to the next gutter. The cats sleeping in the ruins, the pigeons with mangled feet, cathedrals, bridges, cherubs, saints, believers, prayers, protective amulets, holy candles, eight-armed candelabra, and the hunger of these streets, the hunger that drove him in exhaustion back to her domain. Irene wouldn't come from the bar until late in the night, and he was glad of this door that he could close behind him for a few hours.

Then something drove him out again, in the night, the gutters smelled putrid, he saw young men dancing joyfully on a last empty terrace, he passed an encampment, behind a wall were hundreds of dilapidated RVs, lone figures pushing shopping carts and small wheelbarrows with things in them: boxes, goods, the rest of a life or a dream, the half-light, the prostitutes on the corner of a narrow alley, people carrying plastic bags. On a curb, the worn-out face of a woman who looked at him, what else is there, you've been seen, recognized, the cold light of tall streetlamps, he walked.

A few nights he drank so much that even Irene stayed away from him.

+ + +

He'd hardly slept. He sat at the edge of the piazza. Two street performers stood in front of a church, their faces painted white. But the midday heat was so strong that no one walked across the square voluntarily. Behind a man disguised in livery, an angel walked to the steps in front of the church, from under which he retrieved a shabby backpack. They flopped down, legs spread, in the shade on the stone steps, and they smoked and looked wretchedly tired in all the light. *It's like a prison, and you know it.* He heard Mátyás's voice in his ear. They'd fought. It was March. Mátyás had just begun planning his trip. His Andes. The rooftop of what world? The sirens had started to get to them: magenta alarm, yellow alarm, the hurrying to the meeting points, H_2S, the exercises, the routines. The angel brushed a hand through the white of his face. The first stores closed for the coming lunch hour, pigeons walked in the shadows, once Waclaw thought he saw a banded one. He walked as if he, too, were in disguise, as if there were no one left who could tell him who he was or what he should do here.

That evening he sat awhile at the bar, they'd had a broken conversation, from which Irene kept disappearing to pour or mix something or to cut lemons into eighths. He'd tried to tell her about Cairo, about the coops and the sacks of corn that the boys carried up to the roofs for the pigeons, he'd caught himself saying *my boys*, and then, perhaps because it was easier, about the gleaming blue-lit cruise ships on the Nile.

When the door opened and Patrice came in, for the first time he saw that night a flicker of something like interest on Irene's face. Patrice was tall; he grinned broadly and greeted a few of the men, then burst out laughing when he recognized Waclaw, and came over to him. Irene had to stifle a smile, and gave him a sign: she crossed her fingers and pointed to Waclaw. Patrice looked back and forth between them, grinned, and asked what they were drinking.

She went to get beer.

Patrice talked a lot. He hadn't been at it long. Waclaw thought of the Austrians he'd met at the edge of the Sahara. They'd talked only of the heat, of scorpions, of Vienna, of their carports and wooded mountains. Patrice was different. He talked about the gas fields that would soon be tapped. It seemed to interest him.

And do you know what the field is called? he said.

He waited until Irene was back with the bottles. His face contorted into a grin.

Aphrodite, he said. It's called Aphrodite.

He looked back at Irene. His grin stayed the same width.

Aphrodite, Patrice said again. Perfect, right? South of Cyprus.

Again, she gave him a sign. He looked at Waclaw.

And the next field over? Patrice asked.

He reminded Waclaw now of a quizmaster from the nineties, only without a bow tie, and there was no vacuum cleaner to win.

It's named after a sea monster, he said, answering his own question. Now Patrice raised his eyebrows. One of those guys must have been some jokester, he said.

It's called Shithead, Waclaw said.

After which sea monster? Irene asked.

Leviathan, Patrice said. They'll bash each other's heads in over it. Patrice laughed.

Huge fields, he said.

They'll last ten years at most, Waclaw said.

He looked at Patrice. Waclaw didn't know why he made him so angry. He was naïve. He'd jumped on the bandwagon. But he was dumb, too.

Patrice was still grinning.

To Leviathan, he said, and raised his glass.

Irene stared at Patrice. She hung on his every word. On his crew cut.

Waclaw drank.

They will, he said.

He left.

He could hear Mátyás's voice when he sat barefoot in the dark on the sharp cliffs, when none of the lights of the distant freighters were meant for him.

They'd called it Woodpecker Cove because it grew narrow between the cliffs, narrow and straight, coming to a point, like the beak of a woodpecker. The cliffs weren't particularly high, but steep enough to keep other visitors away. It was hard to climb down in the dark. He sat on the edge and waited until dawn began to break.

Only gradually did the black dash become visible, sharpening in the distance like a line someone had drawn with a ruler to divide something. As if there were no movement there, no current.

Mátyás had had a technique, letting the big waves wash over him. He dived diagonally into them, allowing them break over him in order to avoid getting caught in the rollers, which pulled your legs out from under you and dashed you against the ground. He called it floating. Above him, the danger, just gently brushing his back. A light oscillation, like in a boxing match: he floated, he let the waves roll by.

Waclaw had sat on the shore, and here, in the sudden peace of the cove, he'd felt something beginning to work away at him. The images of his accident suddenly resurfaced, though that was all before Mátyás, and he'd long hoped to be able to make a clean break, as if with Mátyás everything would begin anew. But in this sudden peace it all came back. The cot, the numbness in his arm. The big tongs, they said, had sprung back and smashed into his shoulder; his head had hit the derrick as he fell. Waclaw couldn't remember. Perhaps out of carelessness, he'd not secured himself, the carabiner hung useless at his waist. A barely repressible weariness, which was a privilege of the rig elders. He'd known others to whom similar things had happened: the platform slippery in the rain, a warning shot, most didn't come back.

Waclaw.

They'd called him by his first name and pulled him down, his suit was soaked. Then he'd awoken on a cot, even narrower than his usual bed, a light was shone in his face. He'd been fucking lucky, they said to him over and over.

In the following weeks he'd lain in a dim room in Cairo, listened to the noises from the street. The city was a strip of smog and light, his finger lay without feeling on the pillow in front of him, pointing in no particular direction, a long railroad embankment that ran directionless through the land. Perhaps that was the first time he realized that he couldn't go back to her. That was years ago, and he'd wandered through Cairo for weeks before he'd discovered the boys, the coops, the pigeons high above the city. A few times he needed to be close to a woman and went to Farangis—on a platform such addresses were easy to come by. Only much later had he met Mátyás on the safety course.

Here, in the cove, he'd grown uneasy. Sometimes they'd ridden in a motorboat. Along the coast. The water clear. The days stretched.

He was tired after that night. The swimming, when it was barely light enough. The black smoke of a distant tanker. The salt burned on his skin, his linen shoes were torn, he smelled of algae. He could already hear the bells as he was climbing up the cliffs. The distant ringing. He took a detour to the cathedral. St. Paul's. People were streaming through the six columns of the entrance portal, and Waclaw walked around the building until he found a corner—a projection off one of the aisles of the church. He could smell the cool stone as he laid his head against the wall, then he heard the organ, as if behind the wall's foundation lay another room. The resonance was strong, and he remained standing there for a long time. He still had the melody in his head when he carefully pushed open the door to the bar. Irene wasn't there. He went up the narrow stairs and washed the salt from his skin, raised the sheet and let himself fall onto the bed. Everything was still quiet, except for the rumbling of the organ in his head.

It was March, and London was just a stopover. Waclaw stayed in an airport hotel in the southern part of the city: light gray carpeting, soundproof windows. On the way back he'd recognized the specialists who'd been flown in for the borehole measurements. They determined pore space, resistance, and conductivity before the casings could be inserted, they tested the porosity of the rock. They shared a taxi from Gatwick into the city for the evening.

Most of the men wanted to get an early start, so they drank less than usual, and the food and conversation was bland, stale, as if they were just imagining talking to one another. Waclaw left early and started walking south alone, maybe he just needed some fresh air before the night. Then he'd stopped. The street was nearly empty, wind blew through the tall trees. Perhaps he wouldn't even have noticed the melody if he hadn't fought with Mátyás over that trifle a few days earlier. Unlike usually, the bad feeling had lasted awhile, and Mátyás had taken the connecting flight to Budapest in the night. Now the notes floated through the fir trees in the darkness.

They were on the Gulf of Mexico, *West Capricorn*, spring. They'd worked all night, perhaps that had made Waclaw more irritable. In Europe, March was still cold, they could see that on the screen in the television room, and maybe the gray clouds were the reason that the men kept switching back to it. He'd sat wearily on the sofa with Mátyás. Some of the men were watching a bike race, but they changed the channel when ads came on, and those gray clouds returned over and over. A voice spoke very quick Spanish. Mátyás nudged him.

That's Rome, he said.

And then they saw the crowds in St. Peter's Square, a cloudy sky and the rooftops of Rome, gray smoke, the Swiss Guards in their yellow-and-purple gaiters and knickerbockers, plumes of red feathers on their helmets. There was the smell of sweat, and the narrowness of the recreation room, the stained carpet, and while outside the sea grew gray like cold ashes, and far away the clouds took on a bright sheen, over there where the cities must be, where the streetlights were being turned on overhead, the clouds hung low over St. Peter's Square, and Waclaw sat there and couldn't look away. He felt like he recognized them, those pilgrims who had gathered in their thin rain jackets, who stared into the air at some smoke that could only be meant for each of them individually. They all read their own story in that sky. And that story needed a new teller, someone to turn the pages, someone who knew about them, who would accompany them on their journey through the endless cities.

It was the papal election, the bishops had gathered for the conclave, and the other workers sat for a while, indecisive in front of the image on the screen, until it became clear that nothing else was going to happen, no one was coming out, everyone was just gathering around some gray smoke. A few of the men laughed, a few had fallen asleep, and Asle flipped back to the bike race with the remote. He was the driller, he could change the channel, and it took Waclaw a moment before he started to move forward in his seat. He stood in front of the huge flat screen.

Switch it back, he said softly.

At first they were just surprised, but then they started to throw things at him, someone shook a can of Coke and opened it a little bit and sprayed it in his direction.

The evening was saved.

They laughed and lay like a horde of sea lions on their cushions, minus the tenderness between the animals. He could still hear them outside. He tried not to look them in the eyes as he stood up and left. Only Mátyás came after him, he knew where to find him.

What's up, he asked.

We can't lose our sense of respect, Waclaw said.

The argument was short and fierce. Mátyás called him too sentimental, and Waclaw said: Then you just don't understand, and he couldn't explain what it meant that there one hope was being replaced with another one, and all of his father's last prayers.

Later they tried to avoid the topic, but they kept bumping up against it, like a painful spot in the mouth that the tongue keeps running over to test whether it's still there. It was there.

And on that evening in London, among the cold, swaying fir trees, while under the light of the streetlamps double-decker buses drove into their own redness and some homeless people scrapped by a kiosk, Waclaw stood in the middle of the street and listened to an organ, powerful among the firs. Where the music was, the windows were illuminated yellow.

Without the fight, it might not have had any meaning for him, but as it was, he felt a certain emotion, just because of a familiar sound. He could see the miners' estate, the small yellow windows like markings on a much deeper black, the incense, the Polish prayers. At the same time, the whole fight struck him as ridiculous, and he missed Mátyás, who'd grown uncertain in the airplane and had parted from him with a long embrace.

His clothing was still a bit damp, he could hear the vendors outside. In the corner of St. Paul's he'd simply stood there, his ear against the cool stone. Something about the melody was familiar. Now he looked around. On the only plastic hanger in Irene's room hung his jacket with the ivory nut button. He closed his eyes when he heard her steps. She came alone. He didn't know what Patrice had given her. *Aphrodite.* In the bar below he heard something clinking.

15

A Parrot

At the market he bought a glittering watch, the stones were bright on the black armband. He'd withdrawn some money, enough for the next while.

Irene was sitting on the bed smoothing lotion on her legs when he knocked. Her calves were solid and heavy. He looked at her. She rubbed the leftover lotion into her forearms.

She stretched out her legs in front of her.

I can't even touch my toes anymore, she said.

As if to prove it, she bent forward, reached her hands to her knees. The sleeves of her bathrobe were frayed.

What is that? she said.

He gave her the box. She sat on the edge of the bed. The stones gleamed brightly when she lifted the cover. He saw that her brown, scarred knee almost touched the wall. She laid the box down carelessly and looked out the window. The thin curtain waved slightly, it had water stains that had grown brown at the edges.

Do you know what I've been thinking about recently? she said.

I was in my early twenties when I packed my things, it was the mid-nineties. I went to see my grandmother in Berlin, to say goodbye. She'd survived the war and she saw me standing there with my backpack. The wooden floor creaked, it was an old apartment on Warschauer Straße. I probably looked terrible, still some teenage pudginess, my head full of crazy ideas. She put her arms around me because she knew I was leaving. And do you know what she said?

She looked out the corner of the window, over the terra-cotta roofs. Laundry that no one had brought in hung on the fire escape, the building opposite looked lifeless under its rusty antennas.

Irene looked briefly at Waclaw, then looked out again.

She said: It's a big world no matter what.

And then she kissed my forehead and let me go.

That's what you've been thinking about?

That's what I've been thinking about.

She turned her back to him.

I think I'm only just starting to understand what she meant.

She lay on her side and pulled her legs in toward her.

He was careful not to hit his head on the spiral staircase. He saw himself in his first work shoes, in the harbor. And all of a sudden he could smell the faux leather, the little bag in which he'd stowed the sandwiches and a thermos. The street in front of the building lay in shadow, he walked to the same white stones, with the water sloshing against them. He felt in his pocket for the key to the locker. An old tin from his father, papers, letters. The golden initials of a Bremen tea merchant. He would have to wait before he could get his things.

A boat full of tourists had docked: the afternoon ferry. He waited until the last of them had left the shop, he watched almost impatiently while they couldn't decide between all the identical postcards, how their fingers went with greedy determination over the displays of tobacco pipes, linens, and games. Though they couldn't possibly know one another, they seemed to travel the same routes almost daily. From the harbor through the old city to her shop, then across the market square to a café, then to the weaving mill, where their guides awaited them. Beige was their color, and over the years, only their cameras got smaller.

Irene stood smoking under the washed-out awning. Her eyeshadow was thick, and when she saw him she stretched out the two fingers that held her cigarette, like in a film. She did not smile.

He set down the bag to embrace her, but she took a step away. She looked tired, like the village women whose cigarettes smolder down to their filters while the beer foam dries on the glasses and in the distance heavy clouds roll over the fields. Her skin had the brown color of shriveled fruit. She was like him. And then she smiled after all.

Saw his duffel, the suit.

Brushed something from his shoulder with her free hand.

Guapo—handsome, she said, and her eyes didn't laugh along.

Where will you go now?

Then suddenly she looked around her. All the postcards. All the sunsets. She seemed uncertain.

I have the shop, you know.

I know.

He touched her shoulders.

It's a good shop.

You wouldn't want me to give it up, would you?

For a fraction of a moment he saw something in her eyes that he had seen once before, a long time ago, in the eyes of a deer that he'd found near the railroad embankment, the grass warm from its blood, it hadn't had the strength to get up. He felt her long, slightly matted hair on his arm as she leaned against him. He saw that it had grown dull, and he smelled the light bar smell rising from her clothes. He knew that she'd be alone for a long time.

But it's your shop, he said softly. And I have to take care of a few things.

Yes, she said, then more softly, things. Be well.

She seemed tired, too tired for a goodbye; she turned around and walked into the shadow of the postcards. He couldn't have said whether she watched him walk away.

The neon sign was partially out of order, so that from the top down it read H TEL. The O flickered only occasionally. It was a run-down, tall building near the harbor, he paid for a room for one night. The halls smelled of old mops and dust. He thought of Patrícia as he folded a few things on the bed. He heard their last conversation like an echo in his head. *No one's here anymore.*

He walked up the hill. In the light blue of the evening the clouds were glowing orange streaks, the lines of airplanes drew a fine ember-orange light after them; the houses below them already lay in shadow. Chimneys and antennas took on sharp contours. The light of the streetlamps that hung on long cables over the street mingled with the yellow and red of a few neon signs. The seam of his right shoe had split, and he felt little stones. Finally came the last apartment buildings. The cracked asphalt continued on for a while, plots of land with tall wooden fences and heavy padlocks. He walked through the darkening evening until he reached the workshop's big parking lot with its sudden floodlights, the neon light, and the scrapped car bodies at the edges, with the little container, a light within it still burning.

Before it stood a high metal fence. Waclaw pushed the gate open, the metal bar whined over the concrete, somewhere a stray dog yapped. He waited a moment and then walked toward the container.

Before he could knock, he heard a parrot squawk inside. The bird, small and gray with a dark beak, moved excitedly back and forth on its perch as the door was opened. Everything was enveloped in blue smoke, the bird clamored excitedly over a sea of papers, work gloves, half-empty oilcans.

In the midst of it all sat Eugenio with his shiny, sweaty skin and even fewer hairs on his flat skull than last time. Eugenio looked up.

Then he laughed.

I thought I'd never see you again.

They walked through the big, low building with the hydraulic lifts, car jacks, and tools, a few boat motors were lying around and Waclaw saw a sweat mark on Eugenio's light-gray shirt where the back of the chair must have been. It was still warm. It smelled of brake fluid and gasoline and solvents, a welding helmet hung on the wall next to a small door that Eugenio opened. The workshop with its meter-high iron shelves full of boxes seemed chaotic and deserted, so that he sometimes asked himself how they actually made the money.

Eugenio looked around.

You're lucky, I'm late today.

Then he reached his hand through the crack in the door, and they went into a low room with a few lockers. A single construction light hung on a black cord from the ceiling. It slowly warmed into a glow.

Vuoi che ti lascio solo?

Waclaw shook his head.

It was cool in the room, it smelled of concrete and dust.

He took the key from his pocket and opened the steel door. The locker looked like it came from a gym or an old swimming pool, only wider. A few names were scratched into the paint.

He stuffed the cardboard boxes into his duffel, then he took out the tin, a green suitcase, and the boots. The leather was lighter than he'd remembered. Good leather. He'd looked forward to the boots.

They'd begun pumping nitrogen into the big oil field of Cantarell to increase the pressure, he'd gone on land with the others to Ciudad del Carmen, and he'd taken the boots from a young charro. It was Mexico, they sat playing poker, their eyes watered. The boy had stringy hair that he brushed away from his face in embarrassment, he drank the last swig of mezcal with the worm, he had three kings and two queens, full house, but not enough. He put his boots on the table, he said they were good, from his father, when he lost again the tears rose to his face, it was hot. It was the night before the start of the shift, the young charro looked back and forth between them, looked at Pasqual, who'd been a boxer before he started as a roughneck, his neck as thick as two, a tattoo of the Madonna on his arm, an oval that warped when he bent over. The cartilage of Pasqual's ears was ragged, the boy looked pale next to him, he sat there as if he had to think it over, then he stood up, said he would come back the next day and trade the boots for money, but Waclaw never saw him again.

They were faded cowhide with a leather sole and a wooden heel. They looked so much like another, real life that he was sometimes ashamed to wear them.

He felt again over the top compartment of the locker, picked up the tin, and wiped it off with his sleeve. He saw the embossed initials, the packet of letters weighed next to nothing, he set them carefully on top of the other things. Then he took a few bills and the keys and gave both to Eugenio.

Eugenio counted the money, then he looked at the keys in his hand.

There are two. This one isn't mine.

Keep it.

Eugenio shrugged.

Aren't you coming back?

Didn't go so well? Problems?

When Waclaw shook his head, Eugenio clapped him on the shoulder.

Women! he said then.

Waclaw accepted a warm beer in Eugenio's container, he looked at the parrot and its dark red tail feathers and didn't speak of the sea. He said he had a goal: Italy. He took out the tin and talked of a friend of his father, Alois, who'd gone back there, leaving the Ruhr, where they'd been almost neighbors for years, like a kind of uncle, Waclaw said. Eugenio didn't understand everything, but he answered in slow Italian of which Waclaw understood only bits. Eugenio said he'd always known that Waclaw wouldn't stray too far.

What did he want up there.

Colombe, he said, really?

Yes, Waclaw said. *Colombe*. Pigeons.

Then he opened both hands. He'd been ten years old back then.

He closed the door to his balcony before dawn. The streetlights were going out, H TEL, it was growing light. He left the suitcase and most of the things on the bed. He carried the duffel, the straps dug into his shoulder pads. The streets smelled damp, street sweepers sprinkled the stones, cats ran timidly between the garbage cans in the early gray. Three cranes towered out of the fog. He heard the clattering song of the beggars as he waited in the harbor of Valetta. He heard that they were looking for bottles, food, and clothing. He thought that it would be easy to look for things. He thought that he'd looked for things in the distance, but that there'd been nothing there. Nothing for humans. It was a high-pitched sound, and those that heard it started to drink and acted out just to get it out of their ears. Few could bear it. It was like hearing the cosmos, interrupted by the brief, futile throbbing of one's own heart. It was easier to look for things. It was easier to sell lemonade on the beach and not to step any farther than that edge.

He looked down at himself. The light-colored boots. As if nothing else were left, as if they were all that remained from Mexico, them and the fear, and the violet-blue blossoms of the jacarandas.

The trees blooming in the streets, and they were there, they were nowhere, they ate *pollo pibil* and corn, strolled through markets, went to a fisherman who rented his boat out for money, though he didn't like the oil people. None of them. It was as if those days and weeks were inaccessible, like massive villas behind high fences, with blinds that lowered automatically. Sometimes he'd thought of that fisherman, his green shirt and the arm chaps, matted strands hung down his back, the hair over his forehead was already gray. He'd watched them go off with disdain, as if they knew nothing of the sea. He stood on the shore with his short legs, a little sun shelter he'd built himself out of driftwood. Protected by a few sheets, he sat in these shadows surrounded by coolers, he watched them push the boat into the water, his foot was missing the big toe, and they rowed clumsily, Mátyás and he, hardly making any progress against the small waves that rolled toward the beach.

When they pulled the boat back ashore, the fisherman was already standing there in the blazing sun. He didn't even look at them as he took the money.

Waclaw, Mátyás said, wait.

And Waclaw saw him, piecing together his few fragments of Spanish before the man. He was a full head taller than the fisherman, who stood there in his green undershirt over his bony chest. Mátyás talked at him, and the old man looked at him calmly, while his hands were already gliding out of his pockets, as if they wanted to grab something. A paddle. A stick.

Next time, Mátyás said softly, I want a little hole, somewhere under the seats, well hidden. One that opens only when we're far enough out. So far that we can't make it back.

Mátyás bent over him, speaking right in his ear.

And I want you to watch, old man. Watch as we sink. Even though we just do the same damn work. Even though we pay for it, every day, in this shithole.

You brought us here yourselves, Mátyás said softly.

The old man looked at him.

¿Qué? No comprendo, he said calmly.

Mátyás's lower lip trembled with rage.

He screamed the same thing in Spanish. But then he stopped.

No es nuestra culpa.

He said it softly, over and over.

And then the old man came toward him.

Much more softly, Mátyás had told him later, he'd said just this one sentence: Boy, what are you doing out here?

They spent a few nights in a town nearby. As if they had the right to be there. As if everything were just the way it was, and none of them had a choice. Horses, thin as flies, pulled carriages full of tourists past them.

Then an explosion in the Gulf of Mexico turned everything on its head. Helicopters filmed the black clouds south of the Mississippi

Delta, over the Macondo oil field. They saw the platform sink in aerial photographs, but for eighty days the hole in the ocean floor couldn't be closed. *Deepwater Horizon*. Mátyás avoided the cove and the beach, he was almost afraid of running into the fisherman again—he was right, he was fucking right, he said. Their relief when they sat in the plane back to the other side of the Atlantic was almost physical. Mátyás didn't look out the window. But you couldn't miss it. The smoke wasn't quiet.

Mexico was the slow rolling by of an empty freight car, the striking of steel against steel above the swells. It was the droning in their ears in the last hours of the shift, and Asle, whose voice carried over it all when he chided them, the cold sea wind on their necks and their feet icy in their steel-toed shoes. *Peak oil*, he roared, meaning that the men couldn't let up, as if it would be their fault if at four in the morning their strength flagged. They were dog-tired. They could almost see the oil well bleeding out.

16

Northward

In front of him on deck a family was having their picture taken, as if the blue were just a photo backdrop, the walls of the quay with the freighters, the yellow-white of the city, the Maltese limestone that they called *golden* in Irene's store, two cupolas towered over the rooftops. He looked at the water, which was now widening ahead of him. They headed for Catania, the wind on deck picked up. Soon the island was no more than a bright spot. He thought of Troy. He thought of Brent, and how great the business still was when he started. He saw the curved rows of the dolphin's teeth, the split skin and the mouth. Maybe it had never smiled.

And of course Eugenio had lied. In the night, as Waclaw sat across from him in the container, he'd suddenly had the feeling that he really was traveling toward something. He'd told Eugenio of this Italy as if someone were waiting for him there, he'd said Alois's name and saw how Eugenio closed his hands again and again, as if he were squeezing out a sponge: a new tic. He hadn't said that Alois's letters, stamped years ago, perhaps no longer belonged to anyone. His father had left him no more than that. After all the years, seeing Alois's writing had touched him. It was only a few clumsy sentences in the middle of a piece of paper that seemed too big for them.

✦   ✦   ✦

And Eugenio? Eugenio would no more leave his container on that evening than on any other. He would just sit there, would watch the air coming in through the little sliding window as in a boat that was growing heavier, sinking farther and farther into the water. His parrot would tell him useful things that neither he nor anyone else understood. When they reached the open sea, the passengers stopped taking photographs. A strange silence fell over them.

The train station smelled of urine and rusty steel, and he heard a few youths working on a vending machine with a hammer, trying to get a few packs of Camels out of it. The machine was old, and once they'd hacked a hole in the glass and cut the wire with pliers they found two packs, and smoked the dry old tobacco without filters. One of the boys spat the brown crumbs on the platform in disgust.

The train station in Catania was small. From the water he'd seen a few salt flats, the glaring white in the pools. As the train pulled in, it smelled of rust and old iron; his hair was still sticky from the crossing. They traveled north for a long time. The train stopped at small stations, and when they finally rolled into the belly of the ferry that was to carry them from Messina to the mainland, the woman across from him had fallen asleep. She wore a jacket with small embroidered flowers, and he felt her knee fall against his. Then he closed his eyes as if also sleeping, so as not to alarm her in case she awoke. The train continued on land at San Giovanni, and while the mainland's mountains, power lines, its blurry green and large buildings passed by, he concentrated on the jerks and bumps of the journey that pressed her knee against his. When he closed his eyes, it was as if they were traveling together. And while the train traveled up the coast, as passengers got on and off and a few beggars crowded around the doors, it made him think of the parts of the sea that currents flowed around, where the sailors once slaughtered their horses, the eternal doldrums: the horse latitudes, the Sargasso Sea, which is fed from outside, by other currents—Mátyás's laugh, when he tracked down Wenzel in his cabin, when he sent signals with the glass of his watch to the passing freighters—and that now there was nothing there, only the bulbous brown algae that almost broke the surface.

And it was all long ago: the floodlights in the harbor, the lights of the seaside promenades, a low marble bench, their legs, stretched in front of them as it grew light, as the high wore off, and they remained there, sitting, as the first street sweepers drove along the streets, a boulevard that knew of the sea, and the neon signs going out above it. Mátyás, his head on Waclaw's shoulder, no longer laughing the way he had all night, and far away, as if they were still searching for something, their eyes wandered over the same hills and the mist and the light that was slowly rising, for a moment all was golden, all bright.

It was evening when they reached Pescia. It was hot in the train station, he was sticky. In the train the temperature had been bearable, the heat outside the windows seemed far away, it had no color, one could almost forget it. When he stepped onto the platform, his body seemed to expand, his face felt hot, he couldn't stand it. He stayed on the platform; a few times he felt the pressure of an unfamiliar bag against his shoulder.

The train station was big, and light fell through the high, dirty panes. It seemed to come from far away, and the hall with its riveted steel arches seemed to come from another era, as if in a black-and-white photograph, people hurrying along in light coats. A gelatin silver print, and the woman from the train was already gone.

05:32. He stood in front of the departures board for a while, undecided, there were no connections before the next morning. As he left the train station there were hardly any lights visible on the street—it was like in the village where they'd lived for a few years, Milena and he, with roller shutters that clattered down every evening, as if every house were a damn capsule, each its own blind world. Still, it had been hard for him to leave.

It was an evening in late fall, a few days before he was supposed to go out for the first time, from the little village in Poland, on the *Rowan X*, his first platform in Mexico, which was hardly more than a word to him back then. He'd walked with Milena in the little bit of woods beyond the fields, they were looking for porcini where the power lines made an aisle through the pines. I've got one. Milena waved him over, pulled him down to her in the grass, past the mushroom's brown cap. Her light skin against the red of her raincoat, her small, firm breasts. That the world disappeared around them quicker than usual, there was a rhythm and the smell of her skin, and that they lay there, closely entangled, before separating, then the cool air and the trees, coming back.

They walked back very slowly. They stopped only when they reached the gate. I have something for you. Milena stood behind him, buried her face between his shoulder blades, and put something in Waclaw's hand. A wooden handle. A French pocketknife.

A fog had rolled over the fields in front of them, next to them there was only the rusty gate, its paint flaking off, chips of white and red. As he walked through the night, he remembered this rust, the dirty white of the gate. Milena had stood close behind him, as if trying to encourage him to keep walking. But he stood there and couldn't. He wanted the folded knife in his pocket to disappear, he wanted to turn around, he wanted all that and to be back behind the gate in this familiar world, while they were already trudging through the darkness, and soon reached the first streetlights and fences of the village. The empty mushroom bucket hit his knee as he walked, it was still sitting outside the kitchen window when they awoke the next morning. It had filled with rain overnight.

He left the train station behind him, but he didn't look for a room. It was late, and he didn't want air-conditioning, or the colorless slippers, the breakfast, the portioned fruit. He walked. He didn't know where he was. At some point he found himself in an industrial area with large concrete surfaces, a gas station, endless fences, finally a highway and the flash of neon lights, a flat building, the music droned out to the street. He saw the outlines of people through the windows: a run-down bar, two dancing poles like measure lines in the middle of the night. He was thirsty, he went in.

The black welts of countless rubber soles on the metal legs of the bar stools. In a corner, darts players aimed for the middle of a circle, the place stank of sweat and cigarettes, there was the clacking of billiard balls, fiber-optic lamps, a clogged sink over which he hastily washed his face. Through the swinging door of the men's toilet he heard women's voices, their chirping laughter. He stood at the bar. The music was loud, old rock songs, a Lakers game on a TV screen. A woman in yellow edged past him, her skirt so tight that it puckered over her hips. Waclaw ordered a beer, a man thrust himself next to him, did he want a game, he yelled in Waclaw's ear, he had a girl, black as that eight ball. Waclaw shook his head, he held his duffel with one hand, he ordered another beer and drank. *Pepsi*, the man shouted, stretching up to him, *she's called Pepsi*. In the end it was the bartender who nodded to the man to leave Waclaw in peace. For a while he stood there watching the tall man behind the bar, who dropped other people's money into the till without looking.

He had to think of Pippo, their old drilling foreman, whose dry humor had held them all together. You could barely sense it back then, even Francis could work normally. Waclaw noticed the change only when Pippo wasn't there. Without him the whole crew seemed to wear down like a drill head under the excessive demands, and they returned to land leaden and as if wounded. The bartender was a bit older, the skin of his throat leathery, and when he needed to find something, he put on rimless reading glasses that seemed foreign to his face. For a while, Waclaw just drank his beer. The train ride lay behind him like a blurred landscape, he'd thought of the standpipes and of the winter, of the narrow cabins in which they'd told their stories. That time was like a tunnel which was now gradually growing dark.

The door slammed, and a horde of guests staggered out. Soon there was only a small group of men at the other end of the bar. They wore baseball caps and sweatpants, he'd seen their trucks outside in the parking lot, a few locals were with them. Through the window Waclaw could see the outlines of the vehicles, a single streetlamp. He wiped the bar with his sleeve and wrote Alois's address on a scrap of paper. The only light came from a beer sign, perhaps that was why he pressed the pen so hard into the paper. It was pointless. The bartender stood in front of him. He looked at Waclaw over the edge of his reading glasses.

Where did you come from? he asked, looking at the new guest as if he were trying to place him as a certain species, without success.

From the sea, Waclaw said. *Dal mare.*

It was the sentence he'd practiced with Eugenio in the container.

And where are you from? the bartender asked again. Waclaw looked at his glass. It was cool, and gleamed like all the glasses around him. After a while, he shrugged.

It was a long time ago, Waclaw said.

The bartender inspected him, as he sat there on his stool. Waclaw had wrapped his suit jacket tight around him, like a bathrobe, or as if he were cold. But it wasn't cold. Someone called out from the other side of the bar. Waclaw felt for the duffel with his foot. A large digital clock hung between the bottles. 03:02. Outside, the night. The bartender came back, rinsed a few glasses, and kept pushing his sleeves up. I'm Felip, he said, and Waclaw nodded. The weariness inside him was as solid as a piece of wire that divided everything. New names surfaced, too many faces, it had been this way for years. Everything could only wash over him now. He thought of the narrowness of the recreation rooms, the big buckets of grease that the roughnecks smeared like earwax on the ends of the pipes before they were screwed together.

Che hai fatto là—on the sea? the bartender asked, looking into the dishwater.

Waclaw drank from his glass. Oil, he said finally.

He didn't want to talk, fished for some money.

Lately he'd hated running into the others on land. He'd looked for excuses to stay in the hotel.

The bartender looked at him. How long? he asked.

Twelve, Waclaw said. Twelve years, I think. He didn't look up, though the bartender was standing right in front of him.

The bartender went to the last guests at the end of the bar, they sat calmly behind their glasses, the light fell on their hairlines, which had receded over the years. None of them were young. The smoke wafted over their heads like in a snowglobe, where everything happens far too slowly.

He refilled their glasses, then came back to Waclaw. He leaned forward.

Do you know what they remind me of? He gestured toward the men.

Waclaw looked up briefly. He wasn't sure whether he wanted

to hear it. Over the years it had become easy to make jokes. It cost nothing. Someone was always ready to laugh about the Filipinos in the kitchens, or about the management pricks. It always had to be late and they had to have drunk too much. The bartender pushed his glass against Waclaw's. Then he looked over again. But the way one looks out of a train at a place one is leaving. As if he were suddenly far away. Far from the smoke.

When I stand here, it's like birds in winter sometimes. You feed them, and they come close. You can see how fragile they are, how broken some of them are. They come every evening. And they always remind you of the great cold waiting outside in the fields. Maybe that's what makes them so beautiful.

Or whatever you want to call it.

He looked at Waclaw. Waclaw drank. He looked over at where the others were sitting. One of them wore a track jacket and had stood up, he'd started to tell a story in a southern dialect that Waclaw didn't understand, his arms waving as he talked, like a mayor giving a speech. They laughed. And the bartender laughed too. Then he suddenly turned to Waclaw and made a hurried motion toward him with his hand, like a huge spider. That close! he cried, and Waclaw flinched. He could hear him. Once again it was only the laughter of some bartender.

You don't forget that winter, he said. The days stretch over it like thin ice.

Right, Bernie? he called, and walked slowly to the other side of the bar. Bernardo, he called again, tilted a glass and filled it from the tap, slid it in front of the mayor. The bar sparkled like the sharp runner of an ice skate. When he turned around again, Waclaw was gone. He had slipped out the door like a shadow. Like the shadow of a boy with a pocketknife.

17

Everything I No Longer Am

He'd left far too large a bill on the bar. Waclaw left the town behind him, walked down the big street, but not toward the train station. For the first time in a long while he had the feeling of not wanting to go back at all. A milky film lay between the hills, covering the land, the air was cool and he felt the dampness slowly creeping into his clothes. He turned fifty-two that night. There was no lawn he had to mow, surrounding no house filled with voices or familiar smells. There were no quinces and no jam. There was the night and a fog that had come after a short afternoon shower. In the early gray he walked on the asphalt, just to hear his own steps. He was tired, and he smelled the cigarette smoke, his skin felt sticky, his ears like cotton after the din of the bar.

Jagged fields and shrubs in this whiteness. He didn't care. Maybe it was this fog that he'd been searching for the whole time, even back then, when he'd called Milena to tell her he'd not be coming home between shifts. He'd blamed the weather, which was a lie, and then spent two weeks almost motionless on that beach, watching the rich tourist women stretch their legs in the sun, stiff as ikebana twigs, while in the evenings at the bar the girls smiled at everything, not pushing his hand away while they danced over him. He slept with two of them; each time he felt the clumsy indolence of their disconnected bodies as he penetrated them. He'd liked the feeling of sand, the rolling of the Pacific waves, and he'd thought of his father, of their first vacation on the Baltic, of the brown seaweed and the jellyfish that had lain on the sand like clumps of gelatin, and he'd watched himself sink into this distance, as into a stickily sweet bath: just sand, and the gentle feeling of floating away.

It was a fog that had silently settled over whole valleys, over every country he'd known, and even Milena's calls seemed unreal, as if from another time. Only in the nights had he heard the chirping. Her chirping, as she'd greeted the crows that strutted over the furrows like pitch-black cows.

Once he reached the highway he walked for a long time in the grass. A tanker truck passed him without slowing, and it seemed gigantic and as if out of another era. Nothing lay beyond this road.

When the truck stopped, he felt tiny. He had to walk a short distance up to it: the driver had seen him too late. The taillights gleamed like two huge red eyes in the darkness, and a tarp was spread over the flatbed, dirty and old. As he climbed up the three steps and opened the door, he was met with warm air. It smelled sour. The cab was hung with printed beach towels, most of them displaying women. They lay naked, in front of palm trees. The driver said he was going far north, and asked how far Waclaw wanted to go. Waclaw named the city, he said, toward Parma, and the man asked whether he was homeless. What he was doing on the road at four in the morning. Waclaw said that he didn't know the time, and that he was in a hurry, and had no time to sleep. Everyone has to go his own way, the driver said, but he didn't think people had much of a choice in the matter. God created the world anew every day, and to understand that, they'd been given the gift of night. What was he planning?

Famiglia, Waclaw said.

He was going to visit an uncle, and the uncle was old, and he hadn't seen him in a long time. The driver said that the dead weep for the living, who have no time for one another. They drove for a long time, and on the wide, soft passenger seat, he felt how tired he was. His eyes fell shut, and he didn't understand everything the man said. To their left rose the Apennines, and the man named mountains that sounded big and powerful. Waclaw hadn't expected him to keep talking.

That he always drove the same route. That around him things changed, and he watched. That he saw more and more people on foot. That he was enclosed in his cab with radio stations in foreign languages. Everything he knew he'd learned on this road. That he let himself be read.

The women know my body, he said. They can read it. Waclaw looked at him questioningly. The man was gaunt and wore a light blue jean jacket. There was nothing striking about him. What do they read? Everything that I no longer am. He said they could see it: all the missed opportunities. He said that was long ago. That he'd come to terms with it. Life passed before his eyes. That not everyone was granted the grace to participate in it. That the night was like a curtain that opened and closed, but he was no longer allowed entrance.

Waclaw's eyes closed. The motor droned, long and even, and the gray, early land with its distant mountains lay before their high seats. What kind of grace was it that he was talking about? The driver said he didn't know much about it, but that man was capable of things for which he could never forgive himself. Then he was silent. After a while he asked whether Waclaw didn't have something to say to that, and Waclaw said no, that he knew nothing of such things. The driver said that these were the questions that haunt men in the night. That he could hear them, as if they floated above all the sleeping houses.

Il paese. The land, he said, is not ruled by men.

When Waclaw asked him where he lived, he raised his out-stretched arm and pointed in front of and behind him. Then he laughed.

He had a brother in Bergamo who sold tires.

Could he spare a blanket. A blanket?

He had one in the back, to secure the freight.

Waclaw said he could pay for it.

That won't be necessary, the driver said.

Waclaw let himself be dropped off in a town that seemed to con-sist only of a few houses. He passed a sad campanile and came to a square. He sat there awhile. From the edge, he could look down at a valley, with a city of red brick, he could hear motors, and a stoplight shone in the distance. *Ti amo sempre* scratched into the rust of the railing. When the sun was already higher in the sky, a few boys came to the square, walked to a little water fountain, filled their mouths with water, and tried to squirt it at one another. Then they walked away, snorting.

A while later the long line stood in the same place, washing him-self. He went to a small shop. Bread, dry sausage, coffee, a small pot, sugar.

A dog was tied up in front of the store, and it whimpered when it saw him. The dog was old, a white shadow in one eye. He stood there awhile and looked at it. The light fur. The feeling that no one was coming.

◆　◆　◆

That evening he watched the coffee slowly come to a boil in the little pot. He'd walked far out, and between the hills and a few gnarled trees he'd found a tree trunk with a patch of softer sand in front of it. He looked for wood in the bushes, he looked for wood for the night. The coffee was very sweet and strong. Bats hunted among the trees in the twilight.

Only the embers were still warm when he awoke. He spat in the ashes. He ran his finger through them. It made him think of Patrícia. He drew his finger over the tree trunk. The ashes left a dark streak. He turned on his telephone, but there was no service. The land was green and soft and inviting. He rubbed ashes on his mosquito bites. Then he rolled his bundle together and left. He avoided the roads. The paths ran along fields, and the fields were thirsty. He had to buy water, a chorizo. He asked about maps, but the shop with the maps was closed. He asked about a direction, and the woman answered him and looked at his boots and his dusty trousers. She talked with her hands and feet. Finally she beckoned him behind the counter with the cash register and showed him a map on a flickering screen, and on the map, the way. Then she offered him a cigarette. They went outside the shop and sat on a plastic bench and smoked. It was his first cigarette in years. The smoke bit into his lungs.

The woman pointed to the sun and said that he should wear a hat. This light is different. He asked if she had something to eat; she said yes and led him into a small tiled room. There was nothing but a table with two chairs, and a small fan buzzed. The potatoes were cold and turning dark in spots. She asked if he had money. He shrugged. She watched him eat in silence.

◆　◆　◆

He felt his weight and the weight of his things and that there was no weight that could still keep him anywhere. When he walked through suburbs in the evening, they smelled like garbage, and he could hear the clicking of the car hoods as they cooled. Once he heard music that seemed familiar, but he didn't dare stop, nor did he dare go to it. He heard voices resounding through the darkness, and he knew that they weren't voices he recognized. He simply walked on, until the houses and the streetlights ended, and the cars turned on their brights when they spotted him in the darkness, and the rows of vineyards surfaced in the first light, long and even like typescript. *You're in the whole world and I'm in a village, that won't work*, Milena had said.

That evening he lay in the darkness on a hill, looking at the highway in the distance. He must have walked far. During the day he'd taken off the jacket and trousers of the suit to spare them, but he'd felt naked, and his body was thin and white in the sun. Now he lay in his battered T-shirt, and the sand beneath him was still warm. The air quickly lost its temperature. The lights hurtled after one another in both directions through the land. He made a large fire in a hollow, he'd gathered wood and stones. He placed the stones in the embers.

He waited. Then he used a stick to push the stones back into the sand. He laid them in two rows on his T-shirt, some were black from the fire, sooty. He wrapped the fabric around them, and felt the heat through the cloth. Then he pulled the tarp over and lay on it face-down. He pulled the cloth to the level of his buttocks and tried to line the stones up along his spine. It didn't work, they were crooked, a few stones slipped to the side. But it was hot. And it was good.

Mátyás had gone over the dark circles on his back as over the fields in a board game. It had helped, at first. Waclaw liked the sound of the flames being lit, the suction of the cups. The bamboo huts and the feeling that Mátyás was waiting for him. He wanted them to be together in this warm and humid climate, all the plants around them with unpronounceable names.

The Caribbean, too, was salty, and for a while they'd rented a bungalow on an island two hours away by speedboat. On the way they passed natives who had to drive hard against the waves, they left them behind. The trees were big, the heat indescribable, the cocktails so cold that they steamed in the heat. He lay in a hammock next to Mátyás; three times a day, a bell called them to eat. The man at the bar wore glaring white socks and a shirt to match. Most people there shoveled down their food, their heads just above the table. Mátyás undertook little energetic hikes over the island, as if he wasn't ready to give up, under the lianas and coconut palms and the tousled network of the mangroves. He usually came back covered in bug bites. They were close to each other only in the exhaustion of evening.

The refineries grew in wide intervals on these shores, the white tanks like bad jokes over cream cakes. The gas flares in all the heat made no sense, but they forgot that they could forget them.

He lay there like that for a long while. Wind brushed over his arms. He could taste the fire, the smoke hung over the hollow. As the stones cooled, he imagined hands feeling along his back, carefully touching the spots. As if something were broken.

The sky was just turning gray when he got up and raked sand over the fire and continued on in the direction that the woman had shown him. No one travels on foot anymore, she'd said. Maybe you could take a bus, *Signore*. He'd thanked her for the cigarette and

shook his head. *Grazie.* Five days, she'd said, but she didn't know
exactly.

The land grew more lush, and between the hills lay large estates
with sprinklered grass, which he gave a wide berth. When he came
through the villages, he looked for the farm stands and left coins. He
bought honey. That night he drank strong black coffee with honey.
He dunked cookies in it and scalded his mouth. He tried to keep
his fires small. He thought that this land must belong to someone.
He started awake in the night when a dog barked in the distance, he
heard motorcycles. He rolled himself tight in his tarp and listened
out into the night for a long time.

The powerful tolling of the bell in a village on whose low houses
the stucco was old and water-damaged, the pinkish gray, yellowish
gray, the rusty balconies. Tiled roofs grown tired under the weight
of many summers, after hills full of barbed wire, roads with barren
estates.

He heard the tolling of the bells like a long-forgotten language.
He saw chickens running over a harvested field far beyond a farmyard and he found their eggs in the furrows of the field, and when he
cracked them, they were black and rotten.

He lost his way. He walked for days.

When he passed through villages, the old women watched him
out of the windows and the men looked up at him out of the depths
of their gray garages. There were grocers with cracked and blackened
hands, men in suits with linen scarves and crests of white hair who
surveyed him with interest, but then avoided his eyes. Once a boy
followed him and asked if he could be his friend, but Waclaw said he
had enough friends in the world, and went into a shop with him and

watched as he drank a bottle of vanilla milk and ate the sweet bread that the woman put on the table for him. He reminded Waclaw of other boys, of a day in Bucharest in the spring; the magnolias bore huge buds, the land was warming up, and they'd lain in the shade of old subway stations clutching their baggies; they dragged themselves there and could hardly get up. Waclaw was in the city alone; he'd found a park with jungle gyms and a lake encased in concrete, he'd gone to the opera and couldn't make anything of it, he'd walked through the dilapidated villas of the embassy district. This was the time after Milena, and he couldn't tell her or anyone, he never went back. The boy said he had no friends but he had grandparents, and Waclaw said that grandparents were better than many friends, but that he couldn't understand that yet. The boy said that he was bored. Waclaw said that no one could take this boredom away, and that he shouldn't believe anyone who said they could. The boy asked how big the world was. Waclaw said he didn't know. On some days it was bigger, and on other days it was as if it didn't exist at all, even when you flew around it in an airplane. He said he had to find out for himself. But that the world wasn't the globe they showed him in school. The world he would live in one day would smell different and have different colors that the people at school didn't know anything about. Waclaw said he should go with his grandparents, and mustn't think badly of them when he was older. The boy was thin, his favorite color was red. They parted behind the only ice cream parlor. He wanted to accompany Waclaw to the highway, but Waclaw said no and left without turning around. When the city was far behind him, he looked back and there was no one there.

He tried to avoid the fences. The night was cloudy, and in the morning it rained. He rolled his clothes together and sat under a large willow and felt the drops hit his shoulders. He found fruit on the path and boiled coffee in the pot until it foamed brown. He was tired from walking and thought of Alois. He didn't want to think.

And as he lay there, he looked over the meadows as they slowly grew dark, and against the soft black of the hills he saw Mátyás before him, sitting before him and moving, a black body, filled with shadows, and yet it seemed he could still turn to him and speak. But the shadow had no body. He saw how Mátyás trembled.

Later that night he dreamed of a great hall that was connected by escalators with other floors, and it was neither day nor night in the artificial fog, in the spotlights, there was all this sweat on his forehead, they'd swallowed so much of the stuff. Mátyás's steps were leaden, as if the world lay spread out beneath him, a pounding rhythm, the ears were all that remained, and who was this slim, rather wilted man who carried water after him and followed him, his pupils huge, black-light backdrops, his T-shirt sweaty, someone had to bring him water, lots of good, sweet water. And this man stood there, Waclaw, he sang, no one could hear him, the escalators kept bringing up ever more bodies, it was cramped and stuffy and Mátyás was gone, *Glückauf*, Waclaw sang, why this song of all things, *und er hält sein helles Licht bei der Hand*, he sang over a dull, very loud bass, it's the sound of the neighbors' houses, the miners' estate, the well water, it's the "Steigerlied." Suddenly he feels an arm, someone is holding him, he turns and wants to say something and a blow hits his open mouth, a second one on his jaw, then it's quiet.

The shadow of the alder was big and calm.

Far above, satellites with complicated lens systems traveled along their paths. Particles of space debris. It was no dream. Just a night in Antwerp; the next day Mátyás had hummed the melody to him, *what was with you?* But Waclaw pretended not to recognize the few bars that had emerged from his depths.

He spent the day in the shade of a few trees. Tired wooden fences that ended under crags. Greenhouses that shimmered in the distance like some animal's scaly back. Something sleeping, something big and old. He'd walked until midday and then stopped for a while in the shade under a high bridge. The concrete was cool and there was a wind, the joints of the bridge trembled under the weight of trucks. He leaned against the concrete base. His undershirt was sweaty and full of yellow streaks, he had a bad taste in his mouth, like grass. He walked through the night.

The land grew more lush, and at dawn he came upon a large farm with cattle, perhaps eighty cows stood strewn over the hills. Around them was the green, and beyond it was nothing. Some lay and chewed on the grass that they then regurgitated. He saw a few calves pushing greedily at their mothers' udders. As he came closer he saw that their heads were wet with milk.

He walked along the perimeter fence and reached the farmyard.

An old man was tinkering with a tractor.

Waclaw asked if he needed help.

Lavoro? Work?

The man wiped his brow and considered.

There are a few things, he said. But not for long.

Every morning the woman fried eggs and placed a dish of warm flatbread that smelled of rosemary on the table in front of him, and she smiled as she did it and watched him eat, but she didn't say a word. She topped up his coffee and put out a pair of her husband's old gloves for him, black from sweat.

During the days, she sometimes sat on a bench in the middle of the yard and watched from a distance as the clouds above pushed into one another and dispersed above him, while he stooped and stretched new wire for the fence.

After a few days he pulled long boards over the grass, hefted them over the fence and let them fall on the bushes. The hedges held the weight so that he could walk over the little stream, only the scrub and the gurgling of the water under him, and he stretched up for the dark purple fruit and watched that evening as the figs were cooked with sugar in a huge pot, and the smell was sweet and warm, and like no place that he'd known in a long time.

He asked her why she watched him and what made her so happy, and she said that in earlier generations there had been many like him, and they'd rambled and had known songs, and even when she was a child there had still been many who came to them and had even preferred it to the wretched life of a factory. She'd always liked that, and now people were lonely in the countryside and alone in the cities, and the same people were sent out all over the world. She said that she was old but that her memory didn't play tricks on her, and some stories were older than their heroes, the stories really just repeated themselves, but they were now breaking off, and there was no one who could change that.

The cover of the pot lifted, and he heard the hot, viscous mass bubbling underneath it, and she took a spoon and stirred the figs off the bottom of the pot. He said he'd worked before at the foot of the mountains as a fruit picker, but she made a dismissive hand motion and said that was another thing *del tutto*, which no longer made anyone happy. She said that war had mixed life up, but not so much after all. She looked at him. *Non sei ancora pratico di qui, ma imparerei*, she said. He said she had to speak more slowly so he could understand her.

She turned down the little bluish gas flame. She stirred the pot with her powerful arms. The kitchen tiles were large, irregular stones, and behind the thick walls outside the low window, evening was falling. He said that people didn't go out there for no reason, that it was old wishes and expectations that they hoped they could fulfill. He said that they didn't know enough. That no one warned them. He said that the distance got into them, but not in a friendly way. That there was nothing to get out there. She looked at him. Then she said that she didn't know anything about it, but that it had always been easy to lose oneself in something, for there was no end to the wishes other than time, which would catch up with them all. But that the farms were changing too, and soon no one would be needed anymore. She struck her heart. *Come un essere umano.* As people. But then there would always be some kind of work. She shooed away flies with one hand. This here is another world, she said. But Waclaw slowly shook his head. Not another world, he said slowly.

Then she paused for a moment. You remind me of someone, she said. Then she looked at the ground, her husband came in. His steps were small and he hardly lifted his feet. He sat down at the table and looked at them both from his dark corner. He said it would soon be fall and the rain would start. The man asked Waclaw how far he wanted to go. In a few weeks the first snow would fall on the mountains in the north.

Waclaw left them in the kitchen and went into the cold hallway, and it smelled of ripe fruit and sugar, and he knew the smell. He lay in the darkness, and he knew the smell.

After eight days Waclaw packed his things. The clothes were washed and dried. He'd dug a drainage ditch for several days. For the autumn rains, the man had said. Then he'd seen Waclaw's back. They both knew that it wouldn't last. He'd split firewood. A few times he'd thought about how much a doctor would cost. Sometimes he stood leaning forward, resting on the axe handle.

Middays they'd drunk a light wine, and the woman had fried big slices of bread in oil.

The man asked few questions.

He said that Waclaw was a good worker.

Colombe? Waclaw asked. Pigeons? and pointed to the sky.

The man seemed to think briefly.

He pointed to the high trees.

Not here, he said. *Ci sono troppi falconi.*

In the nights, Waclaw had lain awake.

He had the address in his breast pocket and he knew it by heart. Other than that, there was nothing.

18

Hawthorns

The grasses stood like bushy yellow spears, and it wasn't yet late when he found the hut and laid himself on the bales of hay and took off his boots, which were scratched, and the soles worn down. The shadows of the trees shimmered silent and violet.

In the twilight he heard shots from a nearby wood. From the shelter he could see the dry tips of the corn plants, and then he heard a cracking and saw the tall stalks bending, and something running through the field, but he couldn't see the animals. He could smell them. The heavy mineral smell of the wallows in the pigs' bristly skin. They ran. Someone shot at them. He withdrew farther behind the bales and waited, but the shots didn't return. He lay awake in the night and thought of Francis, how he lay there listening, and every step echoed against the taut screen of his fear. As if a person were just a membrane that everything could pass through. The wind pressing against the cabin walls. In his sleep he heard animals panting. He didn't set out until the day was bright. He found fresh tire tracks on a path, but he saw no one.

He came through a ravine between the fields; large beeches grew on its slopes, and a wind came up, the first rain in weeks beat the dry leaves off the branches. A warm, penetrating rain soon hung over the fields, and he walked. That night he'd seen the first winter constellation rising on the horizon, and the Milky Way revolved above him as it did over all.

He'd thought of Alois's brother, Vincenz, who'd given him work in the apple orchard back then, Alto Adige, the summer in South Tyrol when he went to work with Jacek for the money they so desperately needed. When he still thought that Milena. When they were still thinking of names. When they were still making plans that later seemed to him far too large. From a distance he felt that he could look at their time together as if under a glass dome, and at their limits, too. Their inner Königsberg. Milena had picked up this expression. A thinker, she said, who spent his whole life in one place. If there's *us*, then that's enough. He could hear her. Maybe she was trying to convince herself that it was a good thing that they couldn't travel, maybe it was more than that. Their inner Königsberg. What do you mean freedom, she'd asked Waclaw when he brought her earrings of bright green feathers.

The sun was high over the land. He wiped butter off the paper with the last bit of bread, his fingers gleamed. He'd also eaten the boiled eggs the woman had given him. Cars whooshed by not far away. He'd followed the signs, he'd walked along the road for a while, someone had yelled something at him through an open car window, it hadn't sounded friendly. He'd eaten the bread and the ham. There were lots of insects, and the dust of the cars rushing by stuck in his pores. The place he was looking for lay far off in the hills, which in the morning were nothing more than watery shades of green. The sun rose slowly, the stones were still cold. He washed, and then walked the road toward the mountains, freezing. He noticed how slow he was.

* * *

A few times he saw signs pointing toward Genoa. Genova. Cruise ships. The harbor of emigrants, and the harbor for oil, for the supertankers, for liquid natural gas. *Haven*, the tanker that had broken in two off the coast while discharging its cargo. The Ligurian Sea. Ramshackle pipes. Mátyás, who'd stood in front of the square lighthouse, who'd wanted to hear nothing of the pipelines that ran from here to the center of the country. The refineries on the coast. A few mountains separated Waclaw from the harbor in the south. He thought of the key that he'd left with Eugenio. *Haven*. Just like that. What they'd set out for. It was harder for him now to think about the beginning, about the first weeks when everything had suddenly seemed to glow. Mátyás and he, the cozy feeling of a kitchen when they sat in the mess hall, betting a few cents on cards. Secretly Waclaw had thought of the pine bench, of his father and Alois, tired after their shift, under the low hanging lamp.

In the afternoon he came to roads that were narrow and unsealed at the edges. He saw young people jumping off rocks into the river, and the way the water grew dark blue in the deeper spots. Just a sound when the bodies met the water's surface. *Klackklack*.

The roads grew steeper. Fornovo di Taro, he took a bridge over the river. The landscape reminded him of the old women in the community who brought the word *oregano* back from the trips they could finally take as widows, as if the taste alone could hold open a door they'd seen only briefly: a light far beyond the estate. The way they boarded the bus, the hopeless way they spruced themselves up for the journey. *Oregano* had something to do with these hills. With this light, which slowly sank and cast a spell over the landscape. *Klackklack*.

He left the plains and walked northwest toward the mountains. He saw an old mill in a valley. He talked to no one. The sun was already low when he reached the riverbank. Small fish jumped between the stones in the shallow water, the heat had driven the river far into the middle of the riverbed. Soon the whole valley lay in shadow. That night he hung his jacket on a tree, and in the morning he smoothed the cloth, and washed himself thoroughly between the worn stones. He set out before it was light.

Somewhere in the distance he heard a train. Gas stations gleamed like graveyard candles against the darkness of the mountains. He thought of the brightly lit windows that would appear one after the other, and he thought about how this day would have a direction, because he carried an old piece of paper in his pocket. The sun lifted itself above the ridge of the mountains as if in slow motion. Goats. The road was barren and wound up the slope in bend after bend, between hills and slopes marked by this dryness: yellow, crackling, groaning under the light and with the soughing sound of the motorcycles dangerously cutting the curves. Waclaw was thirsty, and around midday he came upon a *paninoteca* where he bought white bread and asked about water, and when the baker brushed off his hands and asked him where he was going, he had no feel for the word that he carried in his mouth, as if he were standing too near a large picture that made no sense close up.

He paid the man and said he didn't know how far it was. As if the place were only a name, like the sign for a town that was long gone. His mouth was dry, as if with great excitement.

The sun burned. A single crow sitting with shining feathers on a heap of sand. The dust on the leaves of the bushes near the road. In the afternoon he approached the place, Bobbio, and soon afterward he saw the house. The light fell uneasily on a narrow dirt road, hawthorn trees stood on both sides, a girl with a light sun hat squatted by a few dried-up puddles and played with stones. Waclaw searched for some clue, something that would tell him he was in the right place, but he didn't know what that could be. It was an old house with a red tile roof; lemon trees stood in large buckets next to the entrance. For a while he looked at the path and the light that fell uneasily through the branches. Then he heard something that sounded like someone hitting a pot with wood. A name was called out. *Enni? Enni!* The girl, who now seemed to notice him, looked up and ran in sandals to the house.

Un uomo!

Beyond the lemon trees he could now see a woman on the steps. She wore a light-colored dress and picked up the girl, propping her on her hip, then looked at Waclaw.

He left the duffel on the edge of the path and walked slowly toward her; the woman remained on the highest of the three steps. She whispered something to the girl and put her down. The door was open and framed them both in darkness.

He greeted them, and his voice was hoarse. He felt her eyes trace downward, the gray dust on his trousers reached to above his knees. He kept his distance, and then said Alois's name. He asked if the address was correct.

Then he showed her the paper.

He came a bit closer, said his name, and held it up to her with his long arm. She looked at the stamps, the address.

A-l-o-i-s? She said the name like a foreign word and looked at Waclaw, uncomprehending. He waited. In the distance, in the direction from which he'd come, he saw a plane flash silent and high in the sky, a metal projectile.

She looked for a long time at the handwriting, small and angular in the middle of the paper, surrounded by a large white frame, like a shy girl pushed to the center of the dance floor.

Then she looked up.

Dio, she said softly, are you serious?

She wiped the sweat from her brow with the underside of her forearm. Her hands were covered in earth.

That's a long time ago, she said.

Waclaw looked at the letter she held in her hands.

Do you speak German?

She nodded her head in the direction of the mountains.

Tutti questi turisti, she said, I have to.

He hesitated.

And Alois—he's not here?

She looked past Waclaw to the duffel that lay on the path.

Enzo never lived here, she said.

He wiped his hand on his trousers and looked at the ground. He felt awkward when she looked at him, and he needed time to think.

But there were no thoughts. There was only an image: he was kneeling on the ground in Alois's loft, holding a pigeon in both hands. Alois sat before him on a bucket, he had a needle and thread in his hand. A crow had attacked the pigeon, and Waclaw held it around the neck, felt the throbbing under its feathers. Clouds trembled in its water dish, and for several moments all was quiet, as if there were only this pounding, ragged, and he listened fearfully for each further heartbeat. How strange that it kept going.

He's not here, he repeated slowly.

No, she said quickly. She took a step toward him.

He wrote down this address because the mail wasn't reaching him at first. Maybe they were too lazy to drive up there just for him.

A-l-o-i-s, she said again. No one calls him that here. You've come all this way to see him?

Waclaw nodded.

But it's far. In this heat, you won't make it to him today.

She looked at him again. His arms, poking out of the sleeves.

I can drive you, she said then.

Enni, dai! We're driving the man to him.

The girl sat in the back seat and chewed on the ear of a stuffed bunny. Elena had introduced herself quickly, brushed some sand off the passenger seat, then rapped the steering wheel with the flat of her hand. You're in luck, she said. The Citroën jolted in zigzags over the narrow curves, stones hit the bottom of the car, and through the cracked windshield the landscape was a juddering green.

In less than half an hour, she drove the way that would have taken him half a day on foot. Elena laid her arms on top of the steering wheel, he could see the light skin shimmering under her armpits.

Visiting, she said, I think you're the first for that.

The air whooshed through the cracked window, a few houses passed. The road rose upward, and he liked it when the turns pressed him into his seat.

I hope you're not bringing bad news?

Elena talked loudly and looked straight ahead. She drove around some potholes, and Waclaw shook his head. Genoa, he said then, he'd worked there, near the harbor.

We're rarely at the sea, she yelled. You're in luck.

Her daughter in the back seat stared at him unswervingly.

Then Elena pointed to a chain of hills and turned with a jerk onto a gravel road. It's up there.

The crags were light and overgrown with the same bushes that

Waclaw had been seeing for days. A single dark stone house stood hard against the slope. As the hand brake ratcheted, the girl pushed open the door, ran across the yard to the house, and pulled the door-bell. They heard the note swell and slowly die away over the valley. Elena wiped her forehead. His car isn't here. You'll have to wait. He nodded. She called to the girl. Then she turned around. He'll call me if something's wrong.

19

The Lantern

The bucket hit the water hard. He heard the echo and pulled it up through the narrow, shadowy cylinder. He washed himself, and the water was clear and cold, and older than the low house and the glow of the province and older than the silence of the meadows all around. The light turned yellow, the jacket lay over his knees. He sat on the edge of the well and waited. Gasoline stains shimmered in every color on the gravel lot in front of the house. He kept his head down, and he could hear the pigeons. The low cooing. He could see the loft: a gable, half-timbering, three compartments, and the landing board. He wasn't sure what Alois still knew about him.

It was late when he heard the engine, and shortly thereafter he saw a bluish cloud shooting up the narrow dirt road. An old green Kadett that braked abruptly on the forecourt. The driver's-side door had been replaced, its paint was a bit darker.

An older man got out and stopped next to the dented metal. He looked in Waclaw's direction, saw the thin man sitting on the edge of the well next to a large bag.

Then he came toward him.

His legs were so badly bowed that his feet almost brushed each other as he walked, and he seemed to have gotten even smaller. He wore a shirt with short sleeves and a collar from a different era. His forehead shone. He asked in Italian what Waclaw wanted here, and Waclaw stood there, tall and narrow as a trellis, and didn't move.

Waclaw gave Alois some time to look him over, time to fish an old pair of glasses out of his pocket, to take the slip of paper that Waclaw held out to him. The skin on his arms seemed almost transparent, and where the old scar from the red-hot oven had been ran a white line to the elbow. The wrinkles on his face gave him the look of an astonished child, harmless, like someone who had never put in all those shifts at the coking plant. Harmless, Waclaw thought, and watched him take the paper and hold it close to his face to read. His glasses were dirty, and he breathed in heavily, as if it were hard for him to understand what he read. Waclaw gave him time to furrow his brow, to turn the paper this way and that and then, slowly, to look up at him.

Alois? Waclaw said.

His heart leaped softly when the man suddenly looked him in the face and embraced him, his head briefly pressed under his chest, light, old, a bright gleam on the back of his head. Damn you, boy, he said. Didn't I say you should have got on home long ago? He ran a hand over Waclaw's back. Then he looked at him and called him too thin and weather-beaten.

Later they sat on a stone bench behind the house, the shade under the grapevines buzzed with warmth. The last insects were flying, and before them in the valley the shadows of the hills expanded and stretched. They could see far, and the darkness came like an old dancer climbing wearily onto his stage. They didn't turn on a light, because of the mosquitos. They drank a dry grappa. It was clear and good.

I didn't think I would find you, Waclaw said.

Alois leaned forward and pointed to his eyes with two fingers.

But here I am, he said, and patted Waclaw's arm. Then he eyed the dark cloth of the suit, and Waclaw just nodded.

They'd put out all the lights except for a little glass lantern, and when they didn't speak for a while, they could hear a dog, its teeth scraping over something that sounded like a hollow bone. It must have been somewhere in the darkness of the meadow.

Alois said: Katrina, Mexico, really? He said: Your father mentioned it back then. Then he shook his head in disbelief. He couldn't believe that Waclaw had been caught up in that business.

Then he lifted his glass. To you, my boy. Who do you drink to? Us?

Don't you have some protector?

They're not Catholic out there. It's a long time ago, Alois.

Yes. Now they call me Enzo again.

And me?

Not you.

They drank.

He thought of Mátyás's unmade bed. Again, the cord of his Walkman. Alois had gotten up, and came back with a cardigan. He put it on, and they sat awhile without talking. They drank.

And who was left, then? Waclaw asked.

The fat butcher lady from the Sauerland. Alois laughed. What do you think. Everyone was still there, really. Only your father left, and then me, later. Have you ever asked yourself how many lives anyone would ever voluntarily spend in that place? Not one. But the heart can't admit that.

For a while the hissing of the gas lamp was all there was between them.

Then Alois set something on the table.

It would have made him happy for you to have it.

He put something in Waclaw's hand, *medalik*, it shot through his head, that and the beginning of the prayer to Mary, *pod twoją obronę*. He took the coin and closed his hand, then looked out into the night.

They didn't talk about the birds. All evening they didn't talk about the birds. As if it would have been too easy. They talked about the sea. About Waclaw's father. About his lungs and the open window by which he'd slept, sitting, in the end. How he'd waved to his mates as they kept going down there. Prosper. The shaft, the third, the fourth level. The Baltic Sea, which he'd seen again only when his body was far too worn out. The waves sloshing against the shore. The narrow room.

Alois listened. He left pauses after Waclaw said something, as if to make sure he'd really finished.

Were you with him at the end? Alois asked.

Waclaw shook his head.

You go on land to Ciudad del Carmen, and then you're still nowhere.

He didn't know how to describe it. He didn't know what to say about a night when he'd sat on the shore until the mosquitos had gotten him all over. It had been all the same to him, and he'd heard the rattling sound that came from the waves, as from a badly damaged lung.

To your father, Alois said, Tomasz, good old Tomek. He drank. I thought a lot about him when I heard. But a trip like that, you know, all alone.

Alois was silent. As if he were listening to something else. As if the sentences didn't simply end. As if they branched out, far beneath what was actually said.

Look at you, he said then. It's summer. And you're wearing a suit.

It's not for me.

You know what I mean. You spent your best years out there.

Waclaw brought the duffel into a small room that was built into the slope and smelled a bit damp. The deep sleep of that night. Alois took bedding out of a heavy wooden cupboard and shook it out with his light arms, *sit yourself down, boy*, and for a moment they were in a cloud of lavender. Alois wanted to close the curtains, but Waclaw said there was no need. He would wake early anyway. But he was still lying in the blazing sunlight past midday. For the first time in weeks he slept deeply and soundly until the afternoon.

Alois sent him up the mountain to the narrow place where the stream crossed the path.

You can wedge the metal sheet between the two rocks, he said.

Waclaw stood under the thin trickle for a long time looking down at the valley; he felt the cold water on his neck.

On the way back, the sun shone on his ribs. And his steps weren't those of a holidaymaker, but rather strangely truncated. From far away it looked as if he were afraid of heights.

Alois was waiting for him outside amid the beans. He said that this year everything was going to dry out. Even the blossoms fall off, he said. And did you see the trees?

Waclaw said he'd seen many trees, and had heard the dry leaves in the night, when he'd rolled over, or when the lizards ran through them, and sometimes the wind drove the leaves in front of him over the dry asphalt roads, and the leaves looked like dried chicken feet, he'd seen them once in—

Alois interrupted him.

Have you eaten today?

A bit.

Alois sliced through the ham with a large knife. He cut many thin pieces, and took cheese out of brine, and fried eggplant in a lot of oil. Waclaw lifted a hand as if he wanted to protest, but then he let the hand sink, and Alois stood across from him in the dark, shady kitchen. He watched Waclaw eat but didn't sit.

He just stood there, as if there was nothing more important in all the world than watching the thin man eat.

Waclaw wiped his mouth.

They heard the deep cooing outside.

What happened to her? Alois asked. Your girl—Milena, right?

Waclaw didn't answer. He brushed the table with his fingers.

It was a miracle, Alois began again, that you came through again at all back then, to the neighborhood. And then you pick her up and you leave, as soon as the borders open, to this Polish village and no one hears anything more from you, just that you're driving for a shipping company, and—

Waclaw shrugged.

I couldn't keep it away from us.

Alois looked past him out the window, as if thinking.

Ah, forget about it, boy, he said then, softly.

You never know beforehand what the price is. And above all, you don't know what you're ready to pay. We can't take these things back.

Come on.

They stood in front of the loft for a long time, now and then Alois pointed with his head to one bird or another, and Waclaw nodded.

He wanted to tell Alois about Cairo, but he didn't know how. He didn't know if he should tell about Farangis, or about the accident. He thought about it while he scratched at the wooden floor with a trowel; he tied a cloth over his mouth, he scraped the droppings out of the corners. Then he saw something. For a while he just stood in front of it. Then he propped his broom against the wall and carefully picked it up.

He found Alois in his folding chair between the vegetable beds. Waclaw held the plastic high.

You still have it, he cried.

Alois turned toward him. For a moment he looked at the thin man, who suddenly stood before him, as if trying to reconcile something, as if he saw again the shed roof and the house, and beyond it himself, still with all his hair, and smoking, in an evening light that made everything stand out clearly: the grout between the stones, the black crevices in his skin, the last fir trees in the distance, beyond which there was no Italy, not for a long time yet, only the dirty Emscher River that had sucked away his wife's dreams and made her sick, and the gray ice that came every winter. The smokestacks of the distant coking plant, this land that they were hollowing out, seven levels, the drudgery, leaving early when it was still dark, returning when it was no longer light, the soot on the tissues when they blew their noses in the winter, and just the pigeons, as if they were proof of something that no one could take away from him.

The dish, Waclaw said, you still have it.

Alois lowered the roll of twine with which he'd been tying up the vines.

I need some compost here badly, boy.

Let me see, he said then, and Waclaw turned the water dish in his hands. It was a circular vessel with a top the shape of a circus tent, with five openings for the birds' heads. The plastic was faded from the years.

What else would I do with it?

Alois wound the string around his hand. For a moment it looked like the whole thing made him uncomfortable, and Waclaw let the hand with the plastic drop.

I just mean, he said.

As he brought the dish back to the compartment for the old pigeons, he thought of the woman from the pet store who'd helped him count out his pennies on the counter. Her fingernails, he still remembered, had been painted blue. The whole way home he'd imagined Alois opening the present. It was the end of March, and his birthday.

That afternoon Alois avoided him. From afar, Waclaw saw him in the kitchen, picking the leaves off herbs, whole mountains of leaves off their stems, far more than he could use.

He was tired that evening, he lay down in the room next to the slope. He awoke in the night. He could feel his heartbeat, and the old disquiet was back. Clouds passed in the narrow strip of sky that he could see from the bed, quickening in the slight moonlight. Fall was coming. Fall was a big thing, and it brought the villagers together. They stood in front of leaf fires with their hands in their pockets, a swig of homemade schnapps, swished around a bad tooth. They spoke little. The fall was what surrounded the people who lived in such places. Places like Wiórek. Places that no longer existed.

He must have dozed off when Alois woke him.

They went out onto the terrace and the stone was still cold from the night when Waclaw sat down on the bench. A large jar of honey and pistachios stood on the table. The first light shimmered yellow in the jar. Alois laid an arm over the back of the bench. Have some. Waclaw dipped a biscuit in the honey. He could hear himself when he bit through the nuts.

The honey was sweet. It tasted unusually strong.

Now come, Alois said.

He waited until Waclaw had stood up. Then he gestured for Waclaw to follow him. He opened the carabiner that ran through the latch pin, and then the rickety wooden door that was steel-plated to keep out the martens. He went inside and looked at the pigeons, one after another. He didn't reach out to touch them. A few picked some popcorn from the flat of his hand, a few sat on his shoulders. Then he opened a hatch, and they came out one after another; they rose hastily, their wingbeats when they lifted off sounded like someone quickly shuffling a deck of cards. Then they flew big circles over the valley.

You're still training them, Waclaw said.

You know me.

Below, low tiled roofs shimmered through the mist while the flock drifted above like a body that was lively and big and very light. The early sun fiery red and distant. Alois lifted the flag on the wooden stick. His whole body seemed to grow larger under the expansive swirls of the birds, and he beckoned Waclaw closer to him.

Do you see the big blue one flying ahead? You try it, he said. Waclaw stood there. The flag in his hand. He noticed how Alois watched him. And for him, for him perhaps, he made the same big motions he'd made as a boy. He stretched out, he waved the flag through the air a bit. Once again, he heard the barely audible whooshing of the wings cutting through the air. And then everything came back.

The weight of the wooden stick in his hand, the desire to leave the miners' estate with them, the smell of coal, unusually strong on one of the first days of fall. And the chill of the meadow, Alois's admonishing laughter when he came to him even before school. And he saw the coal dust mixing with the powdery snow, and over it the voracious flames of the *Esse*—the smokestack.

They changed the water and refilled the feed, and Waclaw saw checkered and barred feathers, and later that evening the shadows of the mountains growing slowly darker. They sat on a stone bench; the dog had begun gnawing at its bone again. Waclaw had only seen it once in the daytime, its fur was spotted, and it lowered its head in fear whenever anyone approached. Alois said it had strayed his way, and sometimes it still stayed away for days on end.

What's with your mother? Alois asked.

Waclaw shrugged. I don't know, he said.

Last time he'd visited her in that home—she'd sung, it was a group, maybe six women. They'd sat around a table and she wore a paper crown; the carer had played a plastic instrument with tiny keys.

She was still up there in that home, Waclaw said.

He didn't know what to tell Alois.

It was so warm in the room, he said finally.

He heard Alois breathe. It was dark, and somewhere in the meadow the dog was gnawing its bone. All day, the house had smelled of leeks and stewing meat. Now the chewing sound was conspicuous, as if the darkness that seemed to come from the hills gave it a sharper contour.

They looked out at the land.

But you have it good here, Waclaw said finally.

Alois burst out laughing.

What am I supposed to do. I'm an old man, he said. Someone everyone likes because all I want is peace and quiet. I can be here. But I can't get my life back. It's still up there.

Alois waved his open hand toward the north.

The *Esse*, Waclaw said.

I haven't heard that word in a long time. But yes.

I couldn't've gotten old there, and like everyone else, my stomach bothered me. You just don't want to eat where you don't feel at home. Only your father left, with his lung.

Alois stretched the *u* in *lung* out unnaturally. It sounded almost comical.

But you have it good here, Waclaw said again. Alois waved the thought away.

I was old when I came back. Look at me.

He spread his fingers.

That's what you bring with you.

He held his hand closer to the little gas lamp, and Waclaw saw his fingers trembling.

I don't want it to be like this for you, Alois said. You're still younger than I was back then. She could get used to you more quickly. Isn't there anyone waiting for you?

Waclaw reached for the carafe. It was empty, and Alois told him where to find the box of wine, and then Waclaw stood behind the heavy wooden door and heard his own breath. He heard the wine squirting forcefully into the carafe, and he stood there for a long time and drank in the darkness and couldn't make up his mind to go back up. He drank so quickly that he had to gasp for breath.

2 0

Snakes

He had to go up the little hill behind the house to make a phone call. It was a dry slope with big stones where the snakes sunned themselves at noon; he banged a walking stick against the rocks and made noises to scare them away. After a few days they seemed to find other places to be.

He now knew the paths that led over the hills, and he sat up there in the mornings and evenings, always at the same times, and watched Alois training his birds. Alois had shown him a whole stack of creased certificates: competitions he'd flown in the last few years, and for a moment they'd both looked at the papers that Alois held in his light arms, and Waclaw had seen how the paper trembled. Waclaw talked little; he listened when Alois talked about the pigeons, about breeding lines.

Patrícia had called, and Sharam had left him messages—he had better take care, Sharam said, *You know what they're capable of. Think of the Gulf*, Sharam said, and no longer seemed to know himself just what he meant by it. *Wenzel*, he almost whispered, and Waclaw held the phone close to his ear. He tried to imagine Sharam, on land, alone with his bottles. He wanted to say: it was never about us, we just wanted to believe that, but he never called back. He looked down at the village. Only the sun, burning down on the tiles.

◆　◆　◆

After a few days he noticed that more cars than usual were driving up the narrow road. Alois said something about a festival, and at the end of the week Elena stood outside the door with the girl. You're still here, she said. He nodded. The girl had the valve of a large plastic tube between her teeth, she let go of her mother's hand and ran to the house, and Elena hastily slammed the trunk.

Are you two getting on all right? she asked, and stood next to Alois. He looked small next to her and just nodded. For a while they watched Waclaw help the girl get some air into the valve. The inflatable animal had a jagged head and wings and the tail of a fish. It was purple. When they'd gotten it blown up the girl lifted it over her head and chased Waclaw through the grass. He ran, somewhat clumsily, and then stopped in the shade with his hands propped on his knees. Later they leaned against the well—Alois had gone into the house—and the girl peered down.

That's deep, she said.

Ask the man what deep is, Elena said.

They looked at him.

He said a number. He had to repeat the number.

Elena had to say it again.

Then he pointed to the mountains.

Twice that high.

What's the mountain called? he asked the girl.

Monte Piccio.

Elena shook her head vigorously. It's called Monte Penice, she said, but the girl remained serious.

Two times Monte Piccio, Waclaw said, but instead of up in the air, down into the ground.

He thought of Sharam. The North Sea is a walk in the park compared to what they're planning. Two miles, Sharam had said.

The water off Brazil is a mile deep, and then that deep again into the ground. Do you want that?

Enni grinned as if she didn't believe him.

Then she looked at the well and ran back to the shallow pond in the garden. She set the animal in the basin and let it float.

They ate on the meadow. Alois had made meat broth again, he took out the bones and threw them to the dog. Waclaw said that in the warmer places there were sharks and big fish that swam around the platform.

Enni lifted her feet off the ground and squealed.

They laughed.

In the afternoon two young men came to talk to Alois and looked curiously in the direction of the chairs where they were sitting. Their hair was combed back and gleamed like the chitin shell of a beetle. The younger one's eyebrows ran together, and a light down grew on his upper lip. Alois nodded to them, and when he came back he said they'd be needing him more often—one of the tractors was broken, the engine sounded like a fireworks display. They wanted to borrow something for the festival. Alois laughed softly. Come with me, he said. Waclaw followed him to a shed. They stood in the open door for a long time. Alois pulled him inside. It smelled of gasoline.

You know, I always wanted one like this, Alois said.

I remember how your father and I took a trip, really we just wanted to get things for Easter in Bochum, but then we stopped after all—good Lord, a huge golf course, I'd never seen anything like it in all my life. Grass cut to a millimeter, all the little flags and hills and a few scattered trees like in an old landscape painting, the couple of twerps in their plaid pants were nothing to me, but I was really taken with those lawn mowers. We still used to scythe the meadows by hand and I told Federica about it later, she thought I was nuts but I told her: one day I'll have one of those. And maybe it was just that afternoon we had together out there, your father and I, on the way back from Bochum, we had a few pilsners and it was spring all around us and we sat in the grass, the tires behind me warm from the first sun. I couldn't tell you what we talked about, but at some point we started laughing like crazy, the whole left half of your father's face pulled upward and I could see into his nostrils, where there was still some soot, and in front of us these bizarre gentlemen with their flat shoes and angular movements. At some point it just got to us, all that fuss for a few little white balls, I dunno, something about it took our breath away, and I still remember the pines around us and the moss and grass and for a few moments everything was so damn real—

He paused and wiped the sweat off his brow with his forearm.

Anyway, he said, then I really got the thing, later, once I was here. And now and then they actually have some use for it in the village. And I drive a few rounds here around the house, you know. Who could've ever guessed that it would be like this—that I'd be careening around a place like this—without Federica. He grew softer. As if it were my born right.

He broke off.

The boy with the unibrow looked at Alois. As if there were still something unfamiliar about him, as if something stuck to the sentences he exchanged with the foreign man.

I'll come along, Alois said. Enni! he called. *Dai!*

Enni, the girl, came running around the corner and climbed up on the riding mower, where she sat down next to Alois and waved. Alois started the motor, and the boy ran beside them.

They watched them go. Elena stood next to Waclaw and for a while she didn't move. Then she spoke to him.

You must be happy to be so far away from it all?

She had high cheekbones and a large, narrow nose. He tried to smile and shook his head slowly.

It's not so far away, he said.

He followed her into the village. She walked quickly. Her steps were limber, it was a long path, a shortcut, she knew every rock, and he felt clumsy next to her. I'm going to show you something, she said.

But he wasn't ready for the procession and the weeping women and Elena, who dragged him into the little chapel where he stood behind the last row while a priest sang, and the few people who'd come looked at the ground and crossed themselves while Waclaw with his high, shiny forehead towered above them, not knowing whether anyone saw him standing there, and whether it would be enough if he thought here about that morning and the mirror-smooth sea and Mátyás's helmet and the sweatband that was still damp when he found it. At first he hadn't wanted to touch it, and then he'd stowed it in Mátyás's duffel, quickly, with the other things. For a moment he'd understood that no one would ever wash the sweaty thing. He could stand in this chapel as if he were in another time, he could imagine the altar boys like an optical illusion on that water, as if they were going out farther and farther, on the exhaustive search for Mátyás in their white, wind-blown robes. He stood motionless amid it all.

21

Snow

The festival was set for the coming evening, and when he came early to the loft, Alois had filled a light blue plastic tub with water, and for a while they watched the birds excitedly fluttering their wings as they bathed. A little way from the barn, a girl was doing gymnastics on the cut grass; she moved differently than the girls from the village, her movements smacked of lessons and the city. Under the knotted turquoise shirt, she stretched her legs unwaveringly in the air. She shone with sweat. It was still early, the first cars were drawing toward the barn where the festival was to take place. A scuffed frisbee lay on the side of the road, forgotten.

After a while, Waclaw lugged the dirty water to the next slope. Then he stood there and watched it trickle away. He knew Alois was waiting for him. He thought of the paper crown and the home, the little mouth organ that the carer had played, and the plastic covering over his shoes, which he hadn't taken off, he was in such a hurry to leave, over the golden fields that lay all around the home. The reaped stalks broke under his steps, he walked, something came undone in him, the carer blew into something that looked like a plastic flute with keys. The melody, the paper crown had followed him in the next months at sea, he'd thought of it when he heard the organ in Malta. For a while it was as if he couldn't think of anything else.

He sat by the loft without any idea what the festival was supposed to be. He saw Alois standing there, small and old, he released the pigeons, as if the whole world were up above. He waved Waclaw closer and seemed excited, though the few people who had gathered by the barn would likely take little notice of his birds. Finally Alois lowered the flag, as if deep in thought. *Mia turchina*, he said softly. My blue. Then he laid his arm on Waclaw's shoulder—light, almost tender. Do you see the big blue one flying ahead?

Listen, he said then.

I want you to take her north with you. You can judge the weather and the distance. She has enough reserves for a very long flight.

Waclaw looked at him. The birds were a distant murmur.

What's the point? You want to race her?

Alois shook his head.

He looked at the shady mountainsides. Then he looked at Waclaw.

Waclaw smoothed his sleeves and looked past Alois into the valley.

You've never done that, Alois, that far. And I don't see anyone here who would voluntarily drive up there.

Alois didn't seem to hear him. He looked at the flock, which was soon a distant point over the hills.

I don't know if you'll make it all the way back with her. But she'll fly, as far as she can. My wife went a little crazy up there, you know that, it took a lot of convincing to get her to change her mind, to come back here. I almost had her sold on it when she died.

And then—a whole closet full of furs she'd poured all our money into. She always had to be warm.

Waclaw remembered a small, shadowy silhouette behind the windowpane, a face that was always too pale and too heavily made up. In all the years, he'd never seen Federica with the pigeons.

But there's nothing there anymore, Alois. I'm not planning to drive back there. I have a life—

Alois pointed to his eyes again.

I've seen you these last few days.

They stood there awhile. Waclaw stroking his chin, seeming to search the distant slopes with his eyes, as if they, or anything on that morning, knew the answer.

They heard the pigeons again. A hint of the coming winter over the mountains. This picture, in which they were both only a tiny part. Just something warm in front of these great slopes, something like a very old melody.

Waclaw didn't look at him.

He said that he had little to take care of, and that time had done that for him, and that there wasn't much there that he could pick up again. Alois said time would take care of nothing and would take away nothing, it was a blind animal and couldn't be relied on. The only thing that mattered was the person, and how he stood, and that he could make promises and give the world meaning, and that was the only thing that extended beyond him.

Waclaw said promises were just words, but Alois responded that that wasn't true and every child knew it. He said children were smarter, and the weak.

Then they were silent.

The picture showed nothing but the cool air that surrounded them. Perhaps a few lizards on the rocks, and grasses, still wet from the dew on this first cool morning.

Drive back there again, Alois said. You're still young. Again he stretched the *u* sound in *young*, but Waclaw could hardly hear it anymore.

◆ ◆ ◆

In the picture, the taller, thinner man moved up the path and up the slope. He walked. A thin film of sweat formed on his skin but only cooled him as his steps grew slower. He walked until he seemed to have arrived in the same picture that surrounded both of them. There was no one. There was the crunching of rocks.

Federica. There's the train station. The shadows behind the low, grilled windows. A pair of buzzards circling slowly under the massive fleet of clouds. The sky a matte light blue.

She stands in the shade under the low metal roof of the train station, half propped on her Enzo, who holds the two tickets in his hand and says the numbers of the seats aloud. Summer 1963, they've booked 23 and 24, next to each other, though they could have lived for a while off the surcharge for the reservation. Seat numbers, so Federica doesn't have to stand on this journey, when she can't lift any of the three heavy suitcases.

She wears a simple suit that's a bit too big for her. Enzo, her husband, wears a plaid flat cap. His shoes gleam. They're both a bit nervous and they both know that the others are just getting up, and that they'll be missed in the fields.

It was only four weeks ago, and she still has pains. No, my Enzo, we must go, we must. She can't stand the plantation any longer, the swampy ground near Bolzano, the mice that nibble the hard-won harvest.

The nearby factory like a threat.

She can still see the faces of the two women, the cellar with the green cloths and the hot needles. They were used to the girls shaking with fear when they spread their legs. Federica had suffered unthinkable pain. When they changed trains in Bochum, everything was only just healed.

Alois tried hard. They found a little apartment on Bocholter Straße, hardly more than a room. He couldn't stand it underground for more than half a year, then he switched to the coking plant. The flames were hotter than anything he could ever have imagined. They thought Federica just needed time. But she wasn't in shock. At first she prayed like a crazy person.

But after they'd been there awhile and Federica could understand the news and also that there was a pill that could have spared her all of it, she decided that the priest was to blame. They'd been too poor for a child back then. Over time she became convinced that the whole country was to blame. *Ridotta in questo stato dal paese!* That's how she put it. On Sundays she went to church nonetheless, when the bells rang—how else could she have met the other women.

That evening Alois took Waclaw with him to the village, there was a dance in the dim light of the little hall, in the fiddle tones of a few violins, in the offhandedness of cigarette butts held in wrinkled hands. Men with day-old clothes on their bodies, who knew each other in a wink, in the color with which they called out a name in greeting.

A puppet show was performed on an improvised wooden stage: pig, witch, Kasperle—representing a media mogul and a corrupt parliament—and between them a monkey, feverishly trying to save the world. In the end, even Waclaw had to smile. And there was Alois, among them, but quieter, Alois, who didn't clap or keep the beat with his foot, peering out of the barn door, a mild darkness over the hills. You won't get free of it, he said, and sat with Waclaw at a table at the edge of the festivities. They drank anise schnapps, glass upon glass.

The high notes of a violin.

Outside on the meadow a fire was lit, people clapped. Waclaw found their clapping too loud.

They looked out.

Do you remember the old bowling alley? Alois asked finally. You earned your pocket money down there. Setting up all the pins.

He spoke softly, as if what he said was meant only for Waclaw. The smooth wooden lanes under the Birkeneck.

He didn't look at Waclaw.

I'm still there. The ball rolls and rolls. But there are no pins. You all drank your share down there.

Alois laughed.

Yes, but that doesn't change anything.

Again, Alois looked at his hands. And then you come back, he said, and there's something different about you, it's like a smell you bring with you.

Some schnapps sloshed over the edge of their glasses when they clinked. And Waclaw wasn't tired. He'd heard Mátyás's voice as he snorted the stuff, it was a last little bit, sewed into the seam of a hoodie, why did he just remember it today, little crystals, *snow always helps*, Mátyás had said, *amphetamine, speed*, and how else were they supposed to manage the last hours of the shift, again and again. There was the clear smell of lavender in Alois's room, and Waclaw snorted the stuff and was no longer tired. He'd unpacked the animal and set it on the windowsill, *take her north with you*, then came the snow, bright and light, and he was no longer tired. He watched the animal begin to snarl softly, no land, no water, the frog's feet and the lion's mouth, the weathered white stone, hardly bigger than a piece of soap. The underside of the animal sat flat on the wood of the windowsill, its edge marred by a few brown cracks. The animal crouched there, staring forward. A lion's head with ears cocked as if stalking, the mane passing almost seamlessly into its back. But it was no lion. In the front, two teeth stuck out crookedly from its maw, more reminiscent of human teeth, of a hairy human mouth with a wide snout. The brownish filth of many years clung everywhere. The animal had frog's feet, it spread its webbed toes on the stone ground, it laid back its lion's ears as if to attack. It seemed to have come from the water and yet wasn't native to the land. It resembled him. The rolling eyes, the distrust when he spoke with strangers. He saw the lion's fur on the legs. The body didn't seem like that of a lion. There was something sluggish about it, something wimpy, round, as if the tense facial expression didn't transfer to the rest of it. As if there were some weakness, a paralysis, an infirm base. As if the animal that had done no more than threaten for too long were now stuck to the ground. No longer belonging to the one or the other, neither to the water nor to the land. Waclaw looked at the door. He'd heard steps in the hall. Alois knocked, he followed him to the barn, they drank, and he was wide awake when Alois talked about that bowling alley that no one here had ever seen. Not the brown upholstered furniture at the edges of the room. Not the numbers of the digital clock that glowed red after everyone was long gone. The boy with the unibrow stood in the corner and looked at them. Waclaw recognized some faces from the chapel.

You don't have to be scared of my people, Alois said. I know, Waclaw said. And they both knew he'd said it a bit too fast.

They saw Elena in the half-darkness of the barn. She stood at the edge and watched the two older women next to her talking.

You could dance, Alois said.

Waclaw nodded. We could.

But he stayed sitting and felt Alois scrutinizing him, as if he could see through him, all the way to the silent throbbing that Waclaw had often noticed spreading within him, as if it could split everything he saw, and the parts would sink, but there was no bottom to catch them, no image fell into place.

And while the puppets lay limp over the edge of the stage, while babies were carried home through the night and a few couples danced, Waclaw sat there, and only among all the people did he notice how much he would have liked to tell Milena about it, at least about the dry clay of the barn floor where the children ran barefoot until late in the night.

He stood up and went out. The meadow was cut short and even. All day, the girls hadn't been able to wait for the festival, and now the soles of their feet were green and their eyes shimmered with weariness. He thought of his father and of Alois, the greasy eyeglasses, his damned pigeons that couldn't turn anything around for him. What did he want, what did Alois want from him, *take her north with you,* he walked, Waclaw walked, he wasn't tired, and Alois walked with him and time walked with him, and he could see him, Alois, the slight trembling of his hands, he could hear him, *you were never alone with the pitcarts and their steel tails, you never cursed them, the estate and the everyday faces, we formed you from a lump of dust underground, you're made of a cloud that someone blew into his hands in the cold, your parents loved you, how desperately they wanted to give you this world where you didn't belong any more than they did,* Waclaw looked back, *but they didn't want to believe it of you,* he stumbled, *what kind of architect designed these lives, wrapped in your shabby bedroom curtain, he was the shadow under the fork dropped during a dinnertime row, he was the seam of the dress that was let out, he was the dropped cigarette and the half moon over the chicken coop, he was the ringing of the altar boys,* Waclaw scrambled back to his feet, walked on, *and the moped with a full tank at the gas station, he was the loneliness of the darts player and*

the steam that hung over the pithead baths while the men scrubbed one
another's backs, over the heads of you boys he was the silence in which you
pressed your rulers into the paper to underline the theorems you had to
memorize. Waclaw took big strides through the cut grass.

Alois stayed in the barn. From a distance, Waclaw saw a grille
dragged over the embers of the fire, sparks flew, the hills were outlined in dark blue. Two girls held sticks in the flames, whipped
them over their heads, and ran through the darkness with them like
torches.

He hadn't expected her out there. Elena stood close to the fire,
and the wind came from the side and pressed her dress gently against
her, he could see the contours of her body. She looked aside into the
darkness of the meadow, in the direction where the two girls had
disappeared, the embers crackled, and gray wisps of smoke rose in
the direction of the mountains. She looked at Waclaw, and then she
looked aside.

He left. He walked quickly in the direction of the mountains.
In the darkness he took the shortcut across the field, and everything
was light, and everything was spinning, and he wasn't tired, he had
another bottle with him, and the night was a silent melody, there
was Milena, laying fresh sheets on the deck chairs, while the pasty
bodies of the hotel guests floated as if weightless before her in the
hot salt water, underwater music, as if the world had nothing more
to offer them. She stood at the edge, a pretty person who meant
nothing to them, for nine złoty an hour.

Waclaw walked. The meadow was uneven, and he tore his jacket
climbing over a low fence. Then he stopped and stood for a long
time, tracing the tear with his finger.

22

An Artificial Sun

Alois found Waclaw early in the morning at the edge of the field, sunflowers with heavy brown heads, most of the meadows already mown. He found him next to his own vomit, pale and sleeping, wrapped in a mangled suit jacket. Like something that had fallen from far above.

Alois squatted next to him without touching him.

He saw that Waclaw's hair had grown thin at the temples.

My boy, he said softly.

He half-carried him back, the long man, propped on his shoulders, with only the even throbbing of an electric fence beside them.

He lay for days in the little room by the slope. Now and then Alois came to the door, left him hot soup or some bread, he didn't ask any questions.

Behind the curtains there was the noise of the streets, everything came back: the engines, the honking, the call of the muezzin. The night was not dark. It glowed as under a gas flare. As under an artificial sun. Words rose in him, his father's words, he could hear him: *come back home, my boy.* Waclaw could see him. Tomasz, grown old, kneeling, *pod twoją obronę,* the prayer to Mary, the medallion he wore around his neck when he went underground. The low kneeler in the hallway, the prayer at mealtimes, the smell of boiled beets. *Pod twoją obronę uciekamy się*—We fly to Thy protection. The black Madonna and child was embossed on the silver, Polish miners, their societies, his father's cough, he wore the amulet around his neck. Waclaw could hear these snippets, shadows passed between slats of the shutters, and only after a while did he understand that they were pigeons. He drank water, he lay in the cool, shadowy room by the slope.

Once, Elena stood in the door.

Where were you? she asked. Alois said you just wanted to go back.

Yes.

Waclaw closed his eyes. The room spun.

Where did you get the stuff?

He was silent.

Alois told me about the pigeon, Elena said. That you might do it, take her with you.

He closed his eyes. The room spun.

And what the hell do you want from me, he said.

Then it was quiet again.

And while Alois set bottles of water by the door, while the shadows of the birds passed by the window, while his back ached and he suddenly knew that he wasn't just refueling to get his strength back, but that something of this exhaustion would remain, he thought of Rotterdam, of the big oil tanks and the shipyards where they built the rigs, repaired steel rudders and propellers, and that that was the only place where he would be sure to find work. *Waclaw,* they'd said to him after the accident, *go home, take a break.* As if it were just a discrete distance with an alpha and an omega, that he could travel back. The wind pressed against the cabins. Maybe he would have given up back then if he hadn't met Mátyás. But maybe he, too—and this thought was like a sharp stone—maybe Mátyás, too, had grown tired, and no longer knew what he was looking for in all those mountains he only ever talked about.

Some managed to stop after a few years. They set aside what they'd earned. Built houses—they returned to those worlds that had lined the insides of their lockers for years, dog-eared children's curls and playground slides, worn photos. Paper that you could take out and look at. Paper that sometimes said nothing other than that time didn't stand still. Not for a picture. Not for Andrej. Not for Pippo. Not for him. Others drifted away. Without knowing where the tide was carrying them. Without knowing. In all of it, Mátyás was one of the few who seemed to swim under his own power: a needle, an inner compass.

When Waclaw awoke, he saw the animal on the windowsill. He knew that outside the September quiet was spreading out from Alois's village. He saw the soapstone and he thought of beaches made of dead coral and huts made of pandanus, but none of it made any sense.

Now and then a car drove by, or he heard the melody of the radio that played softly in Alois's kitchen. Otherwise, it was quiet. They would have cleared out the barn and carried the dead out of the chapel, the gymnasts would have packed up their rings and the men wiped down their bocce balls, no dust from that day. Alois asked him nothing. Waclaw lay in the room by the slope, whitewashed walls, the smell of lavender, the large heavy cupboard, he was in no hurry to get up anytime soon.

◆ ◆ ◆

Now and then he saw before him the dark wood of the pier. And he often thought back to that summer day when they'd crouched so long at the edge of the woods, Milena next to him, in the shade under the trees. The light from the lake flickered in the leaves and sent restless stripes down the trunks. They saw the muscles of the snake slowly, rhythmically moving down its body in a pumping motion. The new skin was dark and fresh. And why, he thought later, shouldn't they sit by a lake, watching an adder shedding its skin there in the thicket, why did everything seem wrong when there was no money for a car or gas or a bus ticket or the newspaper. What could be wrong about that light?

It was much later when she called him on the platform. Milena told him that she'd started brushing her teeth as soon as she finished her coffee, so the enamel wouldn't turn brown—she told him such things. Far away, he tried to imagine her, but he had no feeling for her mouth, or for the place where they'd woken up together every morning. As if a glass wall had slipped between them, without a sound. As if a toothbrush could change anything. They spoke for a long time, and when the sentences broke off, they listened to the distance in the connection, which seemed to have a life of its own, setting itself up between their words.

The winter evenings were cold and dark when he came back, and they sat in front of the stove in the little house, they looked into the night as if waiting for something. When he left after two weeks, he had a feeling again for the place he was leaving, even if this place, this world, didn't need him. The other countries, on the other hand, were exciting, the schnapps was exhilarating, the dance and the music didn't need the slow rhythm that pressed the seasons upon the countryside and between the fence pickets. It was the other side of the

Atlantic. There wasn't the damn war in their heads, there wasn't the rearmament or the fucking mine, none of it. The men sat with their full glasses and awaited the future. They worked their asses off for it. The continents drifted, the oil was millions of years old, the winter was dark in the village. He stroked her belly as he drove.

Later he often thought back on it. It was a touch that happened in passing. It was a touch that then no longer happened. *No boy, no girl, but I'm healthy.* Her letter reached him two weeks later on the *West Aquarius*, he worked, sick, days, nights, he let his ticket expire, the cities were fast and lonely, *don't come anymore*, he tore up the letter, he would later regret that, too. He sat on foreign coastlines, watched the fishermen throwing the last leftovers in their nets to the seabirds, he saw the birds, always that same hunger. The tired waves on the beach. The bartenders, their white shirts. *Don't come anymore.*

He lay in the twilight and saw the animal, its frog's feet and lion's mouth, then he fell back asleep. In the stillness he heard the harsh noise of the needle gun that they used to strip rust off the deck.

The wind drove the clouds that had gathered that morning. It was the first heavy rain since he'd been on the road. The crags were wet, and when Waclaw got to the fork in the road, he had trouble wedging the metal sheet between the rocks, the flow was twice as strong, he felt the pressure on his shoulders.

The water was cold. It splashed against the rocks, the moss gleamed where the little rivulet came down the mountain. He smelled the sweat of the last days on his body, and everything seemed far away. The festival. The damned grass in the vastness of Hungary. The green plastic in Alois's loft. The morning was still milky and dismal and he shivered as he took the metal out of the rocks. He didn't know if it was only the cold. Far below lay the house, lay Alois with his old dreams. *Take her north with you.*

He rubbed his skin with a narrow towel. When he bent over, he felt his back. The third, the fourth vertebrae. He stood on the rocks and waited, while the sun gradually rose higher; he dressed slowly. He could trace the ripped cloth of the suit with his finger and stand with his bare feet in his own boots like a guest.

He looked down to the green beans, the landscape had changed color with the rain. And he walked, Waclaw, with stiff steps, past the low canopy under which Alois sat—he saw his fragile hands and the concentration with which he peeled an apple in thin strips. There you are. Alois tried to smile.

That afternoon Waclaw stood at the window and looked out at the loft. The rain had returned, and he watched the pigeon.

In the morning he was already waiting for Alois when he came out of the house. Waclaw saw him coming in his slippers, and he could hear that Alois was out of breath from the few steps up the slope.

Alois sat down in the big folding chair where he always sat. It was patterned with stripes like something out of an old ad for a VW Beetle.

There you are, he said softly.

Yes, Waclaw said.

They didn't speak while Alois opened the hatch and let them out, one after another. They circled the loft once before making their large loops. Here was the whooshing of their wings, here was the silence over the miners' estate, and within it, the soft murmur of prayers. His mother, the aunts, the rosaries. Always, the fear that it wouldn't be enough. A wind howled in their faces, even when they sat in the warmth making lace bedspreads. He thought of the Filipinos who sought out services in their native tongue in every port.

Alois had both arms on the arms of his chair. His breath gradually grew calmer.

How far is it? Waclaw asked.

Alois turned to him slowly. His eyes looked small behind the angular frame of his glasses. He watched Waclaw for a while in silence as if trying to read something. Then a smile came over his face. My boy, he said.

But Waclaw opened his hand, as if expecting an advance payment.

I checked, he said. It's over six hundred. Plus the headwinds. Plus the mountains. Plus the night. Are you sure?

Alois looked at him. Come, come, he said.

He told Alois he didn't need a car.

How else are you planning to take her?

A friend of Alois's with long, thin forearms and a homemade concrete pit, whose edges were crooked and irregular and full of oil stains, took care of it. Flavio grimaced when they pushed the pickup into the yard. An old white Fiat Fiorino; the bed had once transported straw and silage.

Over the course of days, Waclaw could see his arms in the gap between the pit and the underside of the car, a restless lamp, sometimes he heard Flavio curse.

Alois showed him the feed, the bird's papers. And of course he'd trained her. Marcello, a cousin of Elena's who drove a tractor-trailer nearly weekly to Brescia and Bergamo, had taken her with him and let her out high over the Brenner Pass. Everyone who'd ever seen Alois when the pigeons returned knew why Marcello always did it for him. She's used to the mountain air, Alois said.

Waclaw walked to the village. He bought little cakes and pastries for Enni at the bakery, took the dusty road and went up the lane with the hawthorns to the house. He saw the light shimmering uneasily under the feathery leaves, and while they sat on the terrace with cake and lemonade from the lemon trees, they looked toward the mountains a few times, and Elena asked how long he was going to stay and when he was going to set out, and for how long, and Waclaw said: I don't know.

But why are you two doing this thing with the pigeon? Elena looked at him. He smoothed the paper on which the cakes had stood. It was coated with gold.

You know, he said, when you've been out there for a long time, you think about what you're going to eat when you get back to land, and where, and with whom, and you wait for the mail from the mainland, even when you know there won't be anything. A ship docks, or they fly in the mail when new workers come. There's a kind of cult around the mail sacks. You have no reception and no personal telephone. And when something comes, no matter what it is, it becomes incredibly precious. You don't read a letter only once, and when they send you something—a little cake like this one, maybe—these huge guys stand there like it's Christmas. Or Jeff gets a Matchbox car from his four-year-old son. For his birthday. He carries it with him all week, and puts it next to his plate when he eats. It's the worst when there's nothing to do. When the bit's stuck. Then a fear rises in you. And then you just want to wait for the mail and think about what there will be to eat.

He smoothed his trousers.

Alois was up there almost twenty years.

Enni bit into a cookie with red filling. She looked at Waclaw under the brim of her sun hat.

Do you know what she calls you? Elena asked.

Calls me?

Elena grinned. Waccio, she said.

Big Waccio.

Waclaw swallowed. Then he took a sip of lemonade. He could see the cherry trees. He could hear them: children calling his name, sitting hidden up there in the treetops. For a moment they both looked at the girl.

After three days Flavio emerged from the pit and from under the hood. The real Flavio, with a head and neck and a face, emaciated like dry white bread but more angular and oily. He thumped the metal with the flat of his hand. It's ready. Alois raised his eyebrows.

Then you'll be off soon, my boy. Before fall comes. Do you know how quickly it gets cold up there?

Waclaw nodded.

The next day Alois sat in the dusty room with the feed sacks, busy filling old cans with corn and lentils and coarsely ground peanuts. The precision with which he let everything flow through his hands before filling the tins was reminiscent of a secret formula, calculated for all the paths and dangers of the journey. Waclaw leaned in the doorway, he saw the fabric of the folding chair stretched under Alois, the aluminum frame groaned slightly when he moved. The rims of Alois's glasses shone chestnut brown, and it seemed like he had only put them on to underscore the precision of his process, while his hands found the right proportions blindly. Waclaw had watched quietly, and the word *patient* came to mind, though he wasn't sure whether either of them could be patient, whether it wasn't much more that they felt that something was at their heels, a vague haste, as if the winter that would come over the mountains, the winter that everyone just talked about, were something more than *just winter*. Maybe this snow simply made clear that there were edges, beyond which everything known threatened to break off, shrouded in huge, mighty whiteness.

There were six old cans, feed, to strengthen her for the flight, the journey back, as if Alois had forgotten something up north. He bound them together with six-pack rings, the kind that often lay around on beaches. Animals could get tangled in them, Waclaw had seen once on a hotel television, near the beginning, and he'd fallen asleep late to the thought that sea animals could drown. Alois stowed a few cans in a special box, he'd wrapped them with a red band: these were feed for the evening just before the flight. Then he lifted the sacks back into the plastic barrel and screwed on the top. It made a soft snap, like a child that has to practice snapping its fingers, and he flopped back into the folding chair in the semi-gloom. He seemed twice as heavy as before.

What did Elena say? he asked softly.

He seemed to strain to see Waclaw in the bright doorway.

Cos'ha detto? Alois asked again.

She says it's dangerous.

A bit of air hissed through his teeth. Is she from animal welfare now?

Waclaw shook his head.

No, she means for you.

She says that?

Alois clenched his jaws.

She must think I'm a pretty sentimental old codger. That I didn't dare to let a single bird fly the whole way all these years, didn't you wonder why? The Silesians, the Prussians, that's all they did— long-distance flights from Königsberg or Danzig, and what did they care? This way I could always convince myself I was just a good plane ride away.

Alois looked up.

Last year I had mice in the feed. They could kill her. Or mold. But for the rest, she has her good wings. One on each side. And her feathers are perfect. Now stop your nonsense and lend me a hand.

Nuts and lots of fat and always clear water. Don't take too long. He drummed it into Waclaw: to pay attention to the weather, to the airports with their strong radar, to the winds, to birds of prey in the skies. You know how important the release is, he said. Everything depends on it.

Then Waclaw went to pick up the truck.

Flavio sat on the edge of his pit and let his legs dangle. It was hard to guess how old he was. His dungarees were covered with stains, he was agile, but his teeth were bad and his skin lay thin over gradually receding muscles. Flavio looked at the Fiorino as if to go over it all once more, every wire. Waclaw saw that he'd washed the truck, or at least the windshield. A few pieces of baling twine still hung in the grille between the cab and the truck bed. Flavio saw him coming and slowly stood up. It was hard for him to show how proud he was, so he stood almost motionless, with a suppressed smile, listening to what Waclaw had to say while he walked around the pickup, marveling. They took it for a test drive, and Flavio let his elbow hang out the window. Then Waclaw asked about the price, and Flavio shook his head.

Per Enzo, he said. And you came on foot.

Waclaw protested, he just had to fetch the money.

But Flavio shook his head again. He wouldn't accept anything. He pounded the metal.

You won't need the heater, he said. Then he cleared his throat. He'd looked at the route on a map. He hadn't known it was so far.

Do you know how important this is to Enzo? he asked.

Then he looked at his hands and spoke more softly.

You could let her out earlier. You could wait a few days—get a room halfway.

Waclaw looked at him.

Why?

What do you mean?

Why should I do that?

Flavio laughed.

Sei esattamente come lui. You're just like him.

Waclaw bought capers and a chicken and tomatoes and garlic and he cooked the chicken and took the broth with the tomatoes floating in it, and they poured it over the potatoes and sat in front of her house, the light of the candle flickering, it wasn't yet dark.

Elena praised the food, and he said he hadn't cooked in a long time, and she asked why not, and he said they'd gone out to eat, he didn't know how it all worked anymore. Her laugh reverberated through the big, nearly empty house, and then she led him to the door in her sandals and waved after him for a long time. He'd declined to take Alois's old Kadett. But before she knew it, the body of the Fiorino had imprinted itself, and it drifted through her mind over the next days like a shadow whenever she looked at the long, bright lane.

The pigeon basket was made of wicker. Waclaw traced the emblem branded in the wood with his finger as he set it on the passenger seat. Safe Return Pigeon Club. He remembered the stack of pigeon boxes, the vans, the cooing before they were released. The pigeon club, the timing clock at the start of the race. *Jupp, are the pigeons back yet?* Waiting. Sunday mornings. The lattice on the crate could be pushed aside, a few of the wooden bars had been replaced, the floor was covered with sawdust. The basket was as wide and high as two shoeboxes. Alois had added poles in the middle, the pigeon sharpened its beak on the young wood. Its neck shimmered green, the pattern of its wings, black-and-white checkered, was smooth and shiny. Its eye seemed made of glass but for the red glints, and he could feel its warm red feet when he weighed it experimentally in his hands. The bluish plumage. It looked at the three men and the woman who stood in front of the carrier box.

She's used to this, Alois said, she knows it's time now.

The girl climbed out of the Fiorino. A string of plastic beads swung from the rearview mirror. She grinned.

Waclaw slept uneasily that night. He'd thought of his father, of his thin legs and his raw knees in the domain of the *Esse*. Short pants, pencil case, and the conjugations of a language where the word *Esse* meant "being," or "life." It seemed a region where possibilities could be imagined without one's having any claim to them, as if they had to be lost, like the little dog they'd led through the estate on a long rope one summer and then buried with the neighbors' children at the edge of the meadow. Life and *Esse*, life among the *Esse*, the place always seemed to mean something else, as if it had long since turned away from those who lived in it, toward this darkness that began with the heat. The marl layer in Westphalia raised the temperature by three degrees a hundred meters down, the coalfield region with all its darkness and dust arose from a fire, a heat that they knew nothing about. The *Esse*, always only a subjunctive form of life, days in three narrow heated rooms with a view of the curb and the newly built sewer system. Everything was progress, two pubs, a regional football club that, it was said, recruited its players from the area. It was a struggle with the *Esse*, at least for some.

In the morning Waclaw watched the birds circling one last time. Alois, who embraced him in his light arms, he stood there in a checked cardigan and flat slippers, he'd stowed the feed cans with a water container on the truck bed, with just the two cans with the red band in the glove compartment. His eyes gleamed as he lifted the pigeon basket onto the passenger seat.

And suddenly Waclaw saw him, sharply outlined, short, with his watery eyes and a fear in his old heart of which he, Waclaw, was the subject, and it was like the rustling of the trees, and briefly he thought that it was possible, that it might just be possible, for Alois to disappear in this rustling. Waclaw loaded the rest of the things. The duffel. The suit. The water. The blanket. Alois's rather fragile figure as he slammed the tailgate.

Waclaw turned around once more.

It's possible that you'll wait for nothing.

Alois seemed taken aback, and stood there, still. Then he looked up.

He came back to him again, laid a hand on Waclaw's shoulder

to support himself, while with the other he seemed to reach toward Waclaw's chin, but the movement dissolved into the air.

He looked at him. He pointed again to his eyes with two fingers and looked up at him.

No, Wenzel Groszak, he said. Do you understand? That's not it.

He stood there, hardly different than when Waclaw had seen him twenty years ago. He did not say: Of all of them you're the only one who remembers. Just stood there and waved a simple wave.

He didn't start the engine of the Fiorino, just released the handbrake and let out the clutch and the pickup rolled down the little hill. The pigeon basket sat on the seat next to him, covered with a plain, dark cloth. But the way Alois had smoothed it said that for him it was more than just a flight. His bare feet in the slippers, the blue of his veins that early morning.

He would check his loft each day. He would wait. Waclaw rolled down the narrow path and looked back until Alois disappeared. His waving in the rearview mirror: that remained, amid the greenish yellow of the roads. They drove north. They were on their way.

23

And the Alps Were a Horse Rearing Up

The engine hummed, wind brushed his temples. He heard the gravel crunch. He took the small roads, they grew steeper, and he left the fields behind him, the dry edges of the ditches and the rustling of small animals at the side of the road. They were under way. He brushed the lattice with his long fingers, and when the turns pressed the pigeon to the side, he felt its feathers through the bars. Something light. It seemed as if she were leaning against his hand.

He now scanned the sky with concern, looking for birds of prey. The first time his father went for a treatment he had brought Waclaw back a simple, diamond-shaped plastic kite with a bird of prey printed on it. That day the pigeons didn't come back to the loft for hours. Waclaw thought of falcons, diving down from high crags. Sometimes even at sea his eyes had searched the sky, as if something could still come from there, a shadow, a flash, nothing more. The whole Strait of Hormuz, it was said, was guarded by falcons.

The villages he passed through were small and old, there were long-disused arches and towers, fountains, traffic circles and flower beds, colorful as a model railway that someone had laid out with great care, someone with the power to decide what belonged in his world and what didn't, a craftsman with miniature chisels and a powder to make the water shimmer, paint to color the stones and the eternal summer. There were no storms here, nothing was lost. He drove.

The walls were terra-cotta red, and bells hung in the towers like a forgotten choir, soundless. Few people. All day the peaks of the alps towered in the north like the foothills of another world. He didn't drive straight toward them. In the evening he lay down not far from the truck at the edge of a flat, bush-covered cliff. The few towns he had seen during the day glowed weakly in the twilight, a thin film lay over the countryside like an arch of dust. He took out the pigeon and held her wings together and pressed her gently to his chest. He let her pick grains from his hand and ran his hands through the feed. The sun soon sank behind a rock face. He had no light, not even a lighter. There was only the soft cooing, and he almost had to smile because the evening, everything about this evening, seemed so simple. His clothes would get clammy, and the tarp would surely be too thin for a night at this elevation. When the meadow grew damp, he lay down on the truck bed.

Rain pelted the roof of the truck during the night, he heard it getting stronger and then abating. Through the small crack he'd left for air, he could hear how the drops made a sea of the slopes, it swelled and undulated, there was the brown of that night, but only briefly. It sounded like a long recitation in which days and nights began to resemble each other, the same steady beat, as if the meanings, too, were starting to match, there were no more towns, just the pelting that surrounded him, and the bird that slept beside him.

At dawn he sat in the driver's seat with a bottle of water, next to him Enni had her head in her feathers. The sun was stuck behind the mountains. He'd dipped water from a stream, and the gurgling between the stones, which slowly ate a path through the rock, was like a great echo of something he didn't understand. He'd sat

wet and shivering on the cliff. Why can't you just drive. Idiot. He
wanted to hear his own voice. How long had it been since he'd heard
Milena's. He remembered the airport departures board, in front
of which Mátyás had tossed a coin, how they'd bought everything
they needed when they got there and then left it behind in the hotel
rooms, and always the clear feeling that he was leaving more behind
than just those things.

He could see the estate again, the pigeons in their big circles,
a falcon that swooped down from on high, and how the flock dispersed in all directions, but differently, like something that would
find its way back together blindly. A single feather fell down through
the gray summer sky of the mining town.

The bird waited on the passenger seat. The shadows wandered. But
no trace of moon or sun, just the high crags against this early blue.
It was different than on the sea. The mountains, everything about
these mountains, was more powerful than he'd thought. Power
lines. Trails.

The tractor-trailers still had their lights on, they came straight
out of the night. He drove on side roads, he wasn't in a hurry to get
north. He turned on the radio. A man with a guitar sang *that red
rose empire*.

The road wound up the slope in hairpin turns, and there were
few trees, and he was tired when he saw two people in the distance
standing at the side of the road. He'd put Mátyás's old cassette in the
tape deck, and it droned away, as if struggling to draw a clear outline
around their time together. He steered the pickup far to the other
side of the road as he approached them, he didn't want to slow down,
even though he saw that they were looking in his direction. They
seemed small under the high cliffs, a man and a woman, stooped.

They were dressed warmly, coats bulged over their shoulders, and underneath, what looked like various layers of wool. He didn't want to stop. He saw their hands, drawn upward by the thumbs, and he drove more slowly and finally the pickup came to a stop on the slope with its rear end sticking up. He listened to the last notes of the song before rolling down the window.

Next to the driver's side stood a small older woman, her face half-buried in a tower of woolen layers. Her hair lay on her coat collar in a flat braid, and she smiled up at him uncertainly, without opening her mouth. He turned off the engine. She pointed in the direction of the pass that led left into the mountains and north, and he nodded. But then he pointed to the seat next to him. *Non c'è posto per voi*, he said. *Uno*, he said, one seat. The woman waved the man over. He had remained by the rocks, looking shyly toward the Fiorino as if he expected it to start moving at any moment. As he came closer, he seemed hardly to lift his feet off the ground. She whispered something in his ear, and pressed his hand, and he nodded.

They helped him onto the truck bed. He, too, was wrapped in many layers of fabric, and his hair was thin and gray. The woman tucked her coat around his legs and gave him a cloth to wind around his head. The clothes were faded, and the yellow patches on the coat were gray and dirty. Waclaw showed him how to sit, he looked small on the truck bed, and held on with hands that looked like they were used to hard work. He smiled at Waclaw, but Waclaw looked past him. He didn't know why, but later, after the woman had sat down next to him and he had released the handbrake and they had the first few kilometers behind them, he heard himself using the few fragments of Polish he'd learned from his father, this language that belonged nowhere, for which he no longer had a place, only the smell of quince drying in the oven, perhaps of hay, perhaps the crackling of hay.

He told her that he had no other language, and then he looked straight ahead, as if the space beyond the steering wheel were an unreachable place. He shrugged when the woman asked about his route, or about the bird, to whom it belonged, what he was planning to do with it. *Gołąb*, he said, pigeon, and nodded, and left it there, later, too, when she tried to tell him something, about a festival they were coming from. He wondered where they'd spent the night and why they had so much clothing on, but he didn't ask. The woman asked him what the bird was called; he thought about it for a moment. Enni, he thought then, but said nothing.

The river he'd seen that morning between the crags now ran next to the road, a washed-out mountain stream in a bed of large boulders. The road rose above it, keeping a respectful distance. He wondered whether the two old people had a name for the river, and whether they knew the area, and whether it would make a difference either way. But the woman next to him looked out with an expression of wonder and some apprehension, and kept turning around to look through the grated window at the truck bed where her husband lay like a black mummy, or like something that had drawn its wings in.

He didn't react when she knocked on the window.

Waclaw's telephone lay in the glove compartment, it was turned off. In the glove compartment was Sharam's voice, and he could hear it. Don't you get it, Wenzel? You take it with you, all of this here. And it was a port, Rotterdam, everything was big and powerful, the Keppel Verolme shipyard, and they were tiny between the pipes, and nearly nothing beside the base of the platform *Saipem 7000*, which was being prepared in dry dock. Sharam had stood there and looked at Mátyás, who smoked, his hands trembling. It eats you up, Sharam said, no one can survive it alone up there. And he'd meant the North Sea, Mátyás's days on *Troll*, his extra shifts out there. Waclaw had listened, but preferred to look out at the water, and Mátyás said: Well, what? Sharam looked at him and clenched his jaws. Sometimes he didn't need to say anything, he didn't even shake his head. Then they left, Waclaw with Mátyás, over the melting tar and through the silent heat of the port, where in the distance the loading cranes drove back and forth as if they were looking for something, like in a shell game where everyone loses. They spent the next few nights out at clubs. The streets were full of fog in the early dawn.

The last firs appeared, glowed in the early light, then no longer glowed, but were gray and dark in their own outlines, then the clouds came. He could hear the stream when they rested. He climbed down once more and filled the bottles and gave the bird water to drink.

They drove slowly, and soon the Avers mountains were to their north and the western Alps to their left, and the woman sat smiling on the seat next to the pigeon basket, and it smelled of goat and wet wool. Before they reached the pass, he refilled the coolant and carefully put the truck in low gear. They reached the pass, where they were overtaken by other vehicles; the ascent began, the first trees had red caps. Half a meter under this asphalt was a pipeline that ran north, what did the two old people know of it, he drove, the Splügen Pass, pipes lay eighty centimeters under this asphalt, well packed, this grass was more than just a meadow for rams and goats. He knew that the new pipelines were monitored by drones: empty retinas, like the animal skulls in market halls, in front of which people played out their everyday dramas. He thought about this when they entered the short tunnel.

◆   ◆   ◆

They stopped around midday, and the man climbed wordlessly down from the truck bed and sat on a rock in the blazing sun. He moved his hands slowly, and the woman took out a pot fastened with rubber bands and plastic, and they ate strips of preserved mutton, and they offered it to Waclaw, and he chewed and chewed the strips, the meat was strong and tasted of herbs. He left the two alone in the sun, and while he looked after the bird, he saw them backlit like two old pilgrims, and they seemed unreal next to the smooth asphalt and the neon-green paint of the motorcycles. He thought of the figures he'd seen in Tangier dressed in cheap blankets with cords around their waists, their gazes fixed on the distance, but not the other-worldly distance of monks, just the crackling of fireworks on the other side of the strait, where Spain was. *Feliz Año Nuevo!*

The church had arranged pilgrimages too, bus trips to the Vatican, 35 mm cameras and rosaries, and back in the Ruhr Valley the pastor read out a list of the people who hadn't knelt before entering the pew at mass.

Before they continued, he saw how the woman rubbed her husband's hands warm, and how the old man took a long look up at the pass. They drove. But only when they were higher up in the dense fog, and the meadows were gray and the roofs little more than outlines, did he stop the Fiorino, and they brought the old man to the front, where he sat next to the woman, with the pigeon basket on his knees. The smell of wool and animals and damp filled the cab, and he opened the window a crack and took the switchbacks slowly. He saw the countryside under him disappear in fog, and the two old people seemed to slide even closer together on the passenger side. Mountain peaks emerged in the distance like the petrified shadows of something restless, something that had pressed the continents together and banished the edges of its ancestral land to eternal ice. The turns were tight and narrow, and the pigeon basket pressed against the man's chest, the bird inside grew uneasy.

Waclaw stopped. He felt queasy, the mountain air came cool through the open window, and the light fell white and silent, like something that had never touched dust, only these quiet heights. It wasn't a road where you could stop. A convertible with the top closed passed him, flashing its brights. Two motorcycles. Below them the road lay like a dropped piece of string. The two old people said nothing, they seemed to be waiting for him to continue. The windows of the houses were small, they were hidden under layers of cloud, to their right a crude wall supported the hillside. They passed cows that grazed wild on the side of the road, everything seemed to crouch on the back of a huge animal or hollow space. He thought of broad beans, war elephants that he'd carved as a child out of the big white beans that his mother couldn't stand to look at anymore, after the hard times. The pachyderms were given packs and adornments, the mountains were his knees under white sheets, he sat under the sideboard in the kitchen and carved elephants out of broad beans, elephants that tumbled from the slopes, somersaulted, they balked at the ice, some lay down gently in the snow to die. The woman reached for the string of beads swinging from the rearview mirror and asked whether he was traveling to his daughter. A daughter? she asked again. The beads clacked between her fingers. If she was looking at him, she didn't move. He shook his head. Then he leaned forward as if he had to concentrate on the road to keep from missing the arched semicircle that led into the tunnel.

He drove more slowly. It was a short tunnel, open on one side. The light flashed between the columns like the shadows of a very slow propeller. The sky beyond them was white, only road, and no more bushes. He drove very slowly through the hairpin turns until another entrance emerged before him, darker this time, and he was hot, he still heard her voice saying the word *daughter* in various languages, like a question, like a question that lay before him, and he grasped the steering wheel and drove into the opening, which immediately began to swallow the light. There were no headlights and no sound, no fleece that no one wore, only the fear that gaped from below, as if the mountain were a hollow space, as if man were a goddamned mountain, filled with black, and there was the fear, it came from below, he braked sharply, stopped the truck, the pigeon basket slipped on the old man's knees, the darkness around them, the lights out, the engine off, the Fiorino silent, just the beads still swinging, clack, clack, a soft heartbeat that disappeared in the blackness. He could smell them, the two old people and the bird. He was alone.

He thought of Troy and how there was always a kind of gap. A way home. An alpha and omega. And that it was more like a ladder, with wet rungs, with the sky hissing between them, and it was hard to hold on. Between the rungs was an airspace of time, filled with names: Jakarta, Mumbai, Seoul, Karachi. Some platforms were connected to each other by metal bridges the men called widowmakers. There were old images of burning rigs that they carried around with them forever, *Piper Alpha*, the *Alexander Kielland*, which went down with two hundred men, an indeterminate fear that followed them all those years. Fatigue fractures in the iron braces, flames that couldn't be extinguished. When Mátyás came it seemed less important, their eyes always found each other first. But Mátyás had stayed beyond these mountains.

✦　✦　✦

A boat headed toward *Clearwater* from the mainland, he'd watched it awhile, a tiny boat that churned up the sea in a bright line behind it, and he was nonetheless astonished when it cut its engine by the legs of the platform. It seemed desperately small with its outboard. It had women on board, and crates. Waclaw had been out barely a year and watched anxiously as the slewing crane began to move, and lowered the big ring. Over the ring stretched a tapered net of stiff ropes, which the workers held on to when they were lifted up. Bringing prostitutes or others onto the platform wasn't allowed; the fear of piracy was great, and the possibility that instead of Caribbean rum the crates might contain a detonator had been drummed into their minds—particularly those of the younger ones.

Next to Waclaw, Philippe spat on the deck in disgust while the ring containing three women was lowered toward the platform. A few guys helped them on deck, the women carried their shoes, and Waclaw didn't want to see any more, no more than a leg that jutted out from under a coat with every long step. He retreated to his cabin and lay uneasily in his bunk bed. Distantly he saw a ship with a welt of rust around the hole for the anchor chain, a wearily circling echo sounder. A detonator out here, that would be it: an immense, inextinguishable jet of flame, a dazzling hot ball twenty-five meters in diameter, a fake sun, extinguishing explosions and burning water. Waclaw lay there, and in the silence of the cabin he began to tell Milena about it, as if everything he said would coalesce as into a finely woven fabric, and the fear would be only one thin thread, and not something that would be with him always from now on, at the sound of every damn alarm.

He hadn't known that a mountain was powerful and quiet enough to make him feel this way. He hadn't known that everything would stop and lie scattered around and that it would take nothing more than the engine of the Fiorino running, the slight smell of gasoline through the window, the darkness of the tunnel before him. The walls were made of roughly hewn stone, and the road ran toward a turn where the light disappeared, as in a well where something fell and fell without a splash.

He hadn't known that no one would notice if no evening came on which he talked of what had happened all those years, a familiar table, the glasses greasy after a long night, the neighbors would just be closing the door behind them at daybreak. Here was only the rock, the tunnel, silent in all directions, and the old couple had begun to whisper. *Luce.* The woman shook his arm, he should turn on the lights. *Signore*, the old man said, and struck the dashboard with the flat of his hand, the woman began to whimper, he should drive, she said, and wouldn't let go of his arm as he reached for the gear shift and the Fiorino slowly rolled into first gear. Mátyás had stayed beyond these mountains. Waclaw didn't know the places he was driving toward anymore, a water stain on paint, running in every direction, black becoming purple, then yellow at the edges, the pigments separated but the original color didn't return. He was sweating. Next to him the old people still stared at the roadway, and the woman had red spots on her cheeks and laughed nervously as the centerline flashed in the headlights, and after another turn the exit hove into view. The old man began to hum a song softly, and he stroked the basket with his old, worn hand, the way one strokes the fear out of an animal's fur.

Once they were out of the tunnel they drove through heavy rain. The panorama was swallowed by clouds that rushed over the mountainsides like large animals.

In some places green shimmered through the fog, and the old man hummed his song, which sounded guttural and ancient, like a three-note chant. Waclaw's pulse was still racing, a dark pounding that opened downward, that was tearing open every moment, he was cold and he looked for a turnout to stop in. Soon they reached the pass and the boundary marker, and the meadows lay above in a somber light, and he could walk a little way into them, and he stood there and breathed in the fog and felt the couple looking at him. His shoes weren't sealed against the rain that came from all sides.

Somewhere in all the fog stood the boy from the airport, silent and serious, as if in the whole evening, in nothing more than the distant shimmer of a city, in the horizon with its lights, he could read something like meaning. Waclaw felt heavy and tired. In the car he saw the faces of the two old people behind the fogged panes like two bright circles, like stars that were contracting, not because a complicated theory told them they must, but because they had glowed once some time ago, together perhaps, bright, and this glow was now, for anyone who looked upon them, no more than a vague sense.

The Fiorino shone in the fog, and beyond, where the road suddenly flattened over a plateau, a lake shimmered gray and still under a layer of cloud. Beyond it a high wall of rock or more clouds, sluggishly letting out their burdens of rain. A light was on in an RV stopped at the side of the road. Cars passed now and then; they, too, were slow and had their lights on. He didn't know how late it was or how to dry his boots or what to say to the couple. He thought of the pigeon basket and the emblem in the wood and that the bird had no chance in this fog. The mountains like giant waves, frozen.

The couple drank from an old jam jar from which a white liquid sloshed over the edge, little bits of cream or fat floated on the surface, and the woman had a milk mustache that she wiped away with the back of her hand as he opened the door. Everything smelled of barn. They looked at him as if he had accidentally disturbed their nest while plowing, with small eyes, thickly wrapped, creatures that couldn't survive outside. And the woman smiled. *Suiss*, she said, and *casa*, and many other words that he didn't understand. Her hair shone a bit greasily. Through the clouds came the muffled sound of an airplane.

The windshield wipers, the headlights, one lake after another, little vegetation. Here the road was less steep. The man no longer hummed. He'd covered the basket with the cloth, and they drove, all three of them, in silence. They could see no farther than the cones of light from the headlights, as if that were all the future could promise. They took the descending turns in silence.

They'd crossed a border, evening was falling. He was hungry. He asked the couple if he should let them out in the next town by saying *stop* and *exit* a few times, but they shook their heads, so he took them with him as he turned off the road and followed a wooden sign and ordered in a tiny pub, now surrounded again by trees. It looked like an old railway car that had been stuck on a wooden floor, he got three of the same dish by pointing at the menu, and he felt half ashamed and half at ease under the low-hanging lamps. The couple ate shyly and more slowly than he was used to, as if reminding themselves to chew every bite. It was potatoes and eggs, and there was some cheese, too, and the proprietor looked healthy, like the other guests, only his nose was flat, like it had been worked over with a mallet.

People looked at them as they couldn't afford to in most places, and Waclaw prepared for a fight, but the old couple didn't seem to notice. He laid money on the table and waited outside. The firs were black shadows, and a dark gurgling could be heard where the river was. No lights. In the distance a few single engines struggled up the slope. He could see the couple standing up inside and pushing their chairs in until the backs touched the table, then their eyes sought the door, and the woman seemed relieved to see him still standing there. He wanted time to think. He took the spare can and filled up the tank and walked around the pickup. The couple watched him, half-illuminated by the light that came through the high window. They held hands, like children afraid of the dark.

24

White Maps

They found a place not far away. The darkness came as quickly as if someone had spread a cloth over them. But it was cold. The Fiorino stood flat, the headlights shone for a while into the larches, and the slate squeaked on the path when they walked back and forth between the driver's side door and the truck bed.

Waclaw gave them the tarp, they slept on their coats, each of them shrouded in all the layers of cloth. Then the tarp. Then nothing. Alpine air, a darkness. They lay close together. He sat in the cab, and he heard them whispering. Very quietly, so he couldn't understand anything. He looked after the pigeon. He talked to her. Still in another language, he wasn't sure why. He left the light on in the cab for a while. He stretched out her wings, he saw her perfect feathers, she weighed almost nothing. Like Farangis had weighed almost nothing, back then, emaciated like him. He'd brushed her hair, she was light, she needed sleep just as he did. He wanted to tell her about the accident, the brush felt almost like nothing in his hand. He spoke to her in a language she didn't understand, no one here understood the few fragments of Polish his father had taught him. Farangis smelled of a sweet perfume, the room was cool, sometimes he touched her roughly, but then he stayed with her, an hour, two hours. He went home changed, as if she'd reminded him of something. Something like a land that he hardly dared set foot in anymore.

It grew cold. His back hurt. The seat was too short to lie down on, and he couldn't sit. He climbed onto the hood and leaned his back against the glass. Before he fell asleep he tried to find the North Star amid the few stars not blocked by clouds. He looked in one direction for a long time, and he didn't know if it was the right direction, and if it was, whether that would mean anything.

In the dawn he sat shivering before a small fire that he'd kindled from wet wood and a splash of gasoline, and it didn't warm him, and the smoke drifted away over the jagged paths. The old man walked stiffly toward him through what looked like a blueberry thicket. He stood next to Waclaw in front of the puffing fire, but he kept his distance. The flames were weak and both men were wet and chilled to the bone, and Waclaw thought of the little coffeepot that he'd left with Alois, and regretted it. Travelers left things behind but they never came back to retrieve them. A pair of shoes in the closet, a bag of souvenirs, mother-of-pearl, for which there was no space or no one to show it to. The old man stared into the smoke and breathed in deeply.

His face was angular, and without the hood and the thick collar he seemed lively, his hair reached almost to his ears and looked like it had been cut with something blunt, his jaw was a sharp line, his eyes alert, and he seemed to be thinking about something, he breathed in a few times as if he wanted to speak. Then he looked at Waclaw and his still-damp boots and asked if he still had a long way home, and Waclaw shook his head a bit hesitantly. The man looked at him.

Then you have to take them off.

He touched his own ankles and made as if to place next to him what were once boots but now were just many bands of leather around his calves. Waclaw nodded. Then he felt naked on the stones, his feet were swollen from the moisture and had a surreal brightness against the earth. He laid his socks in the grass and placed the boots next to the flames that gave off no warmth. He looked at the boots, and then put them in another place, and the man looked at him and at the fire and at the boots and said: wood. And Waclaw nodded: yes.

Neither moved. Finally Waclaw sat, bare feet and smoke in front of him, as if waiting for something. They heard noises from the truck bed, but they didn't turn around to look. The fire died, then flared up again. The treetops on the hill became edged in pink. Waclaw was freezing, but he wanted to stay, like a boy who'd found an older friend. Behind them the woman had climbed down from the truck bed, and they heard something that sounded like rocks being struck together. The old man bent over and picked up a boot, and it was wet and heavy. He weighed it in his hands and gave it back to Waclaw. I can't see where we're going anymore, he said. My wife thinks it's just that my eyes are bothering me, but that's not true. He said that he'd heard the animals in the night, roaming, just like them. His voice was soft, and Waclaw sat awhile and then nodded. They heard steps behind them, and the woman stood behind the old man and bent down to him. Can he understand us? she asked. But he just shook his head.

That morning they gathered firewood that was less damp, and they ate small, sweet walnuts that the old woman had cracked with stones, and they drank hot water that tasted slightly of earth out of one of Alois's empty cans. It was a mountain forest, and the grass was lush and green and the stillness untroubled, and he sat barefoot and saw the pigeon pecking at grains with concentration, one after the other. No one asked what he was planning to do with her.

✦ ✦ ✦

The light fell on the slopes, and the expanse was bluish, no one counted the turns of the descending road, no one counted the little villages and towns they reached and passed through, with their orderly sidewalks and people who waited at yellow-painted crossings, and with other cars and hotels and signs with illustrations of families and canyons and hikers. The man had taken out a little compass, and they followed the roads and tried to head northwest, as new mountains came, and valleys, silent and shining, and no places to stay. The slopes were steep, the crags silent. Conifers pointed toward the sky. The couple didn't say where they wanted to go, but he noticed that it made them uneasy when a road led east for too long. He filled up the Fiorino's gas tank; an endless freight train passed on the track above them while he bought a map and a water canister. None of them tried to read the map or even opened it, as if there was some other kind of coherence, deep beneath the haste. They took side roads and passes, which were crossed by smaller roads and cars like errant caravans that converged by accident, until the hunger grew too strong and they turned into a parking lot above a lake.

Afternoon light. A few white sails like huge moths. They ate at a snack bar with a lighthouse painted on it. There were waves, and tentacles stretching out of them. What these old drawings portrayed, Sharam had told them once, weren't just sailors' fantasies. They knew only too well what it meant to be left alone with oneself. Out there. For weeks. Months. Waclaw had thought then of the pits: out of the deepest mine shafts rose monstrous, poisonous gases. The woman seemed to disappear in her coat, and her feet hardly reached the ground when they sat on the bench: a small lee, out of the wind. She ate fried calamari rings, so slowly that her husband stroked her back, as if to give her courage, so she might hurry up.

◆   ◆   ◆

They looked for a long time for a place where they could stay. In the twilight they sat by the lake and watched the evening coming over the water, silvery bands amid the blue and against the endless black of the slopes, and above them, the embankment and a highway. There was trash on the slope, but the casual strollers didn't come out here with their big healthy dogs and those jackets—thin, but warm enough against the cold that rose off the water. None of them slept that night, the yellow of the streetlights forced itself through the bushes as if to silhouette the sad harbor that was the truck bed, and after a while the man and woman came up front and shook their heads wordlessly. Then they looked at the lake. The woman turned a thin ring she wore on her finger. Waclaw's back ached.

Around four in the morning they sat with three paper cups, and a cleaning cart dragged wet traces over the tiles and around the tables like a sea lion with a dirty, fringed muzzle, and the lights passed by, and the coffee was lukewarm, and the woman cried a bit, against the hurtling of the nearby highway.

They looked at Waclaw, but he avoided their eyes. His elbows stuck to the table, and he didn't know whether they would continue with him, or in another car, or where they were going. He thought of Milena. He could see her, with an open newspaper next to the window, the house in Wiórek, the window frames that she'd sanded alone during his first shifts, the bandage on her arm. She was almost hidden by the paper, but he knew it was her, he saw the dark ends of her hair. But the newspaper was white and it shone, as if from within, unreal, as no paper had ever shone. White maps. She'd loved the old sea maps where only the coastlines were marked and not the countries, as if the world were a territory still to be explored, white land.

He didn't get to think about it any longer, you have to go now, said one of the employees with a scarred upper lip, the bird's not allowed, and he stood there, thin in his red T-shirt with the logo of a fast-food chain, and Waclaw nodded, perhaps they recognized each other for a moment, he'd seen many like him. He stood up, then they went to the Fiorino without a word, the tall man with the basket last, as if it held provisions for a final long journey.

In the truck he turned on the light. The place where the two old people wanted to head lay west of the area his map showed. He wasn't sure whether they were breaking off their trip or whether it was there they had wanted to go from the beginning. He started the engine and they only stopped around midday in a bit of woodland. They'd seen many cable cars going up the mountain, they caught the light and it flashed down off the panes; the land gradually grew flatter. He slept for two hours, and when they drove on, fall collections sparkled in the display windows of the small cities they drove through, it made him think of Zaran, whose daughter worked in a Salzburg boutique, those afternoons he'd spent with her on cast-iron chairs under the chestnuts, while at home in Tuzla the men would never be finished clearing up the rubble.

The old people still looked around restlessly, and they soon started to give Waclaw directions, little churches, apple trees, plots of farmland that grew bigger and bigger, and he drove, the pigeon slept on the passenger side, as if everything were sleeping, everything that lay behind him and everything that lay before them, and Mátyás slept, and the smokestacks slept too. With the two old people, Waclaw got the feeling that he, too, was driving toward something, as if he just had to drop them off, and then continue, with the pigeon, that she would show him the way, like the basket with the emblem.

But the night was big and wide, and the old man had begun to hum again, a song like the one from the tunnel, as if the fear might open up under the asphalt again.

At one point Waclaw walked along the edge of a big field behind a rest stop, and he breathed the cool night air, different than it had been in the mountains that lay behind them, but then he walked quickly back, as if there were a current over the harvested wheat, sucking out toward the dark open field, and he thought of Darya and the night over the harbor, how she'd crouch on the roof and under the distant stars as if she'd simply forgotten to take in the laundry, as if that were the only reason for her to be up there alone.

You tell the girl. Ahmad had looked at him, perplexed. You didn't tell her? No. Go to Darya, please. They'd stood there help-lessly, and there was the strong smell of coffee. These sentences, like gloves that were far too big, with which they were trying to catch hold of a world that had already slipped away.

The two old people waited in the truck, and they laughed as Waclaw walked across the asphalt with big loud steps to get the heavy mud and dirt from his soles. The man drummed his fingers on the basket, they drove on until morning, the woman whispered the names of the villages and seemed to hold her breath as they came to a stop in front of a stone wall, barely taller than the hood of the truck, before a low house with leafless vines on the walls.

They got out, and the sound of the truck door was the only thing around them. They took their things, the coats and bags, and set them down in front of the door. Waclaw stayed in the Fiorino un-til they beckoned him in. Then they sat for a long time at a round, worm-eaten table, they drank schnapps that smelled strongly of pears out of tiny clay cups, and they kept filling the cups, and the intoxication was clear and good, while it grew slowly light outside the window. When the woman had gone to bed, the man thanked him. Waclaw nodded. He had feed for four more days, and he had to hurry, he said, but it sounded as if he were talking about someone else. The walls of the house were made of loam, and they were mended in many places, like a sculpture made by a child's hands, and around midday he lay awake and listened and couldn't make up his mind to get up. Through the window he saw a little telephone booth on the corner next to the property, the glass and the silver cord like a signpost with no words on it. Only static.

The pigeon basket stood on the table where they'd eaten that evening. The pigeon had been fed, and the basket took up almost the whole surface; behind it the woman stood bent over the sideboard. She moved slowly and jerkily, like a music box, she held a big dull knife at hip height, and it cracked against the wood as she cut the potatoes. She smiled briefly when she noticed him. Steam came from a pot, he saw a chicken foot jutting out of the broth, a few feathers drifted light and white over the muck when he went out, and the old man was driving straw out of a low barn that smelled of ammonia, a few goats thronged curiously around a burst bale of hay.

The fence around the property was made of old boards, and behind it stood lilacs that no longer bloomed, and an old brown horse whose hooves were so long that they curved upward. A rusty trailer with a trough. After a while Waclaw went back to the Fiorino in front of the house, and he kicked the tires, though he had tested them only yesterday, and then he sat on the truck bed and took Jány's jacket and smoothed it, as if he were going to need it again now. As if there were poplar pollen around him again, beginning to circle, not around him, not around the middle of some image. The soup was cooking. It was cooking for him and for the bird and for the journey onward. He closed his eyes.

It was the Curonian Spit, endless beaches where amber and washed-up phosphorus were the same color. The nets for the birds, the time just after Milena. He was supposed to count the flocks passing by, but he just stared into the gaps in their formations. That the lines were something he had to construct in his mind out of separate fragile points. That these lines didn't exist, and the beaches told a different story. The munitions rusted underwater as if the ocean had one foot in another time. That summer Waclaw had collected buttons, little metal badges from various vacation destinations, he pinned them on his baseball cap. Weeks later he threw it away in disgust. He went back to work, he went back to land, always a different land, he was tired, so tired that it soon caught up with him, the accident, he didn't care, his arm was still numb, healthy, *zdrowy*, he wasn't that, but he could claim to be, healthy, *zdrowy*, yes, it continued, the cities were fast and lonely, no one asked about it.

The sun shone on his face, and he heard the woman pushing open the door and coming out to him on the truck bed. She smiled when she saw him, still nervous in front of the stranger. Her hair was damp and she'd exchanged her layers of wool for a long brown dress with a few traces of flour on it. For a moment she looked in the direction Waclaw had been looking, but there was nothing there.

He burned his mouth. The broth was hot and good, and she'd cut the meat off the chicken, and she gave him several portions, though he wasn't hungry. She gave him a loaf of bread that was still warm, and socks made of coarse wool, and he pressed the pigeon to his chest while the man went out to clean the basket for him, and the woman ran a finger over the feathers. Only when they set the pigeon basket next to him on the seat and the Fiorino sputtered did he think of Alois, and that he had nothing he could have given him, nothing to bring with him. Somewhere someone had stuck a pin in this map, a distance, a bird, he was the driver, he drove.

It was quiet without the couple, even though they'd barely spoken. The land grew flatter, and it was easier for him here than it had been in the mountains to imagine a bird keeping a steady line. As a boy he'd sometimes gotten angry at his pigeons, always coming back, as if they couldn't fly in some other direction, far beyond the *Esse*.

Now the land lay before him, and he drove all day and all night, highways, a few times he asked for directions, and the women at the gas stations had deep voices and they made jokes in a southern dialect, and he just nodded or shook his head when they asked him something in German. The moon had waxed, and the night wasn't cold. Villages flashed along the roads, and small towns, church towers illuminated like strict teachers in the middle of a much larger night, and he drank coffee and Coke, and at some point he stopped the truck and looked out the cracked window into the moonlight, bright and hollow, just a hunk of rock far in the distance. Just before it was light he took his telephone from the glove compartment and turned it back on, but he didn't listen to the messages that it indicated were waiting, only Sharam's number flashed briefly. It took a long time to get away from the highway, and then he sat on the truck bed and stared at a hill whose grass was so even that in the moonlight it looked like snow. The pigeon next to him, the emblem on its basket, like an alibi, like an identifying mark, a song whose melody he no longer knew. He was twenty-three the last time he'd been there, when he packed his things, with Milena, and steered the shipping company's van carefully around the corners.

He slept, he got stuck in traffic that meant nothing to him, what do you do when you come home, you wash your car, you've made a fortune, the driller comes out of the doghouse, *rounds per minute*, the penetration rate, the cement silos, heavy spar and sample cylinders, there were crates, a library of drill cores, migmatite, red-black rocks, the hydrochloric acid they used to test the samples for limestone, the drill collar and the noise of the mixer, there were the directional drillers, there was Anderson, there were the puffed-up engineers, what does the facility cost per day, what's coming out, *hire & fire*, there were the daughters who got used to farewells, though they couldn't, there were the slips around the drill hole, which kept the pipe from plunging into the deep.

25

Emblem

This was West Germany: overpasses and numbered highway exits, fields with clear contours and houses with straight fences. He passed paper factories, smokestacks, clean-looking from the outside, with white smoke above a green that was new to him. Twilight fell, it lay on the trees and cars. The houses and cars were set up in long rows, as if people could withdraw behind this order, as if they weren't even there.

He stayed on the highway, now and then he ran his hand over the box. Once, tears came to his eyes, but he blamed it on hunger and weariness, and he thought of the coops in Cairo and the boys with their turquoise and yellow colors, all the warmth, their birds flying in high lines over the smog. He'd gone to the seaside with his mother one last time, she'd wrapped a ratty bright cloth around her head, and dropped down onto the sand, too quickly for her age. The dune grass bowed, little lights flashed in the sky, and he wanted to believe her that it had been dragons who had emitted the poisonous gases in the coal mines all those years, she saw the flashes, he knew it, and he wanted to stay, but it was soon too cold. As he drove, these memories popped up, there was no evidence, no photos, just him in his boots on a random highway where everything had frozen, like the gondolas of a Ferris wheel, in midair.

White stucco row houses with black roofs, with red roofs, a

soccer field, few players, spectators yelling something from the side-
lines, a cinder track and more fences and the water-damaged stucco
of a closed movie theater, the streets empty, like after a clearance
sale.

He drove back onto the highway, he saw the supermarket parking lots, hairdos as if time had stood still. And the fashions meant
nothing to him, and the sneakers meant nothing to him, he drove,
he thought of Alois, slaving away in the coking plant, and how
his wife was always cold, even in all her fur coats, how she walked
up and down under the streetlights, Aegidistraße, Velsenstraße,
Rheinbabenstraße, and Waclaw could see himself, saw how these
names came to him again, and she walked, Federica, her outline like
a huge, listless animal that had learned to walk along a narrow curb,
had learned that there is a world underground, and fixed times for
lunch and dinner and church, and still the buzzards circled over the
train station in the bright spring air.

In the dusk the light fell on an old canal crossed by train tracks, next
to it old factories, brick with blind windows and fire escapes. Behind
them, a hulking office building from the seventies, penned in by the
roaring of a train, tired passengers who didn't see him down below,
in the cab of the Fiorino, with the basket on his lap. The little light
under the rearview mirror was on, and he felt the pigeon's heartbeat in his hand. She was very calm. He saw the old smokestacks
and he thought of the smog alert in the winter months, policemen
with signaling discs at the side of the road in air so dirty that any
light in it grew big and round like a balloon, false croup, a toneless
whistling cough, the infants in the evenings, and visibility so poor
that even the slag heaps disappeared. There were the tears in the
eyes of the skat players drinking their shot and a beer, pilsner and

grain alcohol, and the slapping of the cards like feathers, like a beat that would continue forever, and none of them knew that the whole district would lie there like the filament of a light bulb that suddenly burned out.

He drove slowly. No one had welcomed him, it seemed only the stoplights had remained, hurriedly changing, so that whoever came could quickly continue on. He tried to think that he hadn't expected anything else, and he knew it was a lie.

It was a series of never-ending townships. Waclaw had taken the A40 in the dark, then turned north. He'd passed the miner's guild hospital, a vague memory of a high-ceilinged room and a nurse who'd pressed a Band-Aid onto his arm like a medal after the vaccination. Then he'd driven on northward, past the narrow bridge over the Emscher, the sewage canals, the foul sludge they'd steered clear of. The stench was gone, and he took Gladbecker Straße until he could turn right onto Aegidistraße, the old trees along the road that had grown big, the workers' houses—*Vierspänner*, fourplexes with little adornment, red brickwork, protruding plaster bases, and behind the narrow plots, long gardens, three concrete-block steps outside that he'd always taken as one. He stopped the Fiorino on the side of the road. Rheinbaben, the worker's houses. The asphalt gleamed wet under the streetlights, otherwise all was dark. A few windows cracked open.

He left Enni in the car and stood next to the Fiorino for a while, undecided. A thin layer of leaves lay in the gutter, the streetlamps spaced far apart. He walked a bit. The lace curtains, same as back then. Some houses were newly painted: mint green with white roller blinds, while the other halves stood there looking naked in their old brownish gray with smooth plaster. The estate had even survived the damn war, when housing was scarce they'd renovated the attics, *Vierspänner*, miners for the country's reconstruction, protests against rearmament, dismantling of the remaining industries, a 10,000-ton forging press on its way to Liverpool, but everyone kept on, the streetlamps, the sewer system, the residential districts, high rates of silicosis, a car of one's own, steel girders for the Westfalenhalle, sports and horse races, grunts, unskilled workers, hammer and pick and the eternal *Glückauf* in the pubs, where the men drank standing, when no one could imagine that oil and gas from overseas would one day be cheaper than domestic coal. Alois had come when everything was still in full swing, he'd moved in not far away, on Rheinbabenstraße, which ran dead straight toward the mine, and was one of the few streets without trees. Waclaw walked slowly. The heels of his boots against the asphalt. The old houses for the functionaries on Nesselstraße, two stories, with wide front gardens. But their sheds were useless, Alois had said, too small for pigeons.

He turned around. A few windows glowed with an unreal brightness behind the trees on the corner of Sydowstraße, as if this night shouldn't exist, in which a man looked up out of the darkness, without expecting anyone to ask him *what were you doing all this time.*

A bit later he stood under their old window. The splatter shield over the pan, the cutlets, and the pine bench, the dish towel on the shiny plates, the green of the frozen peas. He could even smell his sports jersey, drying on the heater in the winter, could hear his mother biting her nails as she leafed through the ads. And he heard the coughing. Brick walls, open windows, the men with their old pride, suddenly feeble, the dark coal field inside them. How they took slow walks in little groups, tiny dogs on leashes. But in the early gray, everything was still.

✦   ✦   ✦

Dawn found him rolled in Jány's jacket under the tarp on the truck bed. The air was damp, and a light haze hung over everything; the first birds hopped between the garbage cans lined up in a straight row. The Fiorino carried dust and mud in its wheel wells, and the neighborhood lay still and seemingly forgotten, while in the distance the engines began their roaring. Waclaw slept, and above him the day opened its eyes, the bells tolled, to the beat of old Stresemann suits, to the beat of old factory gates, like a metronome that no one listened to anymore, like a pulse deep inside a big, motionless animal.

He drank from the water canister and washed himself and rubbed his temples, he should have gotten a room, his back said, and he folded the tarp and took one of the tins out of the glove compartment, the red band, he saw how Enni pecked at the nuts, and he looked down the street. That's all, he said, and the bird understood not one word more than it had the day before.

The woman who opened the door was much smaller than he remembered, and she seemed too tired to even lift her eyes, so that she was talking to his chest, to the dirty seam where he'd done and undone his buttons. She said, I'm not buying anything, before he could say a word. The entrance to the house on Aegidistraße was on the garden side, the door to the adjoining building was open a crack, Waclaw saw junk piled up to the ceiling. On the kitchen table behind the woman was an oilcloth cover, a plate of rice with brown sauce which wasn't finished. Her eyebrows had grown colorless and her eyes looked for nothing. He said: Good morning, and she said: My husband is dead, you'll have to ask my son.

It sounded as if she herself hadn't understood the words she spoke. A smell of carpet and cigarettes wafted from the back of the apartment; he could no longer imagine how six of them could have lived here together, his friend Rodlo, he'd always just picked him up and they'd gone to play outside, in summer as in winter. Waclaw gave his condolences, and the woman nodded without understanding that he'd known her husband, Rodlo's father, who'd started in Mathias Stinnes after the war, shaft 2, nine levels, and that raving madness that Rodlo had told him about. This man who then sat in his shed, his sweaty brow, model airplanes, true to scale, British, French, the precise emblems on the finish, until perhaps his hands grew too shaky. All the tools, files, saws that he could no longer use. Waclaw had never particularly liked Rodlo's father.

The woman considered him now. Her stockings had slipped down, he saw the dry skin of her calves, her legs were little more than lines. Wait, she said. She turned around and went into the next room. Waclaw waited. The same cupboards and the same white veneer. Then she stood before him again. She gave him a scrap of paper that looked like it had been saved for exactly this situation, a copy, an address, a phone number. My son, she said again, ask him.

Then she looked almost apologetically behind her into the room and at the table. A used fork lay next to the plate. Sauce clung to the fork. It's for the hedgehog, she said.

As he drove through the streets, he saw everything from a great distance, as if it were a place in the future that stood there, abandoned. Nothing more to see, sweetheart. He drove as through a ghost town in a Western. The air was clearer, the Colt was no longer smoking, the villains and the good guys remained in black and white. Rows of shopping carts that pulled lost-looking people behind them, a soccer field that had seen some investment, where boys ran around in jerseys, the colors off, as if they'd been treated with chemicals.

And then again the closeness of the houses, white window frames, privet hedges. He thought of Cairo, the bags of trash on the roofs, the junk, the grayed satellite dishes, a long wait for the last decisive signal. He gave the bird water to drink.

26

Gladioli

The beer sign next to the Birkeneck was torn down, it was a big building with a hip roof and dirty red roof tiles. The stucco was dark with damp. All the windows were still whole, and the curtains closed behind them, old lace, yellowed with the years, with a lighter stripe where a cord had once held them back. Now even the curtains looked fragile, as if one were only allowed to whisper in the room. Or as if behind them the men were still playing one last round—the Pröses from the pit, who'd tanked up here every week; the eldest had drowned himself in the rain barrel. Thursdays bowling with the pastor, Sunday-morning pints, they staggered out of St. Ludgerus, across from Wacholderweg, just a couple steps down Birkenstraße, then a round of Dortmunder Kronen, collars undone, the incense forgotten. Those with black lung kept smoking anyway, the men stood at the bar or played Doppelkopf in the corner, and whoever could, bought a round: grain alcohol, beer, the pastor, the undertaker, the roofer, and between them young Willi Pröse, who couldn't stand it down there and spent his daily wages as quick as he could, never any daylight, the bad air, Willi, who drank too much, always.

Waclaw had seen them all, he'd set the pins back up. Little Willi and the men who stood at the bar too long while dinner was already on the stove back at home; the soup, the roast, and they still stayed a little longer, let the women wait, stood there, *duhn*, tipsy, suddenly calm, without a word to say about the mate who'd kicked it, out of the game, the rattling coughs.

Now it was quiet in front of the Birkeneck. The narrow sidewalk, privet, the old firs and the lawns. As he drove on he passed a boy, an eye patch bulging beneath his glasses, he wore a neck pouch and had his hand pulled up far inside the sleeves of his sweater. The street in front of him seemed endless. There were fewer children here than before, or they stayed inside. And there it was again, the smell of the *Esse*, like someone had drawn on the street with a piece of coal on a hot summer day.

Waclaw drove the Fiorino slowly, as if walking, he left Fuhlenbrock behind, drove down the Quellenbusch, the bells of St. Suitbert rang no more, excavators were digging up the churchyard, they were building, and he was tired, and his mouth was dry. In the rearview mirror someone looked at him, someone who'd learned to withdraw far behind his eyes.

He bought liverwurst and rolls at a butcher shop, and he asked about a guesthouse, but the man just shook his head. There was the old iron gate of the car repair shop, behind it a bluish light, he thought of Alois and his Kadett. All the gasoline stains in front of the house, the dark green of the driver's-side door. *I'll drive it as long as I can.*

The flower shop was across from the cemetery on the Westring and it was closed. Lunch break. Women and men with walkers came toward the gates from various directions. The light was bright on their faces, long shadows on the sidewalk. A woman lifted a rosary to her face and kissed it.

He thought of the seventeen-meter-high wooden cross that they'd set up on Prosper out of old shaft guides, a huge rotting crucifix for their pope, John Paul II, who visited the mine after the warm April days had passed, 1987, the Prosper-Haniel pit. The miners' choir sang while it rained, and the faces were proud, as if that alone could save them. Waclaw's father had stood in the rows in his miner's uniform with its gleaming brass buttons, he had no more air for the notes, he joined in softly for the *Glückauf*, and the image of that day remained stretched in front of the open window where he then sat all the time.

The crucifix was a last hint of the tracks underground, all the oil cans, mile-long shafts that no one would see again, not the women, not the children, and not the man from Rome with that white coat that he couldn't share and couldn't throw over them before he left.

Around one, the sign on the door was flipped, and a woman pushed out a cart with flower arrangements that all looked quite robust, as if they ought to be left outside, fir sprigs and boxwood and red berries, meant to last a long time. On a long table next to them were grave candles in various sizes.

The shop was a low red brick building with deep-set windows, and the woman was changing the water in the buckets for the cut flowers when Waclaw came through the door. She looked over her shoulder at him. Just a sec, she said. Then she went into a little side room, he heard a switch, and a fluorescent light on the wall went on. Underneath it the flowers shimmered in all their colors: yellowish, bluish, reddish, but like at a carnival stall, the colors all looked wrong and green-tinted. He'd seen flower stalls in Bucharest, two-wheeled carts between rows of Ceaușescu-era apartment buildings. The tarps over the flowers billowed in the wind, as if only the thin sheet of plastic could hold the light in.

The woman stood obliquely behind him, she waited. A tall vase of gladioli stood in the corner and he pointed to it. She put on an apron and went quickly to the bucket.

I'm afraid they're not so fresh anymore, she said.

She pointed to the lower blossoms, which were dark red and wilted. Can you take them off? he asked. She nodded. He said he would take all of them, and then the woman smiled. She put on glasses and cut the stems with a sharp knife. Her perm was half grown out.

I'll give you a deal.

Waclaw watched her and waited. What's with the Birkeneck? he asked. Doesn't anyone go anymore?

The woman cut the flowers.

It's been like that for ages, she said. Are you from around here?

Suddenly a voice came from the back of the store. That's all over and done with.

The woman turned and gave Waclaw an apologetic look.

Come up here.

Waclaw went up the two steps. To his right stood shelves full of empty vases, colorful rods, decorative bits and bobs for floral arrangements. On the left were a few flowerpots, a big chest that hummed like a refrigerator. Behind it was a small grated window and a man sitting on an old stool, both hands propped on a cane. Waclaw saw the silver pommel with the big hands folded upon it like tired animals. The man's head and upper body were obscured in darkness.

You must come from here, asking questions like that? he barked.

Waclaw stood and tried to make out more of the man in the darkness.

The bars of the window were distinct shadows.

The old man leaned forward.

Am I right?

My father was here. He heard his own voice. Hewer in Prosper.

There was a pause. Waclaw's eyes began to adjust to the darkness, and he saw the man's crooked jaw.

It's all going to be filled in, he said. It'll be gone soon, it's all ending.

He heard a suppressed cough. Breaths like steps dragging across the floor. The woman cleared her throat.

Excuse me—

She rustled the paper for the gladioli.

Excuse me, she said again.

Would you like plastic film or paper?

Tell him where your flowers come from, the old man began again. It's all from elsewhere, and the mine's going to be flooded.

Flooded? Waclaw said.

Give it a rest, the woman said.

Paper. His own voice sounded hoarse, and he turned around.

I'll take paper.

The man banged the leg of the table with his cane.

It's over here, no one's needed anymore. They're pumping water in, and it won't ever come out. It's over.

And what will happen then? the old man whispered, his voice suddenly harsh.

Processions, he said. The pit ponies, their long blind shadows, freed of the weight of the carts, will come in darkness over the land. Where else are they supposed to go?

Waclaw tried to make out his face more clearly, but he couldn't. Behind the silver cane the darkness was impenetrable as a curtain.

The woman touched Waclaw's arm.

Excuse me, she said again.

The old man nodded.

Go, he said. Just go. There's nothing you can do.

Come, she said. I'm sorry.

She pulled him over to the cash register, she named a price.

That afternoon he got lost in the streets and he parked the Fiorino and bought a newspaper. He took the basket under his arm and walked past tennis courts that were new, he took the old paths between the gardens, then walked along Rheinbabenstraße—single wooden doors with transoms, bases with red bricks—down to where the old freight tracks had once been.

He walked hunched over, and he could be seen from far away, the tips of the gladioli bobbed against the basket, it smelled of fruit and compost heaps and dug-up earth. Now and then someone nodded over a fence, and there were red dahlias with big, full heads, and he knew their brilliance and knew that winter would follow them, heads of cabbage and then snow. At some point he found Alois's house, small like the others, with a carport instead of flower beds, a lawn instead of the loft, and a terrace where the rabbit hutches had been. New windows and the old fence, blue window frames, rusty wire, and the sky empty, over the remaining gardens as well. No pigeons on the ridge of the roof. Not even the familiar metallic clanging of the railway cars behind the embankment. Maybe there were no more tracks, or nothing to be loaded.

In a hotel room he'd once seen a report on British miners, their protests, their songs, Billy Bragg walked across the screen with his guitar, and he'd thought of his father, his dutiful *Glückauf* till the very end, the silent red of the dahlias.

He sat for a while on the grass, then tore the paper and propped the flowers against the fence post. The sour cherry had grown huge. He looked at the tree and tried to engrave it on his mind, and imagined telling Alois about it. He stroked the pigeon's breast with a blade of grass, he said: You'll make it, old girl. The top of the cherry tree looked like a squashed Easter egg that had been painted under a strobe light, all the leaves, the light behind them. In the distance, the shadow of the slag heap, no different than it had been years ago, when they'd set out together, with that vague expectation, as if the Ruhr Valley were only a door that you had to push open to get to the real life that began beyond it, something different than the red and white of the altar boys and the golden chalices full of cold wine. Milena's sister had enough space, a little house in Wiórek that they could move into, they could live in the countryside near Poznań for a while off of what they'd saved. They'd both looked out the window, Milena with the cocker spaniel, whose fur had always been gray in winter.

The newspaper predicted stable weather for the coming days, a large boat had sunk south of Malta. He thought of the outboard motor he'd seen at Eugenio's, the big pack of lifejackets he'd seen lying in the corner of the garage as he left.

Waclaw looked at the pigeon. In three days you have to be gone. It would be risky to release her here: falcons between the houses, the complex terrain. Then he fed her and spoke softly to her. It's crazy, he said, we just keep on driving, and we never know when to turn off. He ran his fingers over the grate. He would have liked to take her out. A married couple walked by, the woman's hair was brown and hair-sprayed and she looked at him sternly. Their steps were the same length. Neither of them said hello. He cleared his throat. He placed the gladioli by the fence, for Federica or for all the Federicas, and left.

27

The Slag Heap

Evening fell, and Waclaw took a room near the Pferdemarkt, he'd bought his first train not far from here: Borelmann's Toys. He paid in advance and took a hot shower, then he went back down and fed the bird. He walked in the dusk: tanning salons and cocktail bars, the smell of hookahs, then residential areas. From under the barrel-shaped roof of a gymnasium he heard the squeaking of rubber soles and the bouncing of balls, behind the floor-to-ceiling windows of new buildings he saw tables where fathers, mothers, and children sat. A cat's scratching post in a tiny ground-floor apartment, a little aquarium, the green shimmered behind the curtains. High-rises gleamed distantly beyond poplars, lighting up the district, still as an athlete after the race.

He'd seen other big cities, he could usually find his way, but not here. Here he wasn't sure what held these places together. Traffic jams in the distance, as if it were too early yet to just keep on driving, as if the cars were looking for something in this old darkness that was now beginning. He went to the Fiorino and took care of the pigeon: the water and one of Alois's special cans. He took her out, hardly more than the meager weight of a few feathers in his hand. They drove a little way, there was a bit of rolled turf in front of a snack bar, bright green in the headlights, and on it the outlines of a few men at high tables, their bent backs, the bottles, dull outlines in the light. Where there had once been railyards were now meadows, the coking plant snorted in the distance like an old horse that wouldn't be quieted.

He drove in the direction of Kirchhellen, toward the shadow that the Haniel slag heap cast over the land. On the way he saw his father's old factory gate; bushes and greenery had grown up around it. He talked to the pigeon and threw the cloth over the basket, then he locked the doors of the Fiorino and started up the path.

There were few clouds, and somewhere a bell struck eight o'clock. People taking walks came toward him, he saw bicycle lamps hurtling down the slopes, a man in a black chef's jacket walked with a girl on his arm, they laughed softly. As he walked up the slag heap, the lights farther below seemed to move, the streets, the houses, looked like something floating, distant. He took steep paths, dark earth that bicycle tires had eaten tracks into. Off the path he passed ramps that looked homemade, planks, jumps of barely a meter: all for a brief moment in the air.

The soles of his boots were slippery, the wind picked up as he got higher. He walked the narrow edge of the crest, there were no more bushes up here, the heap fell away steeply to both sides, forming a crater in which an amphitheater had been planted. He could see down to rows of white concrete seats, in the middle lay a smooth circular surface, permeable like a membrane, as if here in the middle of the slag heap was a huge ear. Except that all was completely still. The twilight was red and blue over the land, lights all around, as if from a single large city, without a center. The smokestacks and the fires had disappeared, one district bordered on another, endlessly. He saw the old pit frame next to the Malakoff tower, the glow of the conveyor belts from Prosper. So he sat there, Waclaw, in his cowhide boots, and looked down.

With Mátyás he'd heard the chirping of the lizards as they walked along the walls in search of mates. They'd sat in the court-yards, mango trees, mosquitos. He struck two stones together: it made almost the same sound.

He sat like that for a long time and felt the air getting cooler, and it made him think of Cantarell, of the gigantic fields, which stopped yielding, little by little. Statfjord, even Brent dwindled, in the North Sea. That someone had taken the trouble to name them all, and that they were now withering, petals and stamens collapsing to leave huge hollow spaces. At some point all that came up was sand and water. And that there was only water over them. That they'd take away the rigs. No trace, like none of it had ever existed.

The North Sea, Petrov had said, is nothing compared to what they're planning now. Goliath, he said, the Barents Sea, the water is a quarter of a mile deep, and then the frost, the storms, is that what you want? Soon they'll only need specialists. Petrov had loved to talk about the first years. Boats that ran up to the platforms and traded a bottle of whiskey for twelve dollars over the railing. When there was still something like adventure in the air. As if the closeness of the cabins and the lousy grub were some kind of liberation. From what? And who the hell wanted to hear about that now?

It had grown dark, and he was cold. A light wind caressed the crest of the heap. Someone had rammed wooden stakes into the ground, he didn't know why. He walked crosswise down the slope, he slipped a few times, but without fear. The lights had started mov-ing again, the glaring pits, in the distance still a few tall, flashing red smokestacks. He sat down on one of the ramps, dampness rose from the ground, he was tired. His feet dangled in the air, the splintery wood under his fingers.

Far in the distance the highways shone in the darkness, as the silver pommel of the old man from this afternoon had shone. Just wait, he'd said.

At night he saw stars. There were more than he'd ever seen here. He didn't sleep. He'd parked the Fiorino on Fernewaldstraße, he sat in the cab, now and then he ran his hand over the cloth. Enni, he said. The bird was silent. He stared into this old blackness, he thought of the irony with which he'd been told as a child of the bomber squadrons they'd called pathfinders, the "Christmas trees" dropped from twenty thousand feet that had bathed the countryside and the cities and the pit frames of Westphalia in a magical light, cascades of magnesium light that could be seen even through curtains and bedroom windows. Nothing helped against those bombs, that torrent of explosions that was only an echo compared to the havoc wreaked by our own bombers, plaguing, choking, shooting—something as immeasurable as the beauty of these lights, which were followed only by detonation, fire. He'd been told of those flames as if they had also somehow been the last of the light. And then there was just the hope of those first years, when everything was still in transition and the men didn't come to stay, but rather to become something completely different after the pit, as if they had life after life after life that they could bore down to as through the unfeeling stone, as if there were something waiting for them beyond the walls of the estate, something of which later all that remained was the sense that they had long forgotten it.

It was another time, and those who had been there passed it on, this fear, as if it were still the same long night.

He lay on the truck bed, and he felt his back, but he didn't want a hotel. The friendliness, the unfamiliar rooms. Carpets that swallowed his steps. Sometimes he'd been almost glad to be back on deck: the language was more direct, rough, you could believe in it. He waited until it was light, a first blue edge over the houses. The feed, which he weighed in his hands, and the basket with its old emblem. Waclaw could see the illuminated windows in the distance, the low, narrow rooms. What it had meant to come into the same kitchen every day, to sit in the warmth on the pine bench, the green beans from the garden, his father's cough, the daily sound of curtain rods at half past nine. There, at the narrow table behind the cupboard, still sat the boy who'd walked that day to the edge of the estate, hunched in silence over his math homework.

The streetlights turned off before it was even light. He took the basket from the seat, pressed it against his side, and walked up the slag heap, where the ground next to the paths was dug up and the early buzz of the city still quiet. As if with the pigeon he could get to another, earlier world, a source Alois was still drawing from.

All was quiet on the slope. He thought: Just let her have drunk enough. He walked slowly. The sun was to his left and still low, wind blew over the bare crest. He heard Enni's claws on the floor of the box, he slipped, for a moment the basket tilted. He set it on his knee and let the pigeon pick a few nuts through the bars. He walked on. There were hot slag heaps that still smoldered deep within. The last warmth of this big animal, whose breath they'd so long feared.

And then there was a hot stabbing between his shoulder blades, bits of sawdust floated around him, and he watched the pigeon rise in a wide curve over the gray, sleeping land. Just a bird that rose, until it headed in a direction, two o'clock, south, in a sky where the light shimmered like asphalt and the stoplights drew an orange stripe under the clouds. He stood with a few grains between his fingers, and he saw her for the last time.

Waclaw didn't want to descend from this slag heap. There was no descent. Time wasn't a ski slope that one could simply go down again. One could only continue up into this fog; he had a vague memory that it hadn't always been so. That they'd once told each other things. Nights in which they'd talked until it grew light. Milena, their inner Königsberg. Places they'd known together. As if it were enough to simply talk about it. The magnetic sense was supposed to be in the beak too, the seat of language. The homing instinct. They didn't know exactly. At some point everything broke off. *Don't come anymore.* The city lay flat. He thought of the sharp eyes of birds of prey. The hoods that the falconers pulled off their heads.

28

A Pierrot

And it was the weariness and midday and the bells that he'd heard how many times that drove him like a piece of livestock down the eroded slope, thirsty, and somewhat fearful of this sky, which now stretched out on all sides.

His hands trembled when he tried to unlock the Fiorino. He set the basket on the truck bed. He didn't know where to go. For a moment he thought he would call Sharam, and the Persian would pick up the phone, put on his circular glasses, and tell him what to do, where they could meet. It had all gone badly, but all was not yet lost. He would give him the name of someone who could help him. Rotterdam, a job in Rotterdam and a friend of Sharam's who would pick him up from the airport, those tight embraces where they always clapped each other a bit too hard on the shoulders, on like that forever, like the clapperboard in a film, and all the recorded material that they carried around with them, all that could never be told. It would be Sharam's old voice, and it would be the old trust between them, the Persian would point him in a new direction, as if that were all he needed.

He walked through Fuhlenbrock, down Sterkrader Straße and past Gleiwitzer Platz, where the big mine administration buildings were, until he reached the town hall. There were waffles and cotton candy in the square, metallic balloons, a few stands. The noise of bumper cars droned from the edge of the square, it smelled of grilled meat. A few pumpkins lay on a trestle table in front of the brick building, someone had painted *Harvest Festival* in blue on a cloth. He heard a man hawking raffle tickets, for a while he watched the thin metal arms that grasped at little stuffed animals in glass boxes.

It made Waclaw think of the dancing bear on the Curonian Spit. It had pawed lethargically at the air, an excruciatingly hot summer day, a flute player and next to him the caricaturist who sketched Waclaw with charcoal. His face in the drawing was a sad grimace with hanging cheeks and hollows under the eyes, in the time just after Milena. He was tired. Now and then he looked at the sky, into the trees, and at the ledges where the city pigeons sat. The bumper cars were loud, he walked between the stalls, and then he saw him sitting on a crate, the Pierrot, a white clown. He wore a faux-silk robe, and his eyebrows were high black lines on his whitewashed face. He watched a stocky juggler next to him with concentration: six balls, eight, that he kept in the air.

Waclaw stopped and looked at the balls that circled and leaped back and forth. Children had gathered, he could look past them, they all stared at the invisible connection, everything was easy, as if by flying the balls became something else. Then suddenly the juggler faltered and had trouble keeping all the balls up. Waclaw stood still. The plane trees rustled. The Pierrot looked up, his eyebrows seemed to lift even higher, for a moment what he was watching turned to chaos, a few balls shot high up in the air, and then finally fell. But when they fell, they were simply balls, dumb oranges. The balls rolled across the bleak stone slabs of the square, then the children chased after them. The whole scene set itself up again. The town hall, the curved lampposts from the sixties, the smell of bratwurst.

And he didn't know why, but Waclaw was angry at the juggler. The Pierrot, too, had disappeared behind one of the huts.

He now realized that he hadn't slept. He went back to the small hotel, it was from the nineties, with furniture made of wire and glass, and black wardrobes. Again he paid for one night, and the hotel owner looked at him.

You didn't even take the key last time, he said.

No, Waclaw said.

This time he fell into bed. He didn't open the curtains that hung over the panes like a white veil, as if he were a bride, or the world were a bride, or neither of those things. He lay on his back, and he woke up in the same position, one hand under his lumbar vertebrae, when it had long been dark. He didn't turn the light on, and he didn't get fresh water for the bird.

Somewhere in the hall a door opened, someone walked past his room, and then it was quiet again. He remembered the feeling of folding his things on his hotel bed on that first evening, before the first shift on the water. Through a screened window he could hear the gulls shrieking. He walked down the narrow street to the beach, strangely exhilarated. People were driving on the left, and he wasn't sure where he was supposed to walk. A wide bay, the sand was dark, and a distant sun gleamed on the cliffs. The new clothes were unfamiliar on his skin, the stiffness of the pants and the seam of the shirt, which he felt with every step. The wind fell on his face like a damp cloth. He breathed it all in deep. A bit of trash danced between the rocks. That night he didn't call Milena, and he couldn't tell her what it was that he'd found out there.

Later there had been other nights. A pub near Aberdeen, fishermen, deep-sea fishermen and oil people. A helicopter had crashed, it had flipped in the air and had crashed engine-first into the water. It was the memorial service for the boys, young punks, engineers, who hadn't made it in the six-degree water of the North Sea, and they were both there, Waclaw and Mátyás, and they knew that this was different from the artificial smoke and the wave machines from the exercises they had to pass every few years—twelve-seaters, upside down in the training pool. They stood at the bar, it was loud and cramped, and they were there too. It was different from the cities in their safe silence: as if someone had torn away their skin, and something else, something like a soul, showed through. That's what he'd thought. That this word only had a meaning among them. Among the exhaustion and among people who meant something to one another, if only for a night. He'd never felt so much himself, so close to something inside him capable of loving, grieving, forgiving. Maybe they were nothing but a bunch of drunks, maybe there'd be a harsh smell in the morning, and the mop in the water, dirty, stinking of that night, maybe the smell would even remain.

Now he sometimes wished it were so, that there were this place they could all return to, where for a moment they might recognize one another: fragile, vulnerable, and here only for a brief time, though they already knew the dates when they were set to go out again. A helicopter had crashed into the North Sea, they heard the deep voice of Iggy Pop, the music was briefly interrupted, nothing more.

Behind the lace curtains the darkness seemed to be made of a thousand tiny holes. The pillow smelled like flowery fabric softener and the carpet smelled old; it was night. The night was specially marked on all the charts—*unsounded area*—a place where sound sank and never came back.

Cheap beer at the gas station. In the morning he walked down, drank two bottles, but the beer grew warm and flat, and he left the rest under the mirror in the bathroom, brightly illuminated.

And he knew the lattice fences and he knew the low hedges as he walked back north to pick up the Fiorino. The pet store was gone too. The way felt long. The estates. He thought of the paper cutouts in windows, the wood-trimmed gables, the only decoration in front of the tall pines. The great care of the women, who stayed home after the first child, populating their flower stands with orchids, living in apartments with serving hatches, now and then a round of tennis at the company club, days faded and silent like the fruit in a rum pot. Women who later rested a hand on the wall when climbing the stairs and felt how cold that wall was.

Some of the houses still looked like the old ones, but they'd been renovated, little roofs built over the front doors, the plaster freshly painted. Grapevines ran riot on the walls. He remembered how they'd stood at the stoplight back then, he and Milena, the shipping company van filled with their things. He was slightly dizzy, and he turned onto smaller streets a few times and looked around as if he were searching for something but couldn't remember what it was. It wasn't the pigeons, it was something other than the eternal waiting.

He washed the windows of the pickup at a gas station. With long, exaggerated motions and too much water, as if all that mattered were getting off the summer's flies, his own unreal figure on the wet glass. He didn't feel drunk, he had the Mary medallion on a string around his neck, something in him was stretched to the breaking point. He didn't want to wait. The pigeon basket sat on the seat, it was empty in a different way than it had been in the previous days. All those years, as if absence always had to be the larger portion.

It was spring when his father had gone down for the last time, and a silence had hung over the streets, no different than now. There had been fewer cars on the road, laundry hung on the line to dry at the neighbors' houses, white sheets, the first sprouts of green, the whole house had smelled of cake, it was just before Easter. He sat out in the loft and watched through the bushes as his father came up Aegidistraße. His mother awaited him in the garden. In Waclaw's memory the scene was soundless, like in a silent film, though he was sitting there with the pigeons. Perhaps he had looked away for a moment, but when he looked up again his mother, who had just been standing there happily in her flowered dress, had a hand in front of her mouth and had begun to sob quietly. She held up a knee pad, worn down and full of black streaks, and she held it in front of her as if trying to reconcile it with the man who stood before her with collapsed shoulders, embarrassed, suppressing a slight cough. You could still see that he'd once been strong. In more than twenty years working down the pit, his father had never brought anything home with him. His mother looked at the overused gear and slowly shook her head. Over the next days she gave the knee pads, miner's apron, and helmet a wide berth. Waclaw's father sat behind the house in the first spring sunshine. All that light. As if he had emerged from a much longer winter.

He opened the Fiorino. He pushed the seat back and ran a hand over the steering wheel. That morning he'd felt the feathers again, they were soft in his hand, and he felt something in them crack very softly. As if some resistance were giving way. He didn't look.

He could feel it. He could feel the silence over the houses, the same silence. He had lain on his side and looked through the curtains, in the direction where there were no mountains and no more houses that stood hard against the slope, as if they wanted to be part of something larger. He'd clenched the bit of blanket tightly in his hand and wrung it like a neck, he could feel the feathers.

And he remembered the night with Patrícia, in which the silence and dryness of the countryside had been almost like heavy rain, as they'd left the station behind them and walked away from the voices, the restaurant and her red Honda, which they'd driven in the ditch next to the road, while people flashed their brights at them and a tractor-trailer whooshed past, huge in the night, huge against the stars, as if they were only remnants, something that had managed to stay alive in the voracious night, and they walked arm in arm, entwined, the two of them and the schnapps, like the warm waft of something that let them continue on, without turning around, without asking questions, into a tenderness, perhaps, that was new, that they could believe in for a few moments, entwined, hot, until the intoxication and the darkness withdrew, to look in the first early light almost scornfully at the two bodies that lay there next to each other, sweaty and unfamiliar, two unfamiliar smells and nothing left to cling to.

His shirt stuck to the seat of the Fiorino, he ran a hand over the steering wheel. A minibus stopped in front of the gas tank, and a few girls with red-and-blue team jackets got out and walked toward the shop. Their hair was braided. A man with a small bouquet of flowers held the door for them. One of them curtsied, and they laughed. When they were inside, he saw the man take a flask out of his inside jacket pocket. Waclaw could see the way he reeled. The clouds broke and the light crossed the washed-out concrete of the entrance and wandered through the green of the hedges. He didn't want to wait.

29

Rodlo

Next to the door stood a concrete tub for flowers, a gray mass with stones pressed into it. Every window in the house had curtains at half height, the stone slabs were swept and there was not a leaf on the meadow. A single maple stood there, red-topped.

Who's there?

Wenzel. It's Wenzel.

The buzzer sounded. Printed doormats. Cats. *Welcome.* On the third floor, the door was open a crack. The black-and-white stone stairwell. He stopped in front of the door.

It was hot and it smelled of lunch, of cabbage.

Rodlo had gotten heavy, he had an unshaven, doughy face. He was pale. Those gray eyes.

Wenzel?

He nodded.

Can you tell her something from me?

What do you mean?

Rodlo wore loose jeans, above which a round belly was visible; he looked shorter, and his fingertips were yellow. He seemed to consider.

Lina? he said then, softly. Do you mean her? Lina-Milena?

When he said it, it sounded like a song. He smiled as he said the words. But only briefly. Then it looked like Rodlo's round shoulders fell even farther forward, toward a point far in front of him on the floor.

Lina-Milena, he said softly.

You don't know, then?

He looked at Waclaw.

She—must have a new number, Waclaw said, did she move? He paused.

She always wanted to move.

He tried to smile, but Rodlo didn't look at him.

They didn't tell you anything? Didn't you have that post office box? Come in, he said. Please come in.

Rodlo came toward him and touched his shoulder from the side, but Waclaw just stood there and then sat on the stairs that led from the third to the fourth floor. The railing was next to him and Rodlo was in front of him, talking at him, *she's not there anymore, Wenzel, do you not know?* But he sat there as if it were another staircase, and he didn't hear, and finally Rodlo went inside and came back with a bottle of grain alcohol and he held it under Waclaw's nose, but he said, I won't drink, and Rodlo looked at him and said, it's not your fault, it was a trailer, a blind spot.

The apartment was full. It was bursting at the seams. No cupboard matched any other, chests stood around, some of them stacked on top of each other, on top of one cupboard Waclaw saw the tires of an old model car and the wings of a little airplane. Screws, hand cream, tissues, economy packs of pencil lead, old ice cream cartons filled with pens and dusty batteries, copper plates, vases, pitchers, houseplants, few of which seemed real.

In the oven were chicken nuggets in the shape of animals—he saw how the paper moved in the air from the fan. Rodlo went first and laboriously turned on an old floor lamp, but Waclaw stayed in the kitchen. A fruit basket, brown bananas, an open carton of West cigarettes. He could feel that something was wrong with his throat, and he thought of Enni. He thought: I can't do anything more for her. He thought: If only I had kept her. Once he'd taken a walk on the esplanade during a storm, so close that the waves almost reached him. The breaking of the water had made such a powerful noise that it had calmed him. It was the kind of noise one can't understand, a noise much bigger than him. Here, in contrast, everything was quiet, and the quiet made him uneasy.

In front of him, the numeral on the oven jumped.

Rodlo held the tea towel in his hands.

It looked small.

Next to the window stood a potted palm. The sky was white behind it.

She's not responsive.

Does she live alone?

She doesn't live anywhere, Wenzel. She's on life support.

He saw the bare yellow land growing smaller beneath him.

The room was stuffy. He looked out the window at an indifferent lawn, and then there was the pale forehead of Rodlo, who'd gone to fetch something from the other room, something he held behind his back. Waclaw couldn't help thinking of his father's oxygen pump that stood next to the bed. Of how silver it had been, and that he'd sometimes thought it was the color that would stand up to the dark realms inside. A childish thought. Light versus darkness. Rodlo, who stood before him with his heavy jowls. Look, he said. Rodlo took out the hand that was behind his back.

The Italian rooster.

He gave Waclaw a big white mug with a photo printed on it. The colors were almost completely faded, and their faces—Milena, Rodlo, and Waclaw—were yellow spots. They stood in front of a wooden gable, atop which sat a gigantic rooster.

You had it put on a cup?

Rodlo looked at him. When you two were gone, yeah.

Waclaw stood up.

When do you have to go back? Rodlo asked. Waclaw?

Tomorrow. To Rotterdam.

He looked out the window again.

The ships in that harbor are three times as big as your house.

Rodlo tried to smile. Then he looked at him.

Stay a bit longer.

At some point Waclaw stood up, and he walked, a long line, down the well-polished flooring in the stairwell and along the tight twists of the banister to the ground floor. He walked over the flagstones, between which no grass grew, back to the Fiorino pickup, in boots that didn't belong to this world any more than he did. As if he hadn't released the pigeon, but rather it had been the other way around, that he'd fallen, still and soundlessly, until she was only a tiny point high in the sky.

The day did not return.

He saw Milena at the edge of the pool, both hands propped next to her body, little waves lapped over the edge, as if she sat on a strip of some very distant, old-fashioned beach. Her head was tipped forward and her feet in flip-flops hardly touched the ground. They swung slightly, and the water ran down her legs.

That night he lay once more on the same hotel bed. His jacket, which he couldn't hang anywhere. Everything out there was no more: the narrowness and the dirt that belonged to those years, that had meant something. A corner where people waited for each other, or a window one looked up at, just to see whether a light was on. Whether someone was there. No one sang as they hung out the laundry. No one passed a glass of schnapps over the fence, Poire Williams, for the women, secretly. We had our fun too. He wasn't elsewhere, the church was dead, the workers were gone, but no one had started a new story, no one had turned the page. They'd crossed the Alps in buses, a church trip. They'd taken pictures of St. Peter's Square, not understanding that they just needed to look very carefully, that they'd always be reflected in the white plates, the porcelain that grew scratched over the years, little cups on Sundays that they were too careful with, awkward.

In the dawn he dumped the duffel onto the bed. As if preparing for a long journey. He looked at the soapstone, the animal. Half land, half water. The bright screeching of the birds in the Bodhi tree, as he lay in bed with fever. The days when the house and the cherry tree had drowned in a torrent of other places, interchangeable, as if the piers, esplanades, whitewashed rooms with ceiling fans, the smell of peaches in the bathroom, were all made for someone else who was meant to stand there in his place and experience it all. Sometimes it seemed to him that those years had been flung away like bits of clay from a potter's wheel that they touched only briefly, and the middle of the wheel remained empty.

He remembered how in Mexico they'd all looked simultaneously at the young charro, the sweat risen to the oval of his brow, his eyes tearing. But it was as if for a moment they could see behind it, as if they could watch as his whole world grew blurry, a farm that grew smaller in its special light, something carved into a tree, the name of his first love. The boy stood up slowly. His hands useless at his sides, his too-small shirt. Waclaw evaded his gaze as he looked at them, one after another, full of disgust and with the last flickerings of pride.

Then someone had pounded the table: it was like a signal that freed them all from their frozen state. As the noise of glasses and voices returned, the boy put the boots on the table between the cards and walked in dirty socks to the door. He left the casino without turning around.

That night their laughter had sounded like noise in Waclaw's ears, and he got up early that morning and waited in the lobby, though he knew that the boy was gone forever.

30

Brights

The fields were plowed and lay like a huge cloth without a seam and without interruption, just here and there corn and silage under tarps weighed down with car tires. The plots were big. The wind would carry away the upper layers of sand before spring came.

He drove for days. Not in a straight line. Not straight toward it. He'd met Milena when he was already working for a shipping company that allowed him to stop off with his parents on Aegidistraße now and then. The neighborhood parties were big, the streusel on the fruit cakes as thick as the gravel on the paths. That's where he saw her for the first time. At first he visited her often, then they set out together. He steered the Fiorino in that direction.

Across the Polish border, RVs under the highway overpasses, all the signs: love for sale. The car in front of him put on its turn signal in the fog, didn't he know that their shoes would be made of cheap plastic, that their hearts skipped in fear when they saw the brights, even if it was only a little joke? What forsakenness hid in this half-light? All the closed doors, the torn maps, and looks that said my heart can't take this anymore. Only the younger ones were given candies. Do they know how brightly those cellophane wrappers crackle? That it can be the very opposite of sweet?

In the nights he saw station wagons on the country roads that ate slowly into the land, headlights left on at railway crossings, spare cans in the trunk, sleeping families. Trips they were on together, waiting together for the trains to pass, for the gates to go up again. How these lights then ate through the plains, and how warm it was inside.

Rodlo hadn't said much more. Milena had broken off contact, in the end she'd lived in the village again, continuing to work at the hotel spa, then in an amusement park one summer, where the visitors paid to drive their cars between the pens of lions and monkeys. Rodlo said: Imagine that. Waclaw hadn't asked any more questions. Sometimes he drove as if he were in a great hurry, then he would park the Fiorino at the edge of some field or other. He hadn't called Alois, he wasn't interested.

There was the dampness of the villages, where dung heaps steamed in the cold autumn air. He sat in a pub, it was already cool outside, there was little staff in the place, and he looked out at the willows that moved heavily back and forth, already yellow and seeming to know everything about the fall and the armada of big clouds crossing the plains from the northeast. He drank his beer, and it was too warm and had a rusty aftertaste, as if something was wrong with the tap or it had sat too long in the lines, or as if too few guests came to the hobbling barman who kept staring at him and then turning away again and again, as if he had to force himself not to look—perhaps someone had said something to him about it once. It didn't bother Waclaw. He looked out at the willows. Beyond them lay Mendoubia Park, the eucalyptus trees above the green, he could see once more how they lay there, only the swaying of the branches above them, thin and supple in the wind. As if this pub were the other side of that moment, which he had sensed even then. Which he knew about, even then, Mátyás's head on his shoulder, the slight smell of a blacksmith's fire, and on the way back the old cannons under the trees, the graves of colonial masters, the inscriptions that he could read but not yet understand. Mátyás lay next to him on the green. As if there'd been nothing beyond it all but the swaying of the branches. As if he could have seen it even then, if he'd only paid closer attention. Himself, at that dark brown oak table. His hair a fucking mane, that's what he'd thought that morning. The barman tapped a cigarette out of the pack, took a match and struck it, his teeth were yellow, and he squinted, his own smoke getting in his eyes, something making it hard to see.

Waclaw looked out. As if there were an image on the other side of this afternoon that was slowly dimming under a cool, dark gray. As if there were something in the clouds that had to do with him and with everything here. As if there were something like fear there. During the day he'd steered the pickup through the villages. The grapes had turned red, giant pumpkins gleamed atop the muck.

The filter was still burning in the barman's hand when he started the engine.

The village approached. The landscape calmed nothing in him, even when it grew open, wider. He stopped at the old granary. He dipped his hands in the little lake. The water was cold and sweet. He felt his back. The smell of damp earth and fall. They'd seen the shadows of the birds on the high brick walls, a bright, light dance. From here it wasn't far to the intersection where he'd often turned back then to drive rolls of paper from the port south, sometimes to Prague or České Budějovice. There in the harbor a man had told him about the oil jobs, and he remembered the potato pancakes they'd eaten, and the disquiet that he'd felt rising inside him.

On that day he'd had to pick up rolls of paper for a printer, and he'd already loaded them and filled out all the customs documents. There was a little snack bar nearby, the kind that were everywhere in those days, and he got into conversation with the man because they both had to wait too long for their food. It was still early in the day, and the fat in the fryer had to heat up. The woman was just putting on her hairnet when they ordered. The man's name was Erik; after a while they sat down on wooden benches that must have been made for children, Waclaw's knee touched the underside of the table. Erik advised him to apply for work on the water, offshore. He was just passing through, he worked on the North Sea. Mostly that afternoon they compared their salaries.

And only two years later, when, despite the two jobs, they didn't even have enough money for the newspaper, did Waclaw revisit the thought. They'd made a fire in the round iron stove, and they drank the last apple wine of the year. Milena wasn't exactly thrilled by the idea, but they discussed it and weighed the options.

At that point, Waclaw was working as a janitor in an elementary school, big empty hallways, pictures that he wiped off the blackboards every day, the smell of chalk. He had nothing against the work, it was just that the ringing of the school bell between classes had started to bother him more and more. For most people the sound probably would have disappeared after a while, but for him it was exactly the opposite: the shrill sound grew more and more conspicuous, and with it, the monotony of the paths that he took to school and back. It wasn't just the money, it was the feeling of really getting out. Among parrots. The real exotics. The opposite of everything he knew. Like a promise of a voice or a color that he'd never seen before and couldn't even imagine. When they began to talk about it, the possibility of spanning all those distances had seemed like little more than an idée fixe. Sometimes the young guys still reminded him of it, when they came full of expectation, and read the horizon, their shiny helmets under their arms. Looking at it from the village, where the pigs didn't care who brought them their potato peelings, and the headless chickens fought their last battles with death in the meadows, where leaves were burned in the fall and crooked fences let cats slip through the pickets, from there, there seemed to be no reason for all that had come to pass up to that point.

He'd driven that street, over and over again. They bought the gear together. Three streetlamps. At first, they'd counted the days and nights until he'd come back. Milena spoke little of her life, as if the weeks just had to fall through this little neck that was their reunion, like the grains in an hourglass. Yet when he came back, he found the house changed, as if someone had shifted everything by a millimeter, or as if the light that fell on the kitchen tiles in the morning had altered slightly, or perhaps it was just the sound the butter knife made when they set it down that wasn't quite the same.

But with Milena, too, a change had occurred. She had never been loud, but now she was almost uncannily quiet. It wasn't that she didn't say anything anymore, but she had, for example, stopped singing when she did chores around the house. And then what they had consisted of nothing more than these little, everyday things. During that time, they hardly went anywhere together anymore, and only rarely saw their old acquaintances, Rodlo, or Milena's sisters. In any case, the banal wordlessness over the peeling of potatoes made Waclaw think of the birds that were sensitive to gas in the mines, and would fall off their perches, unconscious, when the level grew too high. When such a bird stopped singing, a miner had to run for his life. There were little bottles of oxygen attached to the cages; they were supposed to guarantee a safe exit.

At some point Waclaw could see the waves that came from afar, washing the sea up into the garden, and the spray rose in the elderberry bushes, rose in his throat, and made all the words he reached for look the same. As if they had become blurry to each other. As if this world were no longer enough. Or as if it were still the same village, but neither could find the other there. They began to think about a name for the child that didn't exist yet. The child would be like a home. When he called her from the rig, he spoke the names of exotic animals, papaya trees, vultures, he tried to describe the men he was with. But it felt like he'd been struck dumb. And with every sentence he grew dumber, and the pile of things he wasn't able to tell grew and grew. As if none of it counted next to the rotten fence they had known together, by the corrugated metal garages where the cats lay in the sun.

Later, when it was all over, sometimes sitting in an airplane he'd imagine he saw the house on the little screen, the leaky gutters, and behind it, the river with the blackberry bushes and the diving birds, green land, the route a dotted line, distance to destination in miles, but when he looked out the window, there were only clouds. The light fell on the white, and down below, when they broke, the cities had long become other ones; up there, he felt like a spy, a distant observer. In those narrow seats he'd stared at the illuminated ceiling while stewardesses shook cartons of juice, white collars, braids, he'd thought about all the things he didn't know, a whole life broken off, rows of seats in front of him turning their backs on him, that didn't matter, but what did? The pressurized air high up there, as if he were always breathing the wrong air, some other, artificial atmosphere.

He saw a father and son pushing a shopping cart. They took the narrow path that ran along the train tracks, away from the estate. They looked tired, and dirty.

And the village, nothing but adjacent low stucco houses, a red metal fence, the barking of dogs, as if they wanted to urge him to pass by, there of all places.

He'd seen the men here gradually ossify amid all the wood of their houses and fences and barns. He'd seen Jacek, with his watery blue eyes, and the threads with which he hung the apple rings to dry over the oven, for their late child, Iga's thin body and inward-turned face in the evening, under the rising winter constellations. They would hear the rain that hit the metal of the gutters, and they would stay, and from far away one would see the lights going on and off behind the kitchen windows, and new faces behind those same windows, and how they turned into outlines as night fell.

In the first years he'd been proud of having escaped it. Then he'd seen the men, tired in hotel lobbies, freshly shaven necks with lighter edges below where the hair began. They paid for people to put bowls of potpourri next to the bathroom mirrors, flower petals, as if someone were waiting for them.

Maybe he hadn't believed that this place could still exist like this, the same fences, the same paths between the gardens, a burst tomato lying in the middle. The tired heads of the last sunflowers, brown. It all remained unchecked, it was simply there. They were the same flower beds.

31

The Garage

That afternoon, as he tried to understand, it rained again, a dark curtain across the land. He waited. He saw the dolphin's split mouth and the rows of teeth. And he knew that fall was coming now, and that it would grow cold. He tried to avoid the looks that came from the houses, as he parked the car and walked up the village streets in Wiórek.

To hear about it, in the back room of the butcher shop, to look at Milena's mother, next to an immersion heater covered in limescale and an oilcloth on the table, her legs swollen, her few remaining eyelashes adorned with dark kohl below her hair net, the apron she wiped her hands on countless times while she looked past him at the field, a fallow plot filled with crows. While she talked, too, her gaze seemed to stray, her hands smoothed her apron, under which her heavy body was hidden, her voice soft, plaintive, she's gone, she said, she's there, she said, she's wrapped in fog, sleeps, can't be reached, and again and again: my child, my child. At thirty-nine, Milena lay there and her life lay far beneath anything visible. At thirty-nine, after a not terribly serious accident, she'd suddenly fallen into this kind of coma. She didn't have any other word for it. A few times her mother stood up, and he heard her counting a new customer's money into the till, the chime of the doorbell, the heavy steps into the half-darkness of the back room where she'd left him alone with a few pictures. You mustn't think she didn't miss you a great deal. Listen, she said, but then it seemed that she didn't know how to continue the sentence, perhaps she'd been confronted too often with another finality, with the misery of sectioned pigs, with pigs' heads, out of which she made the aspic that was her specialty—*Móżdżek po polsku, czernina, salceson*—the people came to her for these dishes. Brain with eggs and lots of vodka, blood soup, headcheese. There were feet that went to animal-feed producers, bones ground to light powder. The body is lifeless if we're not able to imagine that it dreams, that it talks in its sleep.

He listened and imagined Milena, how she lay there. He wanted to stroke her face, hold her, rock her. It made him think of deserts where the rock formations surged into the morning out of a bluish grayness like relief panels, the first play of colors in the cold.

He said he would come back to visit her in the afternoon, and he had to force himself to drive there. Her mother was waiting for him, but Waclaw didn't want the sweet pastries. In the dry, overheated living room, she took the cups out of a papered cupboard, he saw the clock again, here of all places. Its yellow face hung over the door. Involuntarily, he felt his back.

November, she said, and pointed to the rain clouds over the land. She pointed to the pickup and said he should put the truck in the garage. Then she walked in front of him and pulled feebly at the big metal garage door and he helped her heave it up. She seemed to be freezing in her green crocheted cardigan and he sent her inside, he'd be right here. He drove the Fiorino into the narrow garage and squeezed out of the door. Then he saw how the light changed and grew darker, and then he heard a creaking and saw the garage door, which had started to move, and roared down behind him and closed with a bang.

After the sound, it was quiet. Only the metal still reverberated, and he leaned against the wall and stared into the darkness. A silent black cube and the humming of a fluorescent light in the corner that gave off an irregular, flickering light. Gasoline. The smell of rain from the Fiorino. The wet metal. Motionlessness.

He thought of Milena. He heard the buzzing of the air conditioners that had cooled his rooms like ice cubes in a big warm drink, just beyond began the muggy air of the cities, homeless people who hid their belongings with ropes in the dense treetops, tattered hammocks and garbage under the bridges, the rhythms of the evenings, the legs of countless plastic chairs, the girls, the pastel faces of the saints. He could close all those doors behind him, and the air conditioners shoveled cold air into this other world, into which he retreated night after night. He could lie there, he could think of Milena, and from a distance Europe was a picture in which all was still, evening over the fields, lines of dykes over which a few swallows flew.

On the other hand, the room keys, live chickens at the markets, he had eggs fried for him, he had rice cooked for him, he could still hold out. The light pollution of the cities erased the stars from the night, it was summer when he realized, it was summer when he booked a ticket for the first time, no longer to her, he went to the Curonian Spit, where he counted birds, where the ornithologist wore his tight leggings, turquoise, pink, and it seemed the rest of the world had been done away with, and soon there would be no one. He was alone for years out there. In every room it grew dark at night, in every room he was with her in the evenings.

✦　✦　✦

He was startled by a light knocking. Someone was rapping against the metal from outside. The sky over the house had changed color, twilight was falling. Her mother stood in rubber shoes in the wet grass, she looked at him, but she didn't say a word.

He didn't know how long she'd been waiting. He brought her to the door, he could smell her hair spray, maybe she'd dressed up for the afternoon. She was small and her cheeks were red, traces of highlights remained in her dark hair. A color like plums.

He embraced her briefly, and she remained in the doorway, in front of the small, overheated living room, and he drove the truck across a landscape in which it had begun to rain, clouds rolled over the mounds of the plowed fields. Feed silos. Pig farms. He drove past Poznań, woods, plains, he stopped the truck at the edge of the woods. He could see the highway in the distance, all the haste, all the faith in geographical distances, he walked, walked half an eternity, until the distant villages were only points in the darkness. No city lights in the distance. Walking, he had the feeling of letting his face slowly ice over: a mask, like the skin of the sea on calm days.

Endless rows of sugar beets, light wisps of haze that covered the land. He could see her lying there, completely motionless. A long, dark hallway and the light on the blanket like a shimmering ring. Who had smoothed the blanket so flat? He heard how still it was in the room. Clouds passed by Milena's window, they glowed weakly. Are you cold? Waclaw asked softly.

He walked a little way along the edge of the woods, in the middle of the path a brown strip of grass, dandelions, here and there a cherry tree at the sides, and the valley, through which the cars in the distance shot like projectiles, as if they could speed up without ever having to fear a crash. He thought of cold water corals in the deepest trenches, whose branched skeletons swayed like feathers against the darkness. It must be very cold.

And a man stands on the earth at the edge of an unfathomably large field, he will form the earth into a clod and throw it, and he will watch as it breaks apart. He will feel the cold in his hands. It will be nothing more than that. The dark earth that can be balled up, and only in the air, in the middle of the throw, does it shatter into a thousand pieces. It's a supernova, the moment when something very small becomes something it had never imagined, something it can know nothing of as long as the smallest bit of what it once was remains. It will happen over and over again. For a moment his lower lip will protrude with a slight quiver, and he will stay there as he last did long ago, his eyes shiny, November is only the first breath of cold over the earth. He will run, just a little way, until his lungs burn, he will stand there, leaning over, bowed, propping his hands on his knees, and then this panting is all there is.

He waited for the sound of the crash, but the field swallowed the earth that he threw almost soundlessly, almost soundless were his cries, there on the plains. Exhausted, not calmed, he walked back to the truck. It's too much to ask. It was supposed to sound like a reproach, but as he said it, his voice only formed a question.

32

Lidia

It's cold. A thick layer of leaves lies under the sycamores. The wait-ress carries the tray with reluctance. Lidia had insisted on sitting outside. Her legs are tightly crossed, she smokes. Her pantyhose give off a bluish shimmer. Her telephone, covered in glittery stick-ers, lies on the table. As if to say: I'll be off soon. I have things to do.

She avoids looking directly at him, but he knows that nothing escapes her, not a single detail. The work shoes that he's now wearing again, below the suit.

On the phone she'd asked where he was living.

She said he'd have to come to her.

Now she was sitting there, barricaded in her thin stockings, coat, and smoke.

Her eyes were pale and rimmed with bright blue eye shadow, her cheeks sagged a bit. She could have been a pretty woman, if only the cheap nylon stockings and makeup hadn't made her look so average. He hadn't planned on seeing her again.

Lidia was one of four sisters, a few years older than Milena, and she'd worked for a cosmetics company, overseeing the big vats where toothpaste was mixed. She wore a hairnet half the day, the tips of her fingers turned yellow in the little shelter next to the parking lot where she met her colleagues to smoke, a rough wind over the industrial park. He didn't know exactly. Just those years that the

five of them had lived alone in the house, had gone to school and
to their apprenticeships, after their father had died. Milena had
been ten. She couldn't talk about it without crying. She preferred
not to talk at all, and kept silent. Leaving the Ruhr Valley together
was the first step. Lidia had helped them back then, and he hadn't
expected that she'd still be in the area. She'd had two children,
he looked at the pictures as the waitress set down the tray, and
Lidia put her wallet on the table. She said she wanted to pay right
away, now. She didn't even look at Waclaw as she said it. Her wallet
clicked open, and he tried to steal a glance at the pictures, at the
second one, behind, half-hidden. A group portrait that he recognized, of the four sisters. He wanted to put a finger on it, but she
pulled it away.

She always talked about you a lot, you know, Lidia said. And
actually, she never told me that you'd stopped coming back. I
couldn't follow what was going on, we saw each other so rarely.
And then there was that wooden elephant she had. It was as big
as a flowerpot, reddish wood, sort of oriental-looking, polished
smooth. And there were lighter lines cut into the back, and a few
white dots on the forehead. It was a nice piece, the tail was made
of real hair, and the sun was shining through it when I visited. We
sat and drank coffee, and she'd gotten so terribly thin. And then
I pointed to the elephant. Where'd you get it? I asked. And she
smiled and looked happy for a moment and pointed to the photo in
the corner so that I knew you'd brought it for her. But I wondered.
For days, I couldn't get that elephant out of my head. She'd said
nothing else about you, but several times during the conversation
her gaze had wandered in the elephant's direction. I didn't dare
to ask anything more about it, she didn't exactly look like you'd

just seen each other. Her days were like always, she said: The little library had no money for books, so she collected some from the neighbors, sometimes she got a few boxes from some elderly gentleman who had no use for them anymore. And so a few weeks later I happened to pass a store, right in the middle of town, it had those sorts of Indian odds and ends, everything very colorful, and at the back of the store I saw a shelf with the exact same kind of carvings. Even through the store window I recognized the outline. I was so confused, I didn't even go into the store. And then for a long time I didn't say anything. I waited for an opportunity to bring it up, and then she told me that Jakob had taken her home a few times, and we went out to the countryside together for our sister Nany's birthday.

We picnicked half the day. The ground was still cold, and lots of kids were running around, the baskets on the blankets were full of meatballs and salads, and everyone was eating with colorful plastic utensils, and Nany danced with Luca, the whole field was full of molehills. We laughed a lot, she sat next to me, only sometimes she looked around a bit shyly, suddenly quiet, as if turned inward. The evening was foggy, and I drove us home. We didn't speak. Everything was exhausted, even the colors. But I was uneasy, and it got worse as we got closer to home. Finally I pulled over to the side, right in the middle of the stretch of road. Behind us there were power lines looming out of the fog, the engine was still on, and she didn't look at me when I pulled the handbrake. She knew something was coming. And I didn't want to make a big speech.

Last week I was downtown, I said, and I walked up a street and past the store with the colorful scarves outside.

What do you care about scarves? she asked quickly. Well, why?

You know, I just happened to pass by and I stopped. I looked in the window. And usually I don't bother much with that kind of thing, but they had some really extraordinary figurines.

Now Milena understood what I was getting at, her mind was racing, I could see it.

But she said calmly: Lots of them aren't real, you know, the ones you can get here—

The whole time I'd been looking at a pair of headlights that were moving steadily across the plain, not much more than a pale shimmer, but now I looked at Milena. And I was horrified. I hadn't asked myself why she'd told me the story. She had her hand tight on the collar of her jacket and she was turned away, completely speechless. She started tugging at the seat belt as if it were smothering her. Suddenly I didn't know why I'd said anything or what the point was: What was wrong with fibbing about a wooden elephant? Why couldn't I let her make up a story that had you in it? Why couldn't I even leave her that elephant? All she'd done was give you a place in her life, and she'd only mentioned you with her eyes. I didn't understand myself anymore, but I couldn't take it back. I felt wretched, as if I'd betrayed her. We looked in front of us at the plain, finally I said something banal like: But some of them are really quite pretty, and I drove her the last few miles home. She got out without turning around, I couldn't even touch her.

No, she was never angry at you. But I was. How could you—

Lidia interrupted herself, looked at her watch. While she spoke, her gaze had been somewhere in the gravel of the garden café. He could imagine it all so perfectly that he couldn't think.

Maybe I shouldn't have told you that, it won't change anything.

She pressed her bag against her stomach and stared ahead of her, as if going over it all again in her mind.

Imagine where I was then, Waclaw said. Imagine that it was no different for me.

She furrowed her brow and looked at him suddenly. No different?

She grabbed her bag and stood up. Your no-different was pretty fucking far away.

He had no means of proving her wrong.

Did you ever talk about it again?

What do you think, Waclaw. It hung in the air, like everything with you two.

He saw her leave, and watched her go. Now, more than ever, when Lidia was angry and trying to walk very erect, her silhouette looked tiny under the trees.

33

Hic sunt dracones

It's dark. He's driven all day and now understands why Flavio spent so much time fiddling with the lights. He drives with the brights on, but they hardly penetrate the rain. It's as if there's nothing else, only this rapid falling, little glowing nails, the landscape dark as a fairground stall where a second-rate puppeteer makes his figures dance. The street so wet the drops seem to spring right back up from below.

He hadn't thought about it. He's freezing, he's wet, soaked. The fan blows cold air, and he turns it on and off and on again, as if that will change anything. He looks thin in his big black jacket, and he's turned down the flaps of his fur hat, in front of him is the outline of a bony face. The pigeon basket is empty on the seat next to him, and on top of it are the gloves that have gotten wet, and the bundle with the soapstone, which has gotten wet. The tropics and all the distant lands are far away, and so is the highway with its smooth surface, bitumen, extracted from oil. That it doesn't matter.

Later in the night, the rain has almost stopped. It's no longer far to the coast. He drives the Fiorino up a dirt road, the clutch grinds when he shifts from second to first gear, and the wood on the truck bed is soaked, the tarp wet with rain. When he tosses the match in the gasoline, the fire flares white and hisses, and the flames are blue, and they buckle in the wind. He waits. The warmth is slight, the smoke like a prophecy of all that's to come.

He'd seen the old stable up on the field. As he gets closer, he sees
the white lines of an electric fence that was put up recently. He won't
be able to stay long. The straw is old and wet, but farther up he finds
a bale of hay that's burst open and dry. Sharam had called him:
Come to London, I left you something, you'll find everything there
that you need to know. Don't give up now, Wenzel, come to London.
For fuck's sake.

He lay in the straw and he breathed the damp air. He thought of
the sparks and the smoke, a brief light on the plain. He thought
of what London was from here. His memories were of a restless,
trundling people who never seemed to arrive anywhere. He lay in
the darkness and he knew the smell.

He'd spent several nights that way. He'd heard other men snoring
through the thin walls of hotels, and he'd seen an indifferent light
shining down on him through the cheap fabric of the curtains. He'd
spent a few weeks on a farm: a room, a high window and hardwood
on the ground floor, a narrow bed and faded wallpaper. Enough to
stow a life, big pale pink flowers trailed over the walls as if they held
something together, something he wasn't sure of when he walked
over the meadows during the days, grassy hills, fields, endless, a rain
jacket, a pair of stout shoes and nothing he could have explained.

Sometimes he wanted to talk to someone. The farm belonged to
two siblings, he saw the girl outside, mending some fence, or bringing hay to the rick. Once he lent the boy his truck. That same afternoon he saw the Fiorino tearing up and down the dirt path of the
adjacent hill, over and over. A dog with white fur ran after the truck,
snapping at a piece of meat tied to the truck bed with rope.

The dog was a boxer, it was deaf and didn't even bark. But the
boy was bent on training it to fight, and that afternoon the Fiorino

looked angry, the way it braked and accelerated, and the animal ran after it and soon grew slower, until finally it stopped and looked around. Through the big window in the kitchen, Waclaw could see the boy in the distance jump out of the cab and run to the dog, who cowered, and it looked like the boy was screaming at him in words that neither Waclaw nor the dog could understand. The boxer simply lay on its back on the gravel road, and even from a distance, Waclaw thought he could see the pink shimmer of its belly.

The big table from which he watched it all was coated with wax, and it was a while before he noticed that he'd started making notches in it. Many thin lines. In the next days, he'd thought sometimes of the falconers in the deserts. Of the radar station in the hills of Tangier. What kind of borders those were.

All that now passed by him as he turned the Fiorino north. That afternoon he'd picked it up from the garage, a young female mechanic had welded the gas tank, and he'd left more money than he'd meant to, just because he could.

34

Bananas

Then he'd driven. A little town on the coast, north of Słupsk, where his father had filled his lungs with sea air those last years. There were dunes, the dim Baltic Sea, the attic room with the oval window. They'd expanded an old military base somewhere nearby, he'd understood that much. They'd sold the house to pay for the place in the home, the paper crown, the plastic mouth organ.

Buildings had sprung up around the little hut and then more buildings, the sea air squeezed between the villas as between a gap in teeth. The ornamental hazel now had a solid trunk. The land at the seaside for which his father had saved for years, the thing he'd been driving toward all that time underground, the place that was supposed to be a home, tiled, a structure without weight.

Bigger houses had been built all around, massive, with high, narrow windows. The sea was only a sense, with the wide sky above it. He drew his legs in. His arms poked out of the sleeves of his anorak. It was a down jacket, and it was new.

The house was even tinier than he remembered. Once he'd driven to Schwerin with his father, they wanted to see the castle, spend some time, it had been Waclaw's suggestion, after he'd been out for months. In the Philippines he'd seen them bury a live chicken before the drilling began. The moths were as big as postcards, and around the floodlights it stank of burned and slowly rotting meat. They walked knee-deep through dead moths, the drill floor was dirty, the cabins small and hot, their teeth red from betel nuts. Sacks of chemicals, the airplanes so old that they had to be started with two wires, like in a bad movie. After that he'd known that he never wanted to work on land again. The jungle seemed more dangerous than the sea. Maybe he'd been a bit homesick out there, the soapstone animal like a protective idol on the windowsill. On land, Waclaw had bought a Land Rover and picked his father up in Słupsk. From there they drove all afternoon to Schwerin. On the drive, his father was so quiet next to him that Waclaw sometimes wondered if he were only imagining him. Sometimes he seemed like a shadow, escaped from the time with Alois. Like the light over the houses on a winter afternoon, which had a different color, white, and weaker, and, perhaps for that reason, strangely beautiful behind the bare branches. His father coughed. Waclaw drove on a field next to the road, kicking up sand behind them. They laughed.

What do you say, Waclaw asked.

There was a long pause before his father answered.

We can leave the road, but only for a little while.

Then he nodded, and they zigzagged over the brown fields. When they finally got out, a biting wind was coming off the water. It was too cold for a walk in the castle gardens. The huge parking lot was empty but for a few cars. Waclaw walked close behind him, and they hardly took any notice of the walls as they approached. Waclaw noticed how tense his father was as they went into the hall to warm up. He studied the menu. Only later did Waclaw understand that his father was considering his order. When the waitress came, he showered her with his best German: blueberries, sponge cake, whipped cream, hot chocolate, coffee, and all he wanted in return was a smile. But she placed their order on the table so indifferently that he hardly touched it. Waclaw tried to talk to him, but it was if there were nothing more to the afternoon than the few recordings of classic Beatles songs and the red armchairs. As they left, Tomek looked at the waitress so coldly that his jaw clenched, as if she were the whole country that didn't want the love he'd saved up in all those shifts deep underground.

A harsh wind was still blowing in front of the castle. The light came in long streaks over the big lake, gristly old trees on the bank, their bare branches striking one another. The wind wasn't strong, just very cold.

The windows of the pickup were fogged from inside, Waclaw had spent the night in it. He'd gambled, the streets were a casino, black, white, the numbers of the highways, he'd driven through forests, foxes lay crushed at the sides of the road, flat land, fields. And the wheel didn't stop, and the ball didn't hit the number. No one watched him through a hole in the wall, there were no black-and-white cameras. He'd seen the old pope with his red slippers on the television, he knew nothing of their Rome or of Mátyás's hand, stroking his back, Waclaw wanted to believe in that hand.

He'd stopped on the coast where he'd thought that, with a little imagination, he'd be able to see Sweden on the other side. But he'd seen nothing. A closed carnival, swans on the rusty tracks of a fairy-tale train.

❖　❖　❖

In the little harbor town, the market was being broken down for the day. Men in thick anoraks walked under the vegetable stands, punching water out of the tarps. It slapped the cobblestones.

He saw how the rain ran into their black fingerless gloves, and he saw the turned-up collars and ragged hoods under which the men tried to protect themselves. They stacked the crates and filled a few of them with rotten fruit. They seemed tired from shouting, and hardly took any notice of the passersby. Behind a cash table stood a gas cylinder with a metal pan, through which little blue flames spat their warmth into the area. Waclaw walked toward it, past the men. The rubber hose that connected the canister and flame was wrapped in flaking silver, aluminum foil, the device had seen better days. Waclaw came closer and stretched his hands toward the warmth. How much does this cost? he asked. He turned slowly to the man in the fur hood who stood next to him. The man laughed. He shook his head. We need it, he said. You can see that. He looked at the square, where the wind was rolling a few empty plastic cups. Waclaw didn't move. I mean, how much does this cost? He pointed at the machine again. The man looked at him.

Waclaw dug in his pocket, then gave him a bill. The man unfolded it. He looked at Waclaw for a while. Then he shook his head again. No, he said, you won't pay that much for it. Anywhere.

How do you turn it off? Waclaw asked, as if he hadn't heard him.

The man helped him carry the gas cylinder to the pickup. Then they stood for a moment and watched as the metal cooled down. Five hundred, the man said again. He fished in his pocket and took out a few crumpled bills, but Waclaw pretended not to notice. The money rustled, and it sounded pointless, like a paper crown. The merchant put his money back away.

After he'd stowed everything on the truck bed, Waclaw sat down in the cab. The man closed the tailgate, then he tossed two crates on the truck bed and waved a banana in the air. Take them, at least.

He drove. He didn't know the way, but he kept heading northeast. He had two crates of bananas and a heater, and night was falling. The stars distant behind the clouds.

35

Falcons

And he was far away, and he sat with his back to the rocks in front of the rolling surf and saw the hoisted red flag and saw the footprints washed away in the sand and he felt the salt on his skin, the salty wetness of the sea that came with the wind.

He hugged the duffel, wrapped his legs around it and rocked it back and forth. Like a child. He'd let himself drop into the sand, and the sand whipped his face, and he gritted his teeth as he had so many times before and he looked over the edge of his anorak and over the edge of the dunes and at the sea, where he could see them rising. With their steely gray feathers like projectiles or like distant flashes in the sky. It made him think of Alois. He'd squeezed himself into a phone booth, rain against the glass, a coin-operated phone. He'd tried to call him, imagined what he'd say. When did you let her go? Yesterday. On a day like yesterday. How's it looking, was she in good form? And he would say nothing and stand there and look into the darkness outside the phone booth and read the many little scribbles on the glass, inside this lit yellow cell. He would read *I love you* and he would read the names and he would hear the coins dropping and think of Alois in his little stone house on the mountainside, and he would think of the pigeon and the lights of the refineries in the night, of Alois's good dry loft with fresh water from the river in the mountains. And he would say: all the falcons. He would say that he'd seen them. The white domes in Tangier. The lights beyond the fence. Perhaps he just stood in the booth and held the dead receiver in his hand and listened to the rain that whipped the glass like something that was coming closer.

He lay on the back seat of Flavio's pickup, covered with a thin blanket. He could feel the warmth in his armpits, his head lay heavy on the rain jacket that he'd balled up. He could smell the dampness and the mineral cold of the earth. It was winter now. The rain mixed with snow, but the flakes didn't stick. Grains of pigeon feed glowed in the night sky. He knew it, but he couldn't see it. The roof of the pickup was above him, it was warm under the blanket, a few feathers welled out of the sleeves of his down jacket, and he could see his breath. His nose was cold. The trees and bushes had been chopped down some distance from the high fence, in the darkness he saw the rolls of wire like hairballs on the Y posts, he looked at the other side for a while, two jeeps drove over the landing strip, and a bit of sleet glowed in their headlights. He looked through the fence as if something would come from that direction, something he'd been waiting for this whole time. Since when. Since Milena was gone. Since he'd stood with Mátyás in the workshop, the wideness of the seven seas before them. Since he'd watched her wrapping potato peelings in old newspaper for the pig. Sometimes it had been nothing more than that he'd awoken in the night and stood in the doorway, looking out into the rain. And that she'd stood behind him for a while. Nothing more. The moon like a flashlight, shining under white sheets. That they needed no more than these wet gardens.

The wind came cold from the northeast. Before him, he knew, a few miles as the crow flies, lay the coast, dead trees rose out of the sand like forgotten markings. On the Polish side there were no tourists searching for amber with rolled-up pants. Not now. Not in the winter. He thought of the unreal light of infrared cameras, the shimmering of the bodies that moved in the darkness between bushes, bright spots, as in a dream. And the ground was soft and heavy, it wasn't yet frozen. What little grass there was suffocated in the continuous rain.

That afternoon he'd walked the path between the dunes once more. The tiny house with the oval window, his father's wheezing, which he could hear as the soft sand gave under his feet. He hadn't stayed long. An unfamiliar child had stuck cutouts on the inside of the windows. The window frames clung to nothing. Then he'd driven through the night. The rain had begun just after midnight. The blades of the windshield wipers were torn, and the oncoming lights blended on the windshield into a diffuse film of grime. He had to stop twice for gas before Redzikowo. The best Pumas flew seven hundred miles on a tank, they whirred high over the Gulf of Mexico, they carried the tired and the thirsty, this wasn't Mexico. The rain pelted like sand.

36

At the Edge

And he walked on the coast and through the bright sand, ground small and fine over the years, sand of parrot cages, sand of the seas, blue for the last faded posters of the travel agencies, he walked.

He'd rolled up the tarp and taken it with him, and on the search for something edible he'd found the last of Alois's red cans, and he took it with him. The light was bright and the wind piercingly cold. Bales of seagrass were washed up. He'd stuck his pants into his work boots and his sweater into his pants, but still it wasn't warm. Summer was long over. For a few days he'd had a cough that kept coming back. The wind pressed against the land, he felt it at his back and on his neck, and there was no one else there, the waves somersaulted over themselves, glided out flat, pulled back, a few seagulls sailed over the water, and he walked for a long time, until he found a spot between the dunes, in the sharp grass, the fine sand came toward him over the crest.

And it was later, after he'd rested and warmed up a bit, that he sat up and looked for a long time at the horizon. He stood up, the can at his side, and the cold penetrated his clothes, all the way to his skin. It required courage, he thought. And he thought, he could go now. And he went. To the edge of the dunes. Only a narrow strip of sand separated him from the sea. And there were no sandcastles and no footprints, just the water rolling in. He had the can at his side, the red can, whose edge had become rusty. He felt its weight, which was slight.

For a while he stood there, freezing. The wind in his face. Then, very slowly, he raised his arm. Closed his eyes. Poured the whole last portion into his hand. The nuts, the seeds. Stretched his arm slowly, very calmly, in front of him and lifted it with closed eyes toward the horizon. Toward where the dragons lived. He stood, and he waited a long time.

No sound. But as he opened his eyes, there was something like a bright flash, which he saw through the crest of his eyelashes. A bright apparition like a mouth that opened and came down toward him. He stood calm and closed his eyes, and then there was a very distinct feeling on his empty hand.

Epilogue

One evening on the way back from Alois's he'd taken a detour and found the door of the gymnasium slightly ajar. As if someone had forgotten it.

He went home. They sat on the pine bench, their dinner in front of them. Red tea and the warmth and the conversations, all the voices that were familiar to him.

In the night, he slipped out again. Pulled an anorak over his dark pajamas with the yellow patches. First he stopped for a while in the bushes next to the gymnasium and listened. Whether there were voices, or someone there. Then he went out through the branches, and in the shadow of the bushes, crouched, he slowly made his way inside. It smelled of the rubber mats and sweat, and he could just smell the leather of the vaults from the equipment room. The wood of the parallel bars.

He stood very still against the wall.

There was no one there.

Then, very quietly, he felt his way forward, until his hands touched the long pole with the hook. He stretched it up. After a few tries he found the chains and let down the rings.

Both of them. His heart was pounding. The chains clinked.

Everything in the big room seemed too clear, and the hall, without light, seemed even bigger.

Again he stopped and listened. Then he went along the wall to the equipment room, to the big dish with the block of chalk. The powder crumbled in his hand. As he clapped it off, he could see the white clouds around him in a strip of moonlight. His hands shimmered white as he went back into the hall. As if they weren't his.

The rings swayed lightly above him on the ropes.

He jumped up.

The wooden rings hit lightly against each other. Then it was quiet again.

His grip was firm.

With his whole body, he swung himself back and forth. Back and forth. Ever higher.

He felt his breath, and how fast he flew.

He flew in the dark. Back and forth.

His arms stretched above his head. He could see the tips of his toes stretching out into the darkness. Back and forth. And then he had the feeling he wasn't even holding on, just a light wind at his sides. He felt a grin between his teeth, and he gained momentum, everything so light.

Acknowledgments

Between the first drafts of this book and the finished manuscript lie countless conversations, journeys, and encounters that have helped me shape and condense the material. Particular thanks go to Phil Jorgensen, Peter Müller, and Miłosz Biedrzycki, who helped me with technical questions and research material, the Else Heiliger Fund for the financial freedom to begin, Frank for accompanying me over the Mediterranean, my family for memories of the Ruhr Valley, Michael Krüger, Elisa Tamaschke, and Dorota Stroińska and Piero Salabè for help with the languages.